USA TODAY Bestselling Author

EVE L. MITCHELL

A GLOW OF STARS & DUSK

For my mum.
Who taught me to believe in myself as much as she does.

Note from the Author

There are terms and words within this book that are not contained with the dictionary. This is a paranormal romance book—I reserve the right to make up names and words at my leisure (as my editor will attest to).

Please note that I am a British author, and although I have tried to make this as universal as I could, there will be some British spelling, phraseology, and terminology that I can't (and won't) eradicate from my writing, and I'm okay with that.

BOOK DESCRIPTION

A Glow of Stars & Dusk

They hunted me down.
Six demons who believe I can cast a spell to lift a blood curse.
But I'm merely a clairvoyant who can summon the dead.

Being thrust into the world of demons is terrifying, intimidating, alluring…
Their leader refuses to believe I cannot understand the spell.
He's infuriating—but there is something about him that calls to me.
An attraction that scares me.

Fighting the magnetism to the arrogant demon leader is hard enough, let alone learning to use powers I never knew I had. But I need to learn how and *fast*.
I'm in over my head, and they know it…

A Glow of Stars & Dusk is book 1 in the Watcher Series and ends on a cliffhanger.
Content warning: please note that there is an incident of sexual deception contained within this story...but you know, they're demons.

CHAPTER 1

THE WIND HOWLED OUTSIDE, WHIPPING FIERCELY THROUGH THE naked branches, causing them to dance wildly in the night. They slapped futilely against my living room window as they were pulled brutally by the force of the gale, but the wind had no mercy to give, and instead, they strained against the firm hold on their limbs.

The rain fell relentlessly. Heavy and hard. I had checked several times at the window to know whether it was rain or branch that struck against the glass as I paced the small living room and waited.

I had been waiting for an hour, and I knew that I should accept that my last client of the evening would be mad to come out in tonight's storm, but my elbow itched every time I went to tidy the small area I had set up.

"You can stop itching," I told my elbow crossly. My hands fell to my work materials, and I began to pack up. I usually saw my clients in the corner of my living room at a small table with two seats. Any additional person got to sit on my worn leather couch and listen.

As I dropped the stones into the velvet pouch, I shrieked when my front door was banged loudly. I froze as I knew that it wasn't just the wind that was rattling my door. Staring in the direction of my front door, I didn't need the flare in my elbow to tell me there was someone out there.

The banging happened again, and again it startled me, yet my feet did not move in the direction of the front door. Instead, I glanced over my shoulder to the kitchen where the back door led to my small garden, the back gate and then the path to the river beyond. Biting my lip, I considered the back way just as the hammering happened again.

Slipping my stones into my pocket and grabbing my other paraphernalia, I quickly dropped them into my leather backpack.

Something knocked my window, and I bit back the yelp of fear at the unexpectedness of it, too loud and rhythmic to be the trees outside.

As I made my way to the kitchen, I stopped when I saw the shadow moving across the door. The door handle was tried, and my panicked brain fought the demanding question to myself to know if I had locked it.

The door rattled, and my shoulders slumped in relief to know that I had locked it. I was forgetful; it wouldn't be the first time that I had woken up the next day to find my back door unlocked and open.

I stood in my living room, uncertain. There was something at my front door, something at the back door, and something tapping on the window.

Three.

There were *three* outside. Maybe more. All my life, I knew that only bad things happened to people like me when *three* came knocking on the door. Maybe I was overreacting, I was nobody. The banging happened again, and fear overrode my rational mind.

I checked my watch.

Shit.

The banging happened again. Hastily I pulled out my phone. The signal was poor, but I still *had* a signal. Quickly I dialled.

"Ruairidh?" I whispered when I heard the line connect. "It's me."

"Why are you whispering?" Ruairidh asked jovially.

"There are *three* outside my house," I whispered quickly. "I need you."

"Are you fucking serious?" Ruairidh's voice had lost all humour, and I heard him moving from the room he had been in. "Get out."

"I *can't*, they're at the doors." The banging happened again and cut off what Ruairidh had been away to say.

"Under the floor, take the cellar, it'll be flooded with the rain, I'll meet you in the garden." Ruairidh hung up, and I eyed the corner of the room dubiously.

The "cellar" was actually my wooden floorboards cut to provide a small hatch in the floor that led into my cottage's foundations. Foundations that flooded every time there was heavy rain, because the drainage of the nearby fields was poor. I lived on a slope, and the drains couldn't take that as well as the excess runoff from the road at the end of my lane.

Mumbling about the unfairness of having to drop my five seven build through the floor, I hastily uncovered the small hatch. Grabbing my jacket, I shrugged into it as the banging got louder and louder. Holy God, they were going to be through the door soon; my front door was vibrating from the pressure exerted by the being outside it. Taking a deep breath, I squeezed through the small opening and then crouched low as I fumbled to recover the opening from beneath.

I banged my head off the floor joists and bit back the curse ready to explode from my lips as I waded through the knee-high water and lamented that my Friday night meant I was going to be soaking wet. I banged my head again as something wispy and webby covered my face and I backpedalled away, barely catching my scream. My hands were in my hair as I did the frantic silent-scream dance in the foundations of my cottage in the vain hope there were no eight-legged *friends* in my hair.

With a whimper, I ducked my head as I travelled to the far end of the foundations, which ran under the house and into the spare bedroom extension, and then I was at the small hatch. Shit, it was small. Had it always been so small? In the dark, I smoothed my hands over my jacket as I tried to gauge whether or not my hips were going through the grate. Crouching down, I pulled the ironwork and hissed in annoyance when it remained steadfast and the rain managed to slash mercilessly against my face.

The scream tore from my throat when a face suddenly appeared in front of me. Thankfully, my fear was lost in the howling wind.

"Why are you taking so long?" Ruairidh asked me in exasperation. "Move, woman!"

Effortlessly, he lifted the grate and unceremoniously hauled my arse out of the foundations. "You're such a gentleman," I bitched as I straightened.

"Be grateful I'm here, I think there are more coming." Ruairidh grabbed my hand, and we started to run from my garden to the river. Glancing once over my shoulder, I saw the dark figures casting long shadows on my lawn as they gathered around my home. With a crashing bang that normal people would assume was thunder, two figures converged into the cottage, and then with a purple flash, the protective ward erupted around them.

I grabbed Ruairidh to stop him so I could watch their impending devastation. Instead, I watched as the protective ward on my house failed. My gran had always told me that the house was shielded against unwelcome guests and that no one who wasn't welcome would gain entry.

My mouth dropped open as I watched the figures shake their heads as if they were merely annoyed by a buzzing fly, and then they carried on into my cottage.

"Move, woman," Ruairidh growled and tugged me forward. I nodded and went to turn to follow when my eye caught the shadow. He stood staring at me, green glowing eyes fixed in my direction as he stood under the canopy of the old oak tree. I could make out nothing of his features, but the stance, the height, the almost casual appraisal of my escape told me he was male.

Male what? I didn't know. Fear clawed at my throat as the power that stood under that tree was immense. The steady perusal of the soft glowing eyes made my feet stay in place until a sudden sharp jerk pulled me forward.

"I'm not dying for you," Ruairidh hissed, and his harsh words snapped me out of my trance. "Run, Star," Ruairidh snarled.

We ran.

I heard the shout even over the wind and knew they were following as Ruairidh and I ran at full speed to the river. The river was swollen with rainwater, the speed of the current daunting, but Ruairidh didn't hesitate. He jumped into the fast-flowing water, and as he still had a death grip on my hand, I had little choice but to follow him into the icy waters.

In the inky depths, I kicked my feet to propel me back to the surface. Ruairidh lost his grip in the strength of the current, and I used my arms to swim to the surface. My head broke through, and I gasped in air before I was taken down again, but this time I was closer to the surface, and my head bobbed out again as I looked around wildly for Ruairidh. Catching sight of his red hair, I started to swim to the other side of the bank.

Strong hands grabbed at my shoulders as Ruairidh dragged me out of the river. Gasping for more air and coughing up some river that I had inadvertently swallowed, I crawled up the bank on my hands and knees. My blonde hair hung around me as the wind slapped the wet strands into my face.

"Up! Get up!" Ruairidh urged, and with a heavy sigh, I pushed myself to my feet. "Keep running."

As I followed my lifelong friend into the heavy woods, I fought back the panic as I ran. Shouted orders roared over the wind as my pursuers followed.

I just wished I knew why they were pursuing *me*.

There are many benefits to living in the Highlands in rural Scotland. It's nice and quiet. Your neighbours are usually sheep. They don't eat much, and albeit they can be rowdy at times, they pretty much keep to themselves. The few people I do see, keep their distance from me and have done since I was a toddler. Tourists wander through now and again, and as long as you keep your curtains closed and your door locked, they keep wandering right past in their hillwalking, mountain climbing and outdoor activity pursuits. The downside of rural life in the Highlands? There were no neighbours to help you, and even the enthusiastic tourists were in their hotels and B&Bs on a night like this.

As the rain added to my already sodden clothing from crossing the River Orrin, I ran over the fields with Ruairidh. I was cursing inwardly that the fields were flat and the trees we so desperately needed to hide our escape were on *my* side of the river.

I could hear the howls, causing my feet to trip over themselves, and I went sprawling into the freshly harvested field. I was marginally mollified to see that Ruairidh had also stopped and was looking towards me. I couldn't see him in the dark of the night, but I knew him better than myself, I knew his stance.

"Hellhounds?" I whispered in shock. "They summoned *hellhounds?*"

"Who summoned hellhounds?" Ruairidh asked me worriedly as he looked over my shoulder, probably imagining a big furry dog coming out of the darkness. "*You* summoned hellhounds?"

What? Scrambling to my feet, I looked over my shoulder fearfully. "Don't be ridiculous, you know I'm allergic to animal hair." I grabbed his arm this time and pulled him. "C'mon, Rue, they get our scent, we'll be dining in the pits of hell."

"Not *dining*," he snarled as we ran, "we'll *be* the dinner."

Despite the surreal horror of what was potentially chasing us,

I fought the laugh as we ran. If we could get to the road, we had a better, surer footing for making it to the village.

"Is Abby's open?" I asked as we ran over the uneven field.

"Yes, where do you think I was when you rang me?"

"She better bloody stay open," I muttered as I hastily climbed the fence and once again fell forward. Strong arms caught me and rightened me, and then we were running on tarmac to the village. All the while, I ignored Ruairidh's claims of me being footless. "We should have run out front, at least we could have made it to your car," I lamented as we ran.

"Yeah, because running *towards* whatever is chasing us, was the better idea," Ruairidh growled.

Fair enough.

The local village was small, a handful of houses, a small convenience shop that housed the post office, and we had one pub. Every village in every corner of the world had a pub, and the village of Slate was no different. Abby's was a picture-postcard pub. It wouldn't have been out of place on a Christmas card, covered in snow, with its low beamed ceilings, uneven walls and original wooden floors.

I avoided it like the plague. The bar owner, Abby, was a screeching harpy who was born to make my life miserable. Being the same age, I had endured the she-demon all during school. When I had escaped the Highlands for a short time to attend St Andrews University, Abi-bloody-gale had followed. Like a bad smell. Thankfully, she had come into some money, left uni to hightail it back to Slate, and bought the village pub. She changed the Harvest Bar, which had been named that since its conversion from a farm building in the year dot, to Abby's.

I was still convinced that was what had caused Frank Summer's heart attack when she unveiled the brassy, shiny, gaudy new sign name.

As our feet pounded down the road, the bright lights of the

pub welcomed us, and I could feel our pursuers slow their pursuit. They were drawing off us, why?

Within moments, Ruairidh was bursting through the front door, causing all patrons to stop and stare at him. I heard the shock dissipate and a few chuckles start up until I followed my friend through the doors, and the return to laughter died on the spot.

The silence was deafening.

I knew I was soaking wet. I knew I had fallen at least twice face down in mud. I knew I had a bleeding elbow and a scraped knee. I also knew that my appearance was not what caused the silence. The stony silence was as a result of *me*, in general, coming into the bar. Hard eyes glared at me, and I automatically stepped closer to Ruairidh, his huge frame shielding me from the stern patrons.

"*Star*? Star *Archer* is that you?"

No, it's flipping Tinkerbell, I grumbled uncharitably in my head. "Hey, Abby," I said instead as I pushed my wet hair behind my ears. "How are you?"

"You look a fright," Abby said with glee as she stood impeccably dressed, her long chestnut hair impeccable, her makeup impeccable, her false eyelashes framing her hazel eyes to perfection. Abby always looked like she was waiting for the reality TV phone call because they had discovered her flawlessness. The village had eleven houses, the youngest person in it was Abby, and the men were mostly taken. We were about forty minutes from Inverness, but still, Abby was too glamourous for the Highlands. I had no idea where she found the energy to get all glammed up every morning. If I remembered to brush my hair, I was doing well.

"Swimming in the river does that to you," I grumbled as I walked past Ruairidh to the bar. At the collective gasp from the other customers, I fought but failed to hide my eye roll. "Ruairidh did it too."

I could almost feel them moving their eyes to Ruairidh. At six feet and almost half as wide, he towered over most of the men in the bar. His bright red hair shone harshly in the artificial light as his pale skin almost reflected the light back. Ruairidh was so white, when we were little, I used to put a gift tag on his toe when he was sleeping and pretend he'd died. Morbid, sure, but in the sticks, you make up your own fun.

"Are you wanting a drink?" Abby asked me, her voice heavy with incredulity as I took an empty stool at the bar. I heard Ruairidh talking to some of the other customers, doing that thing he had, the ability to make people like him.

I didn't own this skill. "Nope, just came to collect your soul."

The silence echoed off the pub walls.

Shit.

Why would I think I was funny? I wasn't funny. I was the exact opposite of funny. Before I could protest and tell them I was joking, I heard it, and the sound had me spinning in my chair.

The long loud cry of a hound baying in the night.

Fearfully, I looked to Ruairidh, who had darted to the window and was peering through the netting. "Star," he said in a low voice. "We need to move."

"The cemetery?" I whispered as I leapt to my feet.

Ruairidh looked at me and nodded. "The tomb."

Despite the uproar we were causing with our conversation, I ran to the door, and then the two of us were slipping out of the pub and running to the small ancient cemetery where no eternally sleeping resident had any living relative left.

"Ruairidh." I halted.

The shadows of the night turned from shade to more corporeal form. I looked around wildly, *where is he?* Four, only four, we could make it.

"Damn it, Star, what the fuck were you doing tonight?" Ruairidh muttered as we slowly advanced to the only hallowed ground in the vicinity, keeping the four in our sights.

"I was waiting for a client," I whispered back. "Do you think they can hear us?"

"I can hear you just fine, *witch*." The voice was behind me, and I realised belatedly, we were surrounded. Hot breath at my ear made me freeze. "You tired of running, or are you ready to scream?"

Why choose?

With a determined cry, I leapt forward, snatching Ruairidh's arm as I did so, and I propelled us across the road and through the gates into the cemetery.

CHAPTER 2

WE RAN TOWARDS THE TOMB AT THE VERY BACK CORNER OF THE small patch of cemetery. The old tomb was crumbling, in dire need of maintenance, and as we ran towards it, I screamed when I felt the hand almost catch hold of my arm.

"Faster!" Ruairidh urged me as he reached the iron gate that led inside. "No!" I heard him yell and then rattle the gates. "They fixed the lock."

Panting and out of breath, I fell against the iron, the gates stopping my run. "Seriously?" I hissed. "Get as much of your foot on the stone," I instructed quickly.

"I'll throw you over," Ruairidh told me as he turned to the approach of our hooded pursuers.

"I won't leave you," I muttered as I slipped my hand into his. "Get your foot on the slab."

We pressed against the gates in the vain attempt to make sure our feet were on the concrete.

The cemetery still had occupants, but the church and the accompanying manse were long gone, if in fact they had ever been here. Like unwanted memories, the headstones lay scattered and broken, and the grass lay unkept. However, no matter the upkeep of the cemetery, the tomb was still consecrated ground. The rest of the cemetery was not, but the tomb? The concrete had been blessed and was still decreed to be holy, and as long as our feet were on the stone, we were safe.

Six figures surrounded us in a semicircle, and I was sure I was going to faint.

Two *threes*.

What in hell's name had my last client been wanting to know?

"How long can you stand on the slip of stone without faltering?" a voice asked me; I couldn't tell which one of them spoke. The voice was different than before. I peered into their hoods, searching for the glowing green eyes, and was met with nothing but darkness.

"Until dawn," Ruairidh told them boldly.

The fact they laughed caused me to shiver. "Are you human?" I asked fearfully.

"Do you think we are?" another voice asked menacingly.

That was a loaded question and one I wasn't prepared to answer on a Friday night with the wind howling and the rain pelting down on my uncovered head, with six male *beings* watching me like I was an evening snack.

Ruairidh slipped his hands through the gate for greater purchase, and I felt him nudge me to do the same. Slowly so as not to draw attention to my hands, I grabbed the metal.

"You think that will stop us?" the same voice asked.

"I think you cannot touch me while I am on holy ground," I answered with conviction. "Now why don't you run off to whatever pit of hell you crawled from?"

I ignored Ruairidh's whispered *Jesus, Star* and stood tall as I hoped to all things holy that they didn't try to pull me off this stone.

"You're bold."

If he could see my shaking knees, he would know I wasn't; I was surprised I was still standing.

"But you make an assumption." The speaker raised his hand, and the snarling hellhounds were suddenly in front of us. "Tell me, *witch*, what do you see?"

I saw three massive dogs, no, not dogs, *hounds*, black coats and fierce like Rottweilers but massive and not as handsome. Their eyes burned red, their ears were pointed and stood upright like a Doberman's, they were gigantic yet sleek. Their jaws hung open as they watched me, their fangs—yes, *fangs*—catching and holding my attention. I glanced quickly at their huge paws and felt my heart stutter at the razor-sharp claws.

"Nothing," I lied. To see hellhounds meant death. The fact I had three of them in front of me did not bode well for my Friday night, never mind my weekend.

"You would lie on hallowed ground?" another of the six asked.

"If I was inside, I would be quite comfortable lying on the ground," I countered. "But it's not the night for an outside nap."

One of them took a step forward. He was taller than the others, and I noticed the hounds stayed closest to him. In the dark of night, his eyes glowed faintly. Green. It was him. The one from my oak tree. Fear like I had never known clutched at my throat.

"You think this is a game." His voice was the one from behind me earlier. It caused me the same shiver as it did when he had breathed in my ear. "This is no game, witch, and you have no advantage."

Ruairidh froze beside me as the six closed in on us.

"Your friend can go, or he can die if he stays." They spanned the entrance to the tomb grounds in a semicircle. There was no way through them; they were shoulder to shoulder and so close I could touch them if I wanted to. I really, *really* did not want to.

"I stay," Ruairidh said with a croak in his voice, and although Ruairidh was a tall guy, the way he slouched his shoulders, almost like he was cowering, made him look small compared to the monsters around us.

"No one need die." I tried to convince myself that the being I was locking eyes with was the leader, or Green Eyes at least. "I'm not a witch," I carried on. I really wasn't. I was a psychic, a poor one at that. Witch? Definitely not.

"She lies again," one of them said to the group. He sounded furious, and I knew this one would show me no mercy.

"Or she does not know," another one said. I didn't recognise his voice, and I surmised he hadn't spoken before.

My gaze kept darting amongst them, looking for any distinguishing feature, until I realised that the rain was not hitting them, the wind was not moving their clothes. I glanced at the dogs, the nearest one so close to me I could feel it's hot breath on me. They were also dry.

"Why aren't you wet?" I blurted. "Why does the wind and rain not touch you?" Silence answered me, and I could feel Ruairidh's panic building. My hair slapped against my face as a particularly enthusiastic gust of wind swirled around us as the figures remained untouched.

"Does she have to come willingly?" one of them asked curiously.

She? I was *she*, wasn't I? Willingly? Oh please say they needed my consent.

"She does," Green Eyes said.

I almost slumped in relief. "I'm not willing," I immediately said as I caught Ruairidh nodding emphatically beside me.

"Kill him," Green Eyes instructed.

They moved forward with a speed I found alarming, and hands grabbed Ruairidh. He yelled out as they pulled him effortlessly from the gate. My mouth dropped open in shock, and then I was surging forward to grab Ruairidh.

"No! Leave him!" I screamed.

"Got you." I was suddenly in front of Green Eyes. He took a hold of my arms, and then I was pulled into him as I heard the snarls of the hellhounds. My fists and feet connected with him as I fought to get free, but he held me tight. "Let me go. *Ruairidh!*" I screamed.

A hand covered my mouth as he spun me to face them, Ruairidh lying unconscious on the ground, the three hounds circling him, their saliva dripping onto the grass. "We can kill him," he said in a low voice in my ear, "or you come with us, *willingly*, and he lives."

The hand was lowered slightly. "Promise you won't kill him?" I whispered as I looked at my friend.

"No."

"Why would I give you my consent?" I tried to escape him again, but an arm that felt like a vice encircled my waist and squeezed the breath from me.

"Fine, I won't kill him."

I stopped struggling, but I looked at the other five. "All of you have to promise not to kill him." I heard their scattered laughter, and I could feel my tears building. "I will not consent," I hissed.

"Say it," Green Eyes barked at the others. I heard their mutters, and then I felt Green Eyes loosen his hold. "Consent."

My eyes closed as I sent a quick prayer to the heavens above. "Fine."

"More."

"I consent," I said, my jaw tight, and his arm tightened around me. "*Willingly*."

I was pushed away from Green Eyes, and I rushed to Ruairidh. Before I reached him, strong arms caught me, and I was lifted and turned away. "Best keep you out of harm's way." It was the quiet one who spoke.

"What? Why?" I frantically struggled until I was facing Ruairidh. The other four were standing over him, while Green Eyes was facing me.

Lightning crackled overhead, and he pushed his hood back. He was a man? Dark hair curled over his ears and hung in his eyes, those green eyes glowing softly as he watched me. Another flash of lightning, and I saw him clearly. Square jaw, straight nose, full lips. A cruel smile was flashed at me. "Do it," he instructed.

My scream rang out in the night as the four attacked my

friend. The one holding me turned me swiftly, shielding me from the sight of the beating Ruairidh was being given.

"You promised," I sobbed futilely.

"Not to kill him, girl. They didn't say they would not harm him." His voice was sad. "Be more careful what you ask of us."

"Can I ask you all to die?" I spat vehemently.

"You may wish it." He sounded almost regretful.

"Make her quiet," the terse voice spoke as Green Eyes strode past us both. "We've wasted enough time."

I felt something soft caress my forehead, and then I was falling into darkness. I tried to hang onto consciousness, but I lost the fight pretty quickly.

A SHUTTER WAS BANGING against the window. It always came loose when the wind was high, and Ruairidh always fixed it with a "quick fix" and then promised he would get it fixed permanently. Then the next storm would come and laugh at his poor handiwork. Last time, Ruairidh pulled the shutter right off the wooden frame in a temper.

Why was it banging then?

Ruairidh…

I sat up in the bed and looked around the unfamiliar room. It was dark still, but it was October in the Highlands of Scotland; it could be any time of day. As last night came flooding back to me, I went to get out of bed before I realised I was no longer wet. My hand reached for my hair and found it to be completely dry. How long had I been asleep?

Quickly checking myself, I was still in my jacket and torn jeans. I felt the dry mud flake off as I ran my hands over my legs, and as I stood, I winced at the pain in my knee. Hesitating, I considered crossing the room to the door and finding out who, or what, took me or lying back down and hoping that when I woke up the second time, I would be in my own bed, in my house, clean and mud free.

I needed to open the door.

I stayed where I was.

They were scary. They had hellhounds. They were all taller than Ruairidh and were obviously descendants of giants. They were cruel. They lied. Okay, they hadn't lied, they were flexible with the truth.

Ruairidh.

They hurt Ruairidh. I stormed across the floor and wrenched the door open with a fury I didn't know I could possess. The bedroom opened onto a small hall and a staircase. I hadn't even registered I was on the upper level. Taking the stairs, I stopped halfway down. A hellhound slumbered at the foot of the stairs.

Well, shit.

The dark of the hallway camouflaged the...dog? Hound? Monster? I studied it. Hound. Dog just wasn't appropriate, and monster seemed harsh as he lay there asleep with his head on his paws.

As I got to the bottom stair, I realised I would need to wake the hound because currently it was too large for me to climb over, never mind step over. My eyes ran over it. I could totally ride this thing. It was like a pony in size. My hand was stroking down his fur as I curiously studied the animal. No, not fur. Leather? Hellhounds were hairless? The hound snuffled in his sleep at my touch but didn't stir. Emboldened, I traced my hand over his shoulders and up to his massive neck. Even in sleep, the ears stood straight. They were a softer touch of leather, and as I rubbed it, the hound snickered. Unthinkingly, I scratched behind his ear, and with a small smile, I turned my head to see his back leg jerk as his head twitched.

When I looked back, glowing red eyes were watching me. My hand froze and my gulp was audible.

The hound regarded me intently. Very slightly, he tilted his head. When I didn't move, it did it again. Realising what the hound wanted, I resumed scratching the ear. It endured my touch for a few more rubs, and then it stood.

Holy blessed mother, had it *grown*? It wasn't this big in the cemetery.

There have been very few times in my life where I have been standing and been eye level with the animal in front of me. That this was a dog…terror was crawling up my throat, desperate for release.

The hound watched me. Patiently. As if it were waiting for my panic to be over, and somehow my own insane inner rhetoric was calming me down. Swallowing down my alarm, I forced myself not to freak out.

"I need past."

The hound regarded me, and I swear if he had an eyebrow, he would have raised it.

"Please," I added hurriedly.

The hound moved.

Ruairidh will never believe this. *Ruairidh!* Abruptly, the hound was forgotten, and I went in search of Green Eyes. Two males were in the kitchen, and a tiny part of my mind registered how absurd they looked in the small space, while the rest of me froze at how utterly terrifying they were. The kitchen light was on, the lightshade removed, and again my brain picked up on the fact it was because they would have kept knocking into it.

Huge didn't cover it. They just ate up the space. One was blond, the other dark. One was light-skinned, where the other was dark. One had a beard, the other did not. One had a scar, the other had two. Both had blue eyes. Both were looking at me. I felt

Hound at my back, and my eyes darted to the door that the blond one was only partially blocking. I could be fast.

The hound snuffed. The hound was *laughing* at me. I turned to look at it, and steady red eyes watched me back. I moved my attention back to the two…beings.

"Why—" My dry throat caused me to choke on my words, and as I coughed to clear my throat, Hound nudged me forward into the kitchen. "Why am I here? Where is Ruairidh? What did you do with him? What do you want with me?"

"How did you say his name?" the dark-haired one asked curiously.

"Ruairidh?" I asked stupidly.

"Slower," the other one commanded.

"Rue-ree," I said again.

"Row-ree," the blond one said, almost with uncertainty.

"No. Ruuuue-ree." *What the hell am I doing?* "Where is he?" I demanded.

"He lives."

I spun to the voice of Green Eyes, who was now behind me, the hound gone. He filled the doorway, and I involuntarily took a step back. "You hurt him."

"Did I?" In the light of the kitchen, he was more striking than in the cemetery. Thick dark black hair fell across his forehead, curling over his ears and lying over the collar of his dark tunic. A tunic? It fell mid-thigh over, wait, was he wearing leather trousers? My eyes lingered on his thighs before running down his legs—legs that had knives strapped to them—and heavy black shitkicker boots. I looked him over again before I forced myself to meet his gaze. That cruel smirk was there again, showing a dimple on his left cheek. His straight Roman nose sat over full lips. Forest green eyes assessed me as I took him in.

"You did." I found my voice again as I looked over my shoulder at the other two, realising they were dressed the same way. "*They* did." The other two were silent, their attention solely on me. "You said you wouldn't hurt him."

"No. *We* said we wouldn't kill him," Green Eyes told me, bringing my attention back to him. "He lives."

"For now."

I spun quickly to the other two. "What do you mean?" I asked fearfully.

A firm hand turned me back to face Green Eyes. "He lives as long as you cooperate."

"What do you want?" My arms wrapped around my waist in despair. "I have no money, I have nothing of value. I have nothing to give you." I could feel the tears threatening. I would not cry. I had to be strong for Ruairidh.

"You have something of great value," Green Eyes said as his smirk returned.

"What?" I knew I looked as confused as I felt.

"Your blood."

"*What?*" My shriek was enough to make him flinch.

"Lower your voice, woman, your screeching assaults my ears."

"My blood? You're going to kill me?" I was backing away from him slowly, the two behind me forgotten in my panic.

"Kill you?" He shook his head. "No."

I heard the snorted laugh from one of them and a muted *maybe later*. I had backed myself into a corner, and I watched the three of them warily as I desperately thought of an escape plan. "I want to see Ruairidh."

"Later."

"Now," I countered.

Green eyes narrowed on mine. "*Later.*" He glanced at the other two and nodded. The dark-haired one drew a very long, very sharp-looking knife and took a step towards me.

"He can slow the fuck down," I hissed at Green Eyes, one hand raised to ward the other one off. "Why do you need my blood?"

"For the spell."

"What spell?" I demanded. *Spell?* Oh Lord above, I had crazies in front of me.

"The spell you will cast for me." He held out a piece of yellowed parchment, and I knew just by looking at it that it was skin.

"I can't cast a spell." My hand was still raised in warning to the other one as my gaze darted around the three of them.

"Why?" Green Eyes asked me shrewdly.

"Because I'm *not* a bloody witch. I'm a clairvoyant, not Helga the Horrible!" I threw my arms up in frustration at the three confused expressions. "Think Emma Thompson in Harry Potter, hardly one of the *Macbeth* witches."

"What is she saying?" the blond one asked as he watched me carefully. "Is she speaking in tongues? I don't recognise the dialect."

I almost laughed, but Green Eyes grabbed my hand, and the sharp sting that followed as he sliced across my forearm with a knife had me crying out in pain. All three of them inhaled sharply, and I looked up from my bleeding arm, into a cold hard stare.

Green Eyes' mouth hooked up in a smirk. "Blood doesn't lie, *witch.*"

CHAPTER 3

"Stop calling me *witch*," I growled at him as I jerked my arm from his grip. "What kind of absolute psycho are you?" I grabbed a discarded tea towel off the counter and held it to my arm.

The blond one stepped forward and tugged the tea towel from my hand. "Dirty."

"I beg your pardon?" Not only was I bleeding, exhausted and scared, but now I was *dirty*?

He held the cloth up and pointed at it. Oh. Well okay then. I looked around the kitchen. Green Eyes was watching me, and it was unnerving. Stepping around the blond, I headed to the sink, and the third one stood in front of it, with his arms crossed against his chest. I stood and waited as my blood trickled down my arm to my elbow and dripped on the floor.

"I need to get to the sink," I bit out.

He looked over my head to Green Eyes, and with a disgruntled huff, he grabbed my arm. His hand encircled my whole upper arm, I marvelled even as he jerked me forward. "Hey!" I protested until I watched him run his hand over my forearm and, like magic, the bleeding stopped.

He stepped away from me as I stared at my arm in wonder. Turning it this way and that, I couldn't even see a scar. "How... what...um"—I swallowed—"what the hell?"

I looked to Green Eyes. "What are you? Where is Ruairidh? I don't understand anything that is happening."

"Why would you?" the one who had healed me asked. "You are merely a child."

Green Eyes ran his eyes over me slowly before looking to his two companions. His glance to them both made them grin, and I suddenly felt naked.

"Stop that," I snapped as I pulled my sleeve down and pulled my jacket tighter around me. "Take me to Ruairidh."

"No."

I closed my eyes briefly. "Now."

He tilted his head as he looked at me, and his eyes narrowed slightly. "Tell me, little witch, which part of this picture makes you think you're in a position to make demands?"

"My name is Star. Not witch."

"I know your name, Star Elizabeth Archer. Daughter of Jean Archer, father Roy Archer. Your mother was born of Ria Gallagher, daughter of Mary Campbell. Mary Campbell's mother was Heather Stewart. Heather Stewart's mother was Elizabeth McClellan, I can go all the way back, *Star*. Ten generations ago, your ancestor was burning at the stake in New England; a few generations before that, your bloodline was burning in Ireland; before Ireland an ancestor was burning in Toulouse, France. Shall I go on? Shall I tell you that ever since the first of your bloodline breathed her first squawking breath, your ancestors have been burning for their *craft*?"

"What?" I shook my head in disbelief. "You're saying that all my great-grandmothers are witches and were burned at the stake as *witches*? New England?" I looked at him with scorn. "Are you implying the Salem Witches? You need to do your research. The Salem Witches were hanged, not burned. There is no record of burning witches at the stake in Salem." I tucked my blonde hair behind my ears as I regarded all three of them. "And rattling off my ancestors' names? Please. Anyone with internet access can use an ancestry website. You want to scare me? Do better."

"Do better?" His smile was dangerous, and I felt anxious. "What do you think we are, Star?"

"I don't know."

"Lie." The corner of his mouth hooked in another smirk. "Let's make this easy for you. We know when you're lying."

"Whatever." I looked away from his mocking green eyes. He was suddenly in my space, and I stared at the leather strappings on his upper arms where more knives were housed. Who needed so many weapons? Did he know what year it was?

"We know when you're lying because we can smell your fear," he told me softly. His head dipped down as he spoke quietly in my ear. "We can hear your heart, we can almost taste your terror, you can hide nothing from us."

My hands pushed at his chest to get him to move away, but he stayed firm, and I looked up at him in anger. "Well, that's not fucking disturbing at all." I shoved at him again. "Get out of my space, you don't need to be so close to me."

He dipped his head again, and his whisper brushed across my cheek, causing my skin to erupt in goose bumps. "No." A hand trailed slowly down my arm. "Now, what do you think we are?"

"Demons," I spat out as I willed myself to remain calm.

I felt his smile against my skin before he straightened. "We are the Guard. Don't ever forget." He took a step backwards, and I took my first full breath since he had encroached on my space.

"She's already panting for you," the dark-haired one said callously.

"It's called getting oxygen," I snapped. "You wouldn't want to breathe in sweat and dead animal either." I looked him over with as much contempt as I could. "Well, with all that leather you're wearing, you probably would." I tried my best to stand tall, although the weight of the confrontation was bearing down on me. "So, you googled me. Big deal. You've decided I am a descendant of a gazillion witches. Whatever. This doesn't tell me anything, and even if it did, even if you *want* my blood, which is so creepy I'm not even going to go there, you get *nothing* until I see Ruairidh."

All three of them turned when another one of them entered the kitchen. His hood was also down, and his light brown hair hung loose around his shoulders. Clear blue eyes met mine with friendliness, and he rubbed his bearded jaw as he took in the tension in the room. "Doing well?"

He was the one who carried me away from Ruairidh. The one who had spoken almost kindly to me. "Where is my friend?" I asked him quickly.

"He is resting." His smile was as gentle as his voice. "Do you wish to see him?"

"Chaz." Green Eyes growled at this more likeable one.

"The sooner she sees him, the easier this task will be." Chaz motioned me forward. "Come, Star, he should wake soon."

I shoved past Green Eyes and hurried after the long-haired male, following him out of the kitchen. He led me to a room off of the hallway, and with a cry, I raced past him to the bedside where Ruairidh lay.

He was unmarked and looked to be sleeping soundly, but his breathing was shallow, his hands in tight fists on top of the blankets, he looked for all intents and purposes like he was struggling.

"What's wrong with him?" I asked quietly.

"He fights the healing sleep." The male stood at the foot of the bed. "It would be easier if he did not."

"If your friends hadn't beat him, he wouldn't need healing." I ran my hand across Ruairidh's brow, pushing his hair off his forehead. "He has a fever?" I asked him.

"The weather has not helped. You both swimming across the river didn't help." He smiled at me briefly. "He will heal. If he relaxed his mind, it would go smoother."

"I can soothe him," I said as I stood and kicked off my boots. I looked down at my clothes, I was still a crusted mud mess. "Don't suppose you have magic cleaning hands?"

"I'll leave you," he said with a smile.

I watched as he walked out the room, closing the door softly behind him. Quickly, I kicked off my jeans and my jacket. I gave a quick perusal of my long-sleeved T-shirt, and then with a shrug, I climbed under the blankets.

"Hey, Ru-Ru, you need to relax," I whispered as I lifted his arm, pulling it under the blanket and curling up to his side. "I'm here, we're...safe." I winced at the lie. "They're trying to heal you, but you need to relax." My fingers curled around his, and I squeezed. "It's okay, big guy, I'm fine. You're fine."

As I spoke quietly to my best friend, I heard the soft padding over the floor. Looking over my shoulder, I saw Hound looking back at me. "Should I even wonder how you got through the closed door?" I asked. The hound snorted and lay down on the floor. "Seriously, that mutt has an attitude problem," I muttered as I curled around Ruairidh once more.

As the three of us lay in the dark room, I heard *them* moving around. They weren't trying to be quiet, but still, I noted that they weren't exactly noisy either. How did this happen to me?

Well, I knew how it happened to me. I had the *gift*, as my gran called it. I had seen spirits since before I was old enough to know what a spirit was.

When I was four, I scared my kindergarten group when I continued to talk to my imaginary friends. All children have imaginary friends, which the schoolteacher tried to discourage. When I started telling my classmates what my imaginary friends were asking me to pass on, I was removed from school, and my parents were advised to seek professional help for me. Four-year-olds were considered "disturbed" if their imaginary friends were claiming to be dead relatives of my classmates. After months of confusion, my mum sat me down and tried to hide her tears when she told me I had to hide who I was.

"Star, baby, you can't tell anyone what your friends tell you anymore, okay? You can tell me and Daddy, well, maybe not Daddy, but tell me," Mum said to me as she helped me decorate the sponge cakes.

"But they want me to tell them, they have so much to say," I insisted as I looked up at her. "They talk all the time."

My daddy came into the kitchen, and with a frown to my mum, he smiled at me and scratched his jaw. "Do they talk all the time? Well, that would be annoying, wouldn't it? Is there any way you could not hear them, munchkin?" my daddy asked as he picked me up and placed me on his lap.

"But I like hearing their stories, Daddy."

"I know, baby, but how about I read you two stories every night at bedtime and you promise not to listen to your friends?" Daddy tweaked my nose, and I giggled.

"Roy, no, she can't switch them off like that, you'll confuse her," my mum said to him quietly.

"Two stories and extra hugs," Daddy said, ignoring Mum.

"What if I want the same story twice? Do I get another story too?" I asked.

"That's three stories," my daddy said as he laughed at me.

"It's only two stories."

"Four years old and she negotiates like a lawyer," Daddy said to Mum with a grin. "We'll see. But you'll definitely get two stories."

"Okay." I smiled at him, and he kissed my nose.

"But you have to promise not to listen, baby girl, for me."

I nodded as I went back to mixing the icing. "Okay, but they won't be happy."

"They'll get used to it," Daddy said with a grumpy voice as he set me down off his lap. "We'll give her a few weeks, Jean, she goes to school soon."

"I know, but this won't help." My mum was watching me drip the icing onto the sponges and catching any of my overspill.

"It will. You have to have faith."

My friends left me when I wouldn't listen to them anymore. Some didn't like it and threw things, but Daddy told me to close my eyes and pretend they weren't there and think of happier things than my friends being mad at me. After a while, they weren't mad, and eventually they simply weren't there.

When I was nine, Steven Carnegie slapped me across the face in a fight after school. He was a bully and a mean boy, and he made Ruairidh cry all the time when he called him *Cowardly Carrot*. I had decided it was my duty as Ruairidh's best friend to challenge Steven to a fight. Show *him* who was a coward. We had gathered at the park behind the school, and with no preamble, Steven slapped me right across the face. I was so shocked and scared that he had hit me, when I slapped him back, he flew halfway across the park. In the stunned silence of the crowd as they all looked at me with fear in their eyes, I had fled their whispers and accusatory hate-filled glares and ran all the way home.

The half-forgotten jibes that had followed me through my early school years came back with a vengeance, and I was once again labelled "the Archer Witch" or "witch freak."

When Ruairidh got his growth spurt around age fourteen, Steven Carnegie wasn't so quick to call him names anymore. School for us both was a different experience. By fifteen, I was noticing Ruairidh in a new way, whilst he was noticing every other girl who walked past *him* in a new way. Ruairidh's dad was a farmer, so even though he had always worked the farm with his dad, it seemed that almost overnight, Ruairidh developed muscles that the other boys didn't have. His biceps bulged, and he wasn't shy in showing them off.

Bonnie Ferguson was a complete and utter cow, I hated her during the latter part of school. She kept the *witch bitch* taunt up right up to my very last day of school. I was in the rec room having one last look around before I said goodbye to Regent Academy when the bitch full on *Carrie*'d me. She and her sidekick Steven drenched me in red paint. Ruairidh finally kicked Steven's arse and burst his nose, but to my fury, that weekend at a house party, he slept with Bonnie.

Too humiliated to go to a party, even if I *had* been invited, I had sulked at my gran's cottage. Ruairidh had gone, and when he stonewalled Bonnie for being the bitch she was, she convinced him to forgive her. Meaning she got down on her knees and gave my best friend his first blow job, and about twenty minutes later, he gave her his virginity.

Dickhead.

Bonnie told me personally on the following Monday when I unfortunately ran into her in town, so I had no problem accepting my unconditional offer to St Andrews University when it came, and I left my two-faced, backstabbing best friend behind.

They say time heals all wounds, but I still smarted over Bonnie Ferguson and her whorish ways whenever I was pissed at Ruairidh.

During freshers' week of uni in St Andrews, I ended up losing my own virginity to a nice English boy called Peter. There was no point waiting anymore. I always thought it would be Ruairidh that would do the deed, but he seemingly had no intention of it ever being me for him. I just needed to accept it. Sex with Peter hadn't been very good, and no matter how many times we tried throughout the first few weeks of uni, the sex didn't improve. When I told my best friend I had finally slept with someone, he didn't speak to me for three weeks.

Hypocrite.

Then suddenly, Ruairidh was in St Andrews and said we needed to talk. We went for a walk through the old cathedral grounds and, standing in the late September sun, as we stood looking down at the cement caskets, my elbow started to itch. It hadn't itched for so long it caught me by surprise. Looking up, I saw the dead for the first time in a long time.

I had caught glimpses of them throughout my childhood and teenage years but had always closed my eyes until they were gone when I opened my eyes again, like my dad taught me to. On the grass, in the shadow of the tower of one of Scotland's oldest medieval churches, the dead returned to me.

"Star? What is it?" Ruairidh asked me with a worried look on his face.

"There are so many," I whispered.

"There are four coffins, Star, calm your tits," he said as he laughed and pointed at the coffins.

"I'm not talking about the coffins."

"Oh fuck off, tell me you aren't re-enacting a nineties movie." Ruairidh looked around the empty cathedral grounds worriedly.

"They're everywhere," I confirmed as I turned slowly to look around me. "My God, Ru, I don't know how we got so far in with so many of them here."

"Close your eyes," he whispered urgently. "Close your eyes and think of happy things."

I shut my eyes, but I felt the soft whisper of something touching me, and I immediately opened my eyes. That was how I knew my gran had passed. She was in front of me under the arch window of the historic cathedral.

"Gran?" Tears were already streaming down my face, and I was holding onto Ruairidh with a death grip.

"You have to let them in, Star, they need you. We need you. You can help so many people with your power. Open your mind, my lass, the world awaits you," Gran said to me as her hand reached to touch my face. "You have so much potential, and I was wrong to listen to the wishes of your mum. I could have prepared you for what is coming."

"What's coming? Potential for what?" I stepped forward, but Ruairidh held me tight.

Gran glanced at our intertwined hands. "He is not your destiny. Let him go, Star, a much darker one waits for you."

"But..."

"Listen to your old gran, lass. He is not yours. Never was." She *smiled at me sadly. "You must learn your craft, you need to be ready. When they come, they'll come in threes."*

"Threes?" I took a step back into the protective reach of Ruairidh. Even as much as I tried to ignore my gran's blathering when I stayed with her, her warning of threes had stuck.

"Prepare. The cottage has all you need. Your dad will fight to sell it. Fight him harder, your mum will back you." She leaned forward, and I felt her ghostly kiss. "I love you with all I am, lass. I will be with you when you need me."

"I need you," I cried as she faded, and I heard her familiar laughter on the wind.

I had done my degree at St Andrews, while mum had stood firm and refused to sell Gran's cottage when I told her what Gran had said. The cottage would be mine on the condition I got my education first. I returned to uni, and one night at a party, while half drunk and free from my usual inhibitions, I had told the girl beside me I could see the dead. Which she interpreted as me being a fortune-teller. When I laughed and went to tell her that wasn't what I was, she offered me twenty pounds to tell her fortune there and then.

What better way to earn some money when you were a student than being a fortune-teller? It's amazing how much people will tell you when they think you are "foretelling." Learn to read body language and facial expressions, and halfway in, throw in a relative who was sitting patiently waiting to talk, and you were golden. Over the years, I got better, less nonsense and more truth. By the time I graduated with a Bachelor's degree in Accounts, I headed back to Slate with a job offer to apprentice at an accounting firm in Inverness and a profitable side business as a clairvoyant.

The "talk" between Ruairidh and me never transpired. Nothing between Ruairidh and me ever happened physically. He became my best friend again and occasionally would look uncomfortable when I spoke to some lingering visitors. Ruairidh listened to all my stories and theories about the spirits, and even though he never saw any evidence of them himself, his faith in *me* was enough to never doubt me.

Of the dead, I was careful. When I grieved for Gran, they overwhelmed me, and it took weeks to convince them to leave me alone until I called them forward. Now, I could summon them at will.

I pressed my forehead into Ruairidh's arm, my fingers interlacing with his. My ability to talk to the dead and an irritable elbow that was my version of a divination stick, hardly made me a witch. Or a person of interest to a group of demons.

"Seriously," I whispered into the dark, "I'm in desperate need of an intervention."

The hound on the floor snorted, and once again I was pretty sure that the hellhound was laughing at me.

CHAPTER 4

I WOKE UP TO BRIGHT LIGHT, WHICH CONFUSED ME BECAUSE I wasn't sure where I was. As I took a moment to remember, I turned in the bed and screamed when I came face to face with Hound.

"Jesus, Mary and Joseph, you bloody stupid mutt!" I yelled as I scrambled backwards from the hellhound. Hound looked at me and tossed his head before he turned and *walked through the door.* My mouth hung open as I watched his tail disappear through the solid *closed* door.

"Thought you couldn't see hellhounds?"

I yelped again as I looked to the corner of the room where Green Eyes sat watching me. "Were you watching me *sleeping*?"

"No."

"Then what are you doing sitting there?" I demanded as I looked around to make sure it was just the two of us. "Where is Ruairidh?"

"Do you ever get sick of asking the same question?" he asked me with a bored expression. "I wonder how much of your life you've spent asking, *where is Ruairidh*?"

"You're a dickhead." I got out of bed and hesitated for a minute as he looked over my bare legs. "Eyes up here, dick, there's nothing for you to see."

His eyes met mine, and his smirk was full of his usual mockery. "You're right about that."

"Oh my God, you're an arsehole." I yanked my torn jeans on and tried not to notice him noticing me. "Can you stop?" I grumbled as I tucked my T-shirt into my jeans. He didn't answer and merely sat there. "So, what do you want from me?"

"Blood and a spell."

"We could have a problem then," I said as I sat on the bed and looked him over. Were shadows *actually* clinging to him? No, I had an active imagination, he was merely a man. *Demon.* He was a demon. "Why don't you have horns? What's a demon guard?"

"Why do you think we have a problem, witch?" He remained unmoving, unblinking and steadfast. I was sure it was to intimidate me, which was pointless, he scared the shit out of me already.

"Are shadows swirling around you?" I asked curiously. They were, it was like he had his own private haze. He didn't need it for dramatic effect. He was drop dead gorgeous and screamed absolute danger; the mist effect was overkill in my opinion.

"You were going to tell me what the problem was?" He carried on as if my questions were nothing.

"Do you just keep going until you hear what you want?" I asked him crossly as I folded my arms over my chest.

"Yes."

"I'm not telling you anything until you tell me where Ruairidh is."

"Are you sure?" He was smirking again.

Hound was back in the room, and his previous casual indifference to my breathing was now replaced by a snarl and exposed fangs.

"Holy fuck, what is *wrong* with you?" I jumped up from the bed and moved across the room. Hound followed. "Mutt, we had an understanding!" I said to the hound as it padded across the room and leaned forward, it's nose inches from mine. A low growl rumbled in his throat, and I turned my head away, screwing my eyes shut as I felt the hound get closer. "Okay! Okay fine, you win."

"Why do we have a problem, witch?" he asked me. His amusement at my state of distress did not help my frayed nerves.

"Because I'm not giving you my blood, and I can't cast a spell!"

A hot wet tongue licked the side of my face, and I cried out in protest as Hound turned and went across to *him*. The hound licked his hand and then departed again. I watched as Green Eyes raised his hand to his nose and sniffed.

"Your fear smells delicious." His grin was wicked. "I wonder if you taste as good as you smell, little witch?"

"You're a sick, twisted individual." I rubbed my hand over my eyes. "So you have low tolerance for questions and a tendency to threaten when you want something." I cast my eyes over him. "Spoiled little diva, aren't you?" He snorted and sat back in his chair, gesturing for me to sit. "What are you called?" I asked, and he looked at me impassively. "What? You call me witch all the time, what do I call you?"

"Master."

I snort laughed in shock at his sense of humour and then realised he wasn't joking. "I'm not calling you master." Rubbing my hands over my face again, I tried to regain a small sense of normal. "Where is Ruairidh?"

Green Eyes scratched his jaw. "It's almost obsessive, this constant, incessant need to know where he is." He looked me over again. "I understand now why he doesn't have sex with you."

"What?" *Did he just say that?*

"Clingy, needy, scrawny." His head tilted as he considered me as he counted off my apparent failings on his fingers. "Absolutely no hips to speak of, breasts are adequate at best. I understand why he prefers the female in the bar."

"What?" I demanded. *Fuck you, arsehole.*

"Repetitive." He nodded as if he was making a mental list. "You have absolutely no attractive qualities at all, do you?"

"Wow." I was on my feet. "This was a great talk. I mean as talks go, this was way up there as one of my highlights. I'm done now." I strode to the door and wrenched it open. His laughter followed me out of the bedroom as I headed to the kitchen.

"Ruairidh!" I breathed in relief as I rushed across the room to embrace him, stopping short as I watched him shovel food into his mouth. "Are you *eating?*"

"Hungry." Ruairidh shrugged. "Chaz made me breakfast."

I looked at the long-haired demon in shock. "How long was I asleep for?" Chaz dipped his head, his face shielded by his hair. "You *spelled* me?"

"He did what I told him."

"Oh you can fuck off!" I shouted at Green Eyes. "You too," I said as I glared at Chaz. "You"—I grabbed Ruairidh's arm and pulled him to his feet—"you're coming with me."

Neither of the demons moved as I opened the front door, and I didn't question the fact that they let me leave until I was standing outside, looking at a brilliant yellow fog that was at the end of the short path. I spun around wildly. I could see nothing except the fog, Ruairidh, and the two demons inside the house. Still, I knew north, I could head north. Anywhere that wasn't *here.*

"Star, wait." Ruairidh grabbed my hand and tried to stop me. "You can't walk in this, Star. I'm no supernatural, but this fog *isn't* natural."

"It's Scotland. In October. Fog won't hurt us, we're from the Highlands." I wrenched my arm free and walked forward.

"It's *yellow* fog," Ruairidh hissed.

I glanced past him to see Chaz glaring at Green Eyes, who held his arm across Chaz's chest like he was preventing him from leaving. I had no idea what was happening there, and I wasn't staying to find out. "It's *fog.*" I walked a few more steps. "I'm not going back in there with that twisted demon." My gaze returned to Green Eyes as he merely watched me.

Stubbornly I walked on. Ten or more steps later, I realised Ruairidh wasn't behind me. He had stayed? It hurt more than seeing him eating breakfast in the kitchen. They wouldn't hurt him—they had healed him—and I was no longer there, so they didn't need him. He obviously felt safe, but why would he stay and let me go?

The grumblings I heard were not only coming from me. Something flashed past me, and I halted where I was. Looking down at my feet, I realised the grass I walked on was dead. Brown grass was not something we suffered in Scotland due to our wet climate. "It's not unheard of," I reminded myself as I started to walk again. If I was on grass, I wasn't on a road, and if I wasn't on a road, then I couldn't be hit by a car.

A dark shadow flashed past me again, followed by an eerie scream, and I closed my eyes as I continued to walk forward. The denseness of the fog didn't lift. In fact, it got thicker; it was almost like a blanket surrounding me and depressingly reminded me of mustard gas that they used in the First World War. Something pushed into me from behind, and I yelled as I stumbled forward, losing my balance. On my hands and knees, I felt the thing pressing down on me. Suddenly, out of the yellow, shadows leaped over me, and I bit back my scream as the force pushing me down knocked me so far down that my face was amongst the grass. I heard the rumble, and in my panicked state, I recognised the shape of a paw on my back.

"Hound?" I whispered uncertainly as I moved my head to the side. The paw flexed, and I went to push myself up when I heard the hellhound's low warning grumble as his talons pressed into my back. Moving my head from side to side, I saw the muted shadows and realised there were more than just the one. There were *three*, and they looked to be fighting. "Hound?" I whispered again. The paw eased its pressure on my back, but he didn't let me rise. Somehow I knew that the hellhound was protecting me.

I heard a cry followed by a chant, and something other than Hound touched me where my skin was exposed on my arm from where the sleeve of my jacket had ridden up. My blood began to burn in my veins. I pushed my sleeve up more, sure that the heat I felt coursing through me would be visible. Sweat beaded on my brow as my body warmed. Hound mewled, and the paw was lifted from me. I flipped onto my back as the burning raced through my body. The scream that left my mouth didn't sound human as I writhed on the ground.

A weight was on me, holding me down. I couldn't breathe, why couldn't I breathe? I stared unseeingly into the yellow fog as screams poured from my throat. I couldn't see. Heavens help me, I was blind. Cool, soothing hands ran over my arms and legs, and I whimpered in relief as the burning receded from my body. Cold hands clasped my cheeks and wiped away the tears that I'd shed in pain. My eyes remained closed, the horror of losing my sight too real, and I recognised the sound of myself crying. Strong arms picked me up, and I felt myself being carried. Unthinkingly, I curled into the chest of the one who carried me. I had no doubt it was one of the demons from the cemetery.

"What the fuck is wrong with her?" I heard the harsh demand and curled tighter into the arms that held me. *His* voice I would recognise anywhere.

"Whatever bound her power broke in the fog. She was like a fucking beacon of light in the middle of the plain." I recognised the bitterness of the dark-haired one.

"How long before she's healed? We need to move."

"Nightfall," was the answer, and I knew that Chaz carried me. "Fuck."

I heard the curses, and then I was being laid on a bed. "Star, you need to open your eyes," Chaz said. "I need to see, Star."

My eyes remained squeezed shut, the heat still throbbing under my skin. "It hurts," I whimpered as I reached for something to hold onto. "Please."

"I thought she would be stronger," one of them murmured.

"Heal her," came the sharp command, and I heard the

answering huff of contempt. "The quicker she is healed, the quicker this nightmare is over."

"We should bleed her and then be rid of her. Ros knows the spell," the dark one who didn't like me spoke in disgust.

"It cannot be done that way, she needs to cast it." That was most definitely Green Eyes.

"She will cast nothing if I cannot get quiet to aid her," Chaz snapped at them. "You shouldn't have let her leave."

"She's stubborn and stupid; she needs to learn stupidity will kill her." Green Eyes' voice was tight with anger, and my eyes tightened from his harsh words.

I heard Chaz sigh in resignation. "Just clear the room."

I heard the door closing, and then the soft cool hands ran across my forehead. "You are safe to open your eyes, Star," Chaz said to me softly.

"I see only blackness when I open my eyes," I whispered to him.

I heard his intake of breath, and then I felt him move away from me. "Sam. I need you."

Sam? Who was Sam?

"What now? Zel's right, she's more trouble than she's worth."

My eyes flew open in surprise, and I looked up at Green Eyes. "Sam?" I asked sceptically. "*Your* name is *Sam*?"

"What of it?" Sam asked me as he appraised me quickly. "Why did you call me?" he asked Chaz.

"Sam's so bloody *normal*." I looked him over. He was *so* intimidating. I was expecting something grander, more bone crushing. "Sam doesn't suit you."

"Did you need me for something?" He ignored me and looked at Chaz.

"Well, I did, but Star seems to have healed herself," he told Sam with mild amusement.

"How long before we can move her?" he asked Chaz.

"Tonight."

"This takes too long," Sam growled as he left the room again.

"Seriously? *Sam?*" I looked up at Chaz who seemed to be biting the inside of his cheek. I felt around my eyes before holding my hands up in front of me.

"Your sight is back?" Chaz asked as he watched my self-assessment.

"Yes." I pushed my blonde hair back from my head as I thought about the yellow fog. "What happened out there? Something touched me, and the pain was…" I shuddered as I recalled it.

Chaz sat on the seat Sam had been in earlier. "Can you talk me through what happened?"

"Um, I wanted to go home, *he's* a dickhead, and I don't like him." I pretended not to see Chaz pressing his fingers to his lips as he listened to me. "Fog is fog, we get it all the time. I didn't sense any danger." I shrugged defensively.

"The fact it was yellow didn't dissuade you?"

"Fog is fog," I told him stubbornly. Okay, so sure, yellow fog is bad. Who knew? How was I supposed to know it was on a worse level than that of yellow snow?

"And when you were in the fog?"

"I saw shapes? Figures? I don't know, I could hear voices?" I drew my legs to my chest and rested my forehead against my knees, realising my legs were bare. "Where are my jeans?"

"They were in a bad state and covered in filth," Chaz explained as he handed me a new pair of jeans. "I think they will fit."

I didn't know what to say to that, so I placed the jeans beside me on the bed.

"What happened when you heard the voices?" Chaz asked me.

"The hound pushed me down onto the grass and wouldn't let me up."

"Hound?" Chaz asked me with a small smile.

"Hellhound," I explained softly.

"So you admit you see them?" Chaz asked me, leaning forward.

"He's kind of hard to miss."

"They are indeed," he answered me calmly as he considered me thoughtfully. "And then?"

"Someone, some*thing* jumped over me, and then it touched me, and all I felt was pain." I shuddered as I met his kind eyes. "Burning pain."

"Touched you where?" Chaz asked as he rose to his feet. I pulled up my sleeve, and he cursed in a language I didn't know before he was at the door yelling for Zel.

CHAPTER 5

Dark-Haired and Bitter entered the room along with the blond one from last night. "Still alive?"

"Chaz." I pointed at the long-haired demon. "Zel." I pointed at Bitterness and then looked over their shoulders. "*Sam's* outside, who are you?" I asked the blond.

"I can be whoever you want me to be," he answered with a wink, and despite myself, I smiled at the small dose of normality.

"Your name will be fine for now," I told him as he grinned at me. He wouldn't look out of place on the TV show *Vikings*, with his blond hair pulled back on top, two braids holding the top of his hair back, and the sides of his head shaved. A blond trimmed beard did little to hide the scar that ran in a curve down the right side of his face.

"Ros."

"Ros?" The way he said it made me think it was like the others' and had a *z* in it. "R-o-z?"

"S."

"Okay." I looked at the three of them and felt the shiver run over my spine. "So where are the other two?"

"We're letting her interrogate us now?" Zel muttered resentfully. His hair wasn't as dark as Sam's, but it was still a darker brown than Chaz's. Zel's hair was cut short, in a low fade, his crystal blue eyes cold and glacial, already startling with his dark skin tone. Adding in the two scars that ran down his forehead and over his eyes but stopped midway down his cheeks, made his eyes more obvious. He was memorable and not in a good way. He was clean-shaven too—it was as if he *wanted* you to see his scars. He was incredibly intimidating, and I couldn't hold his stare for long.

"Where did Ruairidh go?" I asked Chaz.

"We need to do this first." Chaz held my arm up to Zel, who looked at it and then glared at me as if it was my intent to have a red angry handprint on my forearm.

"When?" Zel snapped at me.

"Outside."

"She's a fucking liability," Zel grumbled to Ros. "You better go get him."

"Him, who's him? Where are the other two?"

"There's nothing to say we can't gag her, is there?" Zel asked Chaz with an almost pleading look.

"I can still hear you, you know," I told him with a pointed glare.

"And we can still hear you," Sam said as he stalked into the room. "What has she done now? I don't know why I keep leaving this room only to be called back." Wordlessly Zel held my arm up, and Sam looked at it before he glared at me. "We move now." He turned and walked out of the room, and Zel hurried after him.

I looked at Ros and Chaz. "What's going on?"

"Can you travel?" Chaz asked me as he pulled my sleeve carefully over my arm.

"Do you mean can I walk?" I stood up from the bed. "Yes, I can walk."

"You're the worst witch I ever met," Ros said, grinning at me. "I'll take her," he told Chaz, who looked between us but eventually nodded.

"Take me where?" I asked the blond demon, who was smiling at me as if I were his new toy. "Why am I worried about this? Where is Ruairidh?"

"We put him back where he belonged."

My jaw dropped as I stopped pulling on the jeans. "What?" I looked at Chaz. "Put him *back*? Back where?"

"His home." Ros looked at Chaz with a frown. "That's where I was while you were out screaming in the mist."

"Could he hear me?" I asked as I zipped the jeans, then pretended to concentrate on putting my jacket on.

"Girl, the whole entire underworld heard you." Ros snickered as he walked out of the room, calling for Zel to get two ready.

Two of what, I didn't know and I didn't care. Ruairidh had left me in the fog. He had allowed them to take him home. He hadn't stayed.

"The world of men can be disappointing," Chaz murmured quietly beside me.

"You lived in it long?" I asked as I surreptitiously wiped my eyes.

"Been a long time since I was topside," he said with a soft smile my way.

"Should I be flattered?" I asked as I shook my head.

"No," Chaz replied as he looked at me sorrowfully before he looked over my shoulder. "Your friend is better where he is. He would have caused you harm."

"He left me." I sniffed and rubbed my nose. "What more harm could he have done?"

"They would not protect him had he stayed, whereas you would have been distracted and in harm's way looking out for him."

"Maybe," I admitted softly. "Doesn't make it better."

"I know."

"What do you guard?" I asked curiously.

Chaz looked at me in surprise before looking towards the open door. "What do you mean?"

"Sam." I rubbed my forehead. "Seriously, that's the worst demon name ever by the way," I told Chaz with complete seriousness. "Anyway, Sam said you are Guard? The guard? Demon guard?" I waited expectantly. "So what do you guard?"

"I'll let Sam explain it to you."

We walked out of the small room, and Chaz led me to the back garden where the fog still lingered at the gate. Looking at it now, properly, I wondered if I had been struck on the head and had a concussion or something, because the fact that I had walked out into that earlier with no fear could only be a result of a head injury. No one in their right mind would enter that *willingly*.

"What moves in it?" I asked as I watched the distorted shadows within it. Hound came and stood beside me, and unthinkingly I stroked his leather skin.

"Is she *petting* the hellhound?" Ros asked in an excited whisper.

"I think the more important thing to note is that the hellhound is letting her pet it," said a new voice.

I looked over at the newcomer, who had walked around from the side of the house. Tall like the others, reddish brown hair, which was unkept and almost curly. His thick bushy beard matched his hair in that it was wild and untamed. He had a scar through his upper lip, which cleaved his facial hair slightly. Like the others, he wore the dark tunic over leather trousers, only his arms were so massive they were bare rather than covered by the black undershirt that the others wore. The crisscrossing of scars on his arms fascinated me. Dark blue eyes appraised me before he looked to Sam with a nod.

"Pen?" Sam asked.

"Wiping the friend."

"What does that mean?" I stepped forward as I glared at them both. "What does *wiping* mean?"

"He's removing us from his memories," Chaz explained as he pulled me back. "It is easier for him."

"What about me? What about when he looks for *me*?"

"He won't." The newcomer looked at the others with a knowing grin.

Dread filled my veins. "What did you do?"

"He thinks you're a happy girl," Bushy Beard told me as he winked at the others.

"Which one are you?" I snapped.

"Der."

"Why would my best friend think I am *happy* when I am being held against my will by a bunch of *demons*?"

"He doesn't think we're demons," Der answered with a casual shrug.

"What does he think you are?" I pressed and was even more worried when I saw him fight back his laugh.

"He doesn't think we are anything as he hasn't seen all of us."

"All of you?" I looked around at the five of them, some were trying not to laugh, Chaz was not making eye contact, and one was ignoring the conversation entirely while he checked his weapons and watched the fog. He was the one I was interested in, *he* would tell me. "Sam?"

"Witch?"

"What is he saying?"

Sam turned to me slightly, his eyes once again travelling slowly over me. "He's saying your *friend* is content to give you privacy for a while, you're...tied up."

Zel and Ros started laughing, and I closed my eyes briefly before I took a step towards Sam. "Tied up with what?" I knew the answer, I just needed him to say it so I could justifiably slap someone.

"Let's just say he'll knock from now on," Sam told me with that irritating smirk. "Your little kink may get him into your bed after all."

"He thinks I'm sleeping with you?" I demanded as I spun to confront Der incredulously.

"Fuck no, not me," Der laughed as he slapped Sam on the back, and he and Ros and Zel started to walk to the end of the garden. "And trust me, woman, he doesn't think you're *sleeping*."

"*You!*" I glared at Sam even as I shook my head trying to get the image of me in bed with Sam out of my thoughts. It wasn't as distasteful an image as I wanted it to be. "He'll know that's a lie. I haven't had sex in yea—" I shut myself off abruptly when I saw Sam's eyes gleam with what I was about to reveal.

The sixth one appeared from the back door. "He seemed to be very convinced. In fact, even when we put him in his home, he immediately left it. He's in the public house he frequents right now, telling a very pretty barmaid all about how loud you're screaming for more."

I looked at the newcomer. "So you're number six?" I snarled.

"Pen, at your service." His dark blond hair was cut short, he was almost slim compared to the rest of them. He was also the most instantly attractive. Maybe it was his build, his almost fashionable hairstyle, his rough stubble or the light brown eyes, but with this one, you didn't need to be fighting past terror or apprehension to appreciate his looks.

"Why couldn't you have been the one to sleep with me?" I asked. The garden was silent for a moment before Der and Ros were howling with laughter, and Sam's eyes narrowed on me.

"As much as I am sure the experience is…enlightening…" Pen glanced at Sam. "Some *pleasures* are not for me to experience."

"Did he just say I'm ugly?" I asked Chaz as Pen joined the other three, and they huddled together.

"Come, Star, we need to leave," Chaz said instead of answering as he led me to join the others.

"Little witch, you're with me," Ros called to me over his shoulder. "This should be *fun*."

"She travels with me." Sam's hand came down on my shoulder, halting me from crossing over to Ros.

"I don't want to," I answered immediately as I tried to shake him off and go to Ros's side.

"I don't want to hear you either, but we don't always get what we want," Sam told me harshly as he picked me off my feet and tossed me over his shoulder in a proper fireman's lift.

As I hit his back, trying to free myself of him, he spoke to the others in a language I didn't know. My feet tried to kick him until he slapped my arse so hard I stilled in shock. Sam never stopped talking, and then Chaz was in front of me with an apologetic smile.

"No, I'll be good!" I yelled as he wrapped a blindfold around me before catching my hands and binding them too.

"It's too much," I heard Chaz murmur before he was instructed to "just do it." My cries of protest were silenced when they gagged me.

Blindfolded, bound and gagged, I felt Sam start to walk, and he shifted me lightly on his shoulder, one arm holding me secure.

"You know," Zel said after a few moments, "when she's quiet, you can appreciate her butt."

"Nice and round," one of them agreed, and I was sure it was Ros.

"She can still hear you," Chaz reminded them softly in admonishment.

"And I don't want to hear it at all," Sam growled. "Make sure nothing touches her, except me."

"They won't even get close," someone boasted.

Who was they? I wondered frantically.

"I'm counting on you to make sure that's the case, Der," Sam said with authority. "Der, Ros, in front. Zel, you're behind with Chaz. Pen with me." Sam shifted me slightly again. "Hellhounds?"

"Already in front," Chaz confirmed.

"We travel fast, sure, and together. She'll draw them like moths to a flame, try not to engage. We can always clean up later." I heard them all agree or mutter, but Sam stayed still until they were quiet. "Guard, be swift and ready," he told them once more. I felt him turn around. "Hellhounds, *hunt*."

What followed next was terrifying. As Sam took off at a run, the screams, snarls and cries that all mixed in together may not have been so bad if I could have seen. That may have helped, but the unknown made the whole experience more frightening. Sam never stumbled, his feet stayed true and steady, and his hold never lessened. A few times, I was spun around, and I could only surmise that he was fighting. Fighting *what*, I didn't know, and each time, I felt the huge presence of a hellhound beside me.

"Fuck me, there's a lot," I heard one of them grumble, and my fists tightened on the back of Sam's tunic.

"Witch, hold tight," I heard Sam say before his arm was gone from my legs and he lunged forward. The gag muffled my scream as my legs flailed at the sudden loss of the anchor of his arm, and I started to slide down his body. Without thinking, I wrapped my legs around him and heard him grunt as I hooked my bound arms around his neck, knocking the side of his head with a heavy thump. Sam grumbled at the blow, but his focus was on other things, and I was too scared to take satisfaction in the fact I had just hit him, albeit unintentionally.

My head burrowed into his neck, trying in vain to make myself as small as possible as I felt him move around me and the sound of metal hitting flesh surrounded me. As his breathing increased in exertion, my legs held him tighter until suddenly he was still, and then we were spinning. His yell as he wrapped both arms around me made me press into him more.

The silence was deafening, except my heavy breathing through my nose. A hand tugged the gag from my mouth and instantly covered my lips. "Shh, not a sound, control your breathing." Next the blindfold was removed, and I jerked my head back to glare at Sam, but his other hand moved quickly to cushion the blow of my head hitting whatever was behind me.

I was wrapped around him, one of his hands in my hair, the other over my mouth, his body pressed into mine. I looked away from his forest green eyes and looked over his shoulder, and I squeaked.

We were in a poorly lit small space. I suddenly realised there was nothing *behind* me, it was under me. We were lying down, not standing up. I was so disoriented. Sam waited until I had myself under control, and he slowly removed his hand.

Bending his head to my ear, he whispered, "The ground collapsed, they knew we were coming, nod if you're okay."

"Who are they?" I whispered back.

"I said *nod*."

"I say bite me," I snarled back.

He did.

His teeth dug into my shoulder as his hand covered my mouth again as I cried out in pain. "When I say *nod*, fucking nod," he whispered harshly in my ear. "If I say speak, *then* speak."

He lifted his head to look at me in question, and in the dim light of the hole, I glared at him. My head tried to turn to take in our space. We were buried? I was *buried* alive. With a demon? How deep were we buried? Why wasn't he trying to get out?

His mouth hooked up at the right side. My face must have been showing my panic, and I tried to calm down, even as he tried to hide his amusement at my reaction.

"You need to stop panicking and breathe slowly," Sam whispered almost reassuringly into my ear. "I'm holding as much as I can off of us, but I can't *make* fresh air. Shallow breaths only, witch."

He tried to move and couldn't. Releasing my fingers from around his neck, I stretched them out and realised he had something pinning him down as well as all the dirt around us. I looked over his shoulder at the compressed dirt waiting to fall on us. He was holding this *off* of us?

Lifting my head slightly, I breathed into his ear. "Is it heavy?"

"Don't speak," Sam growled as he placed his hand softly over my mouth again, and I felt him adjust his hips. My head dropped back, and I welcomed the cushion his hand provided.

As I lay there, I realised that my legs were still raised on either side of him. My face flushed as I rather inappropriately realised, in any other situation, we would present quite the provocative image. Was this what Ruairidh thought he saw?

Sam's head dropped onto my shoulder for a moment. "I should be able to move," he told me, and I could hear the fatigue in his voice. "It's not just earth and concrete atop us, something is pressing down on us. I can't move it, all I can do is hold it off. We should get aid to us soon, the Guard will find us."

I nodded and we lay in silence. The longer we lay, the more I realised I was not unaffected by having him pressing down on me, his breath warm against my neck. I had a large, not unattractive male between my legs, one hand in my hair, the other resting to the side of my face. My legs were drawn up, resting loosely around him, and my arms were still hooked around his neck. Sam moved again, and I almost groaned. He sensed it and looked at me questioningly. When I didn't meet his look, he nudged my head slightly. In exasperation, I glared at him and felt my cheeks redden when I saw the knowing look in his eyes. His hips moved again, and I looked at him in alarm. A small smirk formed on his lips, and I stared at them for too long.

"Stop it," I hissed even as my tummy flipped when he pressed into me again. "You're not making this easier," I reprimanded him.

"Demon," he said as way of explanation, and I saw an almost grin appear. However, the near smile was gone as he met my incredulous glare, and he dipped his head slightly in acknowledgement of my reprimand, but I could have sworn I saw the smirk return.

We lay there longer, my body temperature soaring with Sam lying on top of me. His weight was becoming too heavy, and I tried to drag in some air. Sam recognised the problem and tried to lift himself off me, but all he could move was his lower body. He tried a few times, but the friction he was causing was not helping my already heightened sense of awareness of *him*. My hands fisting into his tunic made him stop and look at me questioningly.

"You're very reactive," he breathed softly into my ear. "Are you always this sensitive?" His lower body moved again, and my legs tightened of their own accord.

Was he freaking kidding me? Demon or not, this was *not* the time.

Harsh scraping sounds silenced my words of outrage, and Sam went still as he listened. I automatically held my breath. A bad idea when you're already short of air. The pressure from my lungs was building rapidly.

My cough was loud in the quiet, and I caught Sam's unbelieving look before the rock and dirt erupted all around us.

CHAPTER 6

SAM'S HAND PRESSED OVER MY MOUTH WHILE I SCREWED MY EYES shut as dirt fell around us. "Hold on," I heard him call, and then I felt myself being lifted. My legs were vice-like around him, and I knew he was rising through the dirt, but I didn't know how, because I could feel the ground pressing against me as it fell. "Keep your eyes closed," he ordered me gruffly.

Bright light pressed against my shut eyelids, and I cowered into the crook of his neck as my hands knotted into his tunic. No part of me wanted to lift my head from where I had it buried. He smelled of smoke, sandalwood and citrus. How did he smell like an expensive bodywash when the ground was literally falling around us? I breathed in his scent deeply. As things went, it wasn't a bad smell to die to.

"Just a bit more," I heard him assure me, and then we were moving down. Was he crouching? I screamed when we leapt *up*, as my stomach felt like it had fallen out of my body. Fresh air swept over me, encouraging me to open my eyes and look around. We were in the middle of a field, and it was dusk. The sky looked absolutely stunning with its mix of purples and pinks. I went to unwind myself from Sam when his hand caught under my butt and his fingers dug into me as he pressed me close. "Not yet," he warned me.

Turning my head, I saw the dark shadows surrounding us. I couldn't make out features or actual body shapes, but there were *many*, too many, shadows. "Sam?" I asked softly.

"I have this," he told me with a quick glance.

"There are too many." I tried to move off him again. "Let me down."

"No." His arm held me tight. "It's not me they're interested in, witch."

"My name is Star," I grouched at him while I fitted myself tightly into his hold. "You don't even like me, why not let them have me?"

"Stop talking," he said as I turned slowly to take in the shadows. "Are you tired?"

I thought about it, I was *exhausted*. "Yes," I said honestly. "But I can fight?" With what, I didn't know, but I could and I would.

"I need you to use all your strength and hold on." Sam rolled his neck from side to side as he quickly cut free my hands from their binding. "You're nice and tight around me, can you stay like that?"

My face flushed, and I had to look away from him. Could I stay wrapped around a man who looked like Sam like I was a needy spider monkey in their favourite tree? It said so much about my lack of sex life that I nodded so eagerly. Sam smirked at me in amusement as he assessed his opponents.

"Tell me what you see," he asked me quietly as his eyes took on that eerie green glow.

I looked over his shoulder and peered into the moving shadows. "Nothing. I see..." My voice trailed off as I focused on the movement. They were figures, varying shapes and sizes, and the more I looked at them, I saw narrowly-slitted red eyes fixate on me, and features distorted with hate as they came more into focus. They were nose-less, which was weird, and their skin was dull grey and leathery. Their mouths had me clutching closer to Sam, and I felt his arm flex against me, which I took for reassurance. Their jaws were open, showing rows of razor-sharp teeth, almost like a shark.

I had a really irrational fear of sharks.

"Sam?" I asked him worriedly. "Why do they look so *hungry*?"

"You can see them well?" Sam asked as he loosened his knives.

It was a testament to his strength that he was treating my barnacle impression like I was no more than a backpack sitting on his chest.

"They're coming more and more into focus," I told him as I chewed the inside of my cheek, panic and worry gnawing at my insides. "Why are they coming more into focus?"

"You're lifting the veil." Sam hoisted me further up his body. "I can't let you down, they aren't fans of me, but they really don't like you."

"What are they?"

"Scavengers."

"Who do they scavenge for?" I turned my head as I looked at them poised, waiting. "What are they waiting for?"

"They scavenge for the highest bidder, and they're waiting for me."

I drew my head back to look at him in question. "Did you send them?" I started to loosen my hold on him.

"No, I'm protecting you, idiot." He shook his head contemptuously. "Although usually I *do* send them"—he grinned at me viciously—"especially for tasty little witches."

"You're an arsehole."

I felt his rumble of laughter as he pulled me back in tight. "Be grateful I am, that's why they wait. They're confused."

"Because they know you usually *employ* them?" I grumbled as I wrapped my arms around his neck. "Are you telling me that the shark teeth monsters are considering their future job prospects, even as I'm clinging to you?"

"You like clinging to me," he said with a confident smirk. I felt his hand smooth down my back before cupping my butt again, his fingers kneading the soft flesh of my cheeks. "I could get used to these legs wrapping around me."

"Are you *hitting* on me?" I demanded furiously while his hand pressed me closer. "There is a time and a place, and *this* is not it."

Again, I felt his rumble of laughter before he reached behind him and placed my hands, which had been around his neck, onto the leather straps of his tunic on his back. "Hold on, and for fuck's sake, witch, do *not* let go."

Suddenly the snarling cut off, and I peeked over Sam's shoulder to look at the Scavengers. Light exploded around us, and I could see them so clearly I glanced at the sky to check the sun hadn't popped out, and saw instead they had let off several flares.

Then almost as one, they charged.

Sam started to cut into them, and I didn't know what he was fighting with, but I did know there were too many of them. The Scavengers carried no weapons that I could see, but why would they need to when they had those teeth? Sam spun and fought each attack, and I didn't know how he was managing it. I flinched as a jaw came too close to me, and I wanted to curl my arms against Sam's chest rather than have them hanging over his back, exposed.

I heard the howl, and my head jerked up in hope. Hound came tearing through the Scavengers, ripping them apart with a ferocity that I should have found alarming, but he was a welcome sight. With no warning, Sam flung me onto Hound.

Not into him, *onto* him. I was riding a freaking hellhound like it was a Shetland pony.

My hands had nothing to hold onto, and I had no choice but to lie low over the hellhound's back and circle my arms around his neck. "Where in the hell have you been?" I demanded of Hound just as I looked over at Sam, who was fighting with two swords of fire, and my mouth dropped at the sight.

Sam was fighting with swords of fire.

Between throwing me to Hound and now, he had drawn his hood and looked lethal as he fought the Scavengers. I heard more screams and looked away from Sam and saw the others arrive. All were hooded, all with varying weapons coated in fire.

Despite the hell that was happening around me, I couldn't not notice that they looked magnificent as they fought.

Hound tore through the throng of Scavengers, and the Guard parted to make way so that I was in the safety of their circle. Nothing came close to me as the hellhound paced restlessly while it watched the fight, keeping me safe. I wouldn't have noticed if anything got through the demons' circle until I became shark fodder anyway, because all I could see were the six of them. They fought like one and were relentless. Throngs of Scavengers lay dead at their feet, and still they fought on.

I don't know how long after it started, but the Scavengers finally turned and ran. Hound stopped circling and pacing before turning his head to look at me. Hastily I dropped off his back, stumbling when I landed on my feet. A strong hand caught me, and I looked up at Sam.

"You okay?" I asked. My throat was dry and my voice was croaky.

"Never better." He assessed me quickly before he gave a quick nod and then turned to the others. "How did this happen? How did they know?"

I tried to listen to them as they spoke and watched as some uncovered their heads, but my legs were screaming in protest at being straight again and holding my weight. I staggered as I tried to take a step forward.

"Son of a bitch," I cursed as I winced in pain.

"What is it?" Chaz asked me worriedly, breaking away from the mini meeting to hurry to my side.

"I've had my legs wrapped around Sam for too long," I told him absentmindedly as I rubbed my thighs, trying to ease the tight muscles. "I don't know if I'll ever walk straight again after having him in between my thighs tonight." I rubbed my hands quickly over the top of my legs as I spoke, relishing in the slight relief I was receiving. "He's a big one after all," I added wryly as I looked up at Chaz. His mouth hung open, and I suddenly heard what I had just said. "No!" I protested as my eyes widened in alarm as I looked past Chaz to the others to see that they had *all* heard me.

All of them were looking at me, Sam with a smirk, and then Der and Ros lost it. Even Zel was grinning as Pen watched me with amusement.

"I didn't think you'd been down there that long," Pen said to Sam with a sly smile.

"What can I say?" Sam grinned at him as he pulled his hood over his dark hair again. "The witch had me in a tight grip."

Ros howled with laughter as my face burned from embarrassment. "Oh shut up," I snapped at him as I limped across the ground to the others. "Immature little boys, that's all you are."

"Demons," Sam corrected with a glance at me. He sobered as he looked at the ground littered with dead Scavengers. "We need to keep moving," he told the others.

"Chaz?" I looked up at the night sky, slowly turning as I searched the stars. "Where are we?"

"She's going to overreact," Ros said excitedly to Zel, who grunted with what I took as agreement.

"Chaz?" I asked again.

"Well, you're not in Kansas anymore," Pen quipped, and as I went to correct him that I had *never* been in Kansas, he carried on, "but you're close."

"Close?" I looked at them all. "To Kansas?" Pen nodded. "In America?"

"Hear it comes." Ros was so eager to see me lose my shit he was almost clapping his hands.

"I'm in *America*?" I demanded as my voice and panic rose. "What the hell? Where? *How*?"

"It doesn't matter where or how," Sam said as he strode towards me. "You're not staying long."

"I don't have my passport!" I cried out.

Sam stopped and looked at me, his head tilting slightly to the side as he considered me. "Passport?"

"Humans use them to travel," Pen supplied as he too watched me. "Do you think you need a legal document, Star?" He glanced around the field, the dead Scavengers on the ground, the hellhound sniffing the area to the side of me. "Is that really what you're worrying about right now?"

I whirled on Sam. "You said the ground gave way," I accused him. "How did it *give way* and at the same time we crossed the bloody ocean?"

"We do not have time for this," Sam said as his hand circled my arm. He pushed my sleeve up to expose the handprint that looked redder than before. "This," he said as he pointed to it, "is like a homing signal. You are giving away our location. Now you can either shut up and do as you're told and let us get out of here, or you can stand here and ask your stupid, pointless questions, but I *will* cut your arm off so nothing can track you." His look was grim, the moment of comradery from earlier was gone. "Your choice. Move and stay whole? Remain and lose a limb? Decide, my patience is wearing *thin.*"

Bastard.

"Let's move, what are you waiting for?" I brushed past him as I made my way to Chaz. "Can I"—I stumbled around in my head for the word before I remembered—"travel with you?"

"Of course." Chaz nodded and gently pulled my sleeve down. "Let's move out," he called to the others.

I didn't look at Sam even as I fell in step beside Chaz, although I could feel his hard stare on my back. Hound fell into step beside me, and I reached out and placed my hand on his upper leg. The hellhound looked at me, and I very slightly shook my head. It huffed out a sigh and faced forward. Hound didn't need to see me cry, *none* of them needed to see my tears.

"Are you okay?" Chaz asked me quietly after we had been walking for some time. I nodded, refusing to look at him. "It's okay to be scared." I heard the snort of derision behind me, and I bristled at the arrogance from them. "When we set up shelter, I can talk you through what's happening, but—"

"But you're holding us up with your snivelling," Zel interrupted harshly from behind us.

Turning, I looked at them. Chaz had stayed more or less by my side, whereas Sam and Zel were behind. Ros, Der and Pen were gone.

"Where are the others?" I asked as I looked around.

"Scouting," Sam growled, barely hiding his frustration. "You think, after an attack like this, we would just stroll through the night?"

My temper snapped at his ridicule. "No. I didn't think we would *stroll* through the night. But then, I didn't think I would be abducted by fucking demons and taken from my home after being attacked and then being buried alive with an infuriating demon who tried to dry hump me!" I ignored Zel's choked laugh. "And now I'm on another freaking *continent*! So, no, dickhead, I didn't think I would be on a fucking stroll." I was in his face now. Which some part of my brain registered was dangerous because he was big and scary and I was merely *me*. However, I had my mum's temper, and she stood at five two on a good day, and I had seen my tiny mum take down men twice her size when she was in a rage. The Gallagher temper was legendary.

I stood seething in front of the dark-haired demon as he watched me catch my breath after my tirade. His green eyes were faintly glowing, and his stare was hard. As quickly as my temper had erupted, it was quashed as the reality of my situation came crashing down around me and I met the impenetrable stare of a demon.

Sam ran his eyes over me, then merely stepped around me and resumed walking. Zel grinned at me viciously as he followed Sam, and I was left standing staring into the night.

He was ignoring me?

They were *ignoring* me?

"Nothing?" I shrieked as I turned around to look at their backs as they walked away from me. "You have *nothing* to say?"

"Quieten her," Sam said to Zel as he passed him something.

Zel's head swivelled around to look at me with undisguised glee before he was heading back towards me. My feet were already backing up when I hit something solid, and I looked over my shoulder to look up at Der, who leered down at me.

"You don't need to—" I was cut off when Der grabbed me, and with my mouth open to protest, Zel stuffed the gag in my mouth. As my hands went to grab the cloth from my mouth, Zel tried to catch my hands to bind them. My feet kicked out, and my elbow hit Der in the gut. Zel cursed as I fought him, and my head jerked back, fortuitously catching Der on the cheek, and he grunted just as I raised my foot and caught Zel sharply between his legs.

They may be demons, but they were male, and I'd never met a male who didn't have sensitive balls. Zel grunted in pain, and I relished the sound even as I tried to evade Der.

Rough hands suddenly grabbed hold of me, and I was being lifted through the air before Sam flung me over his shoulder.

"She's like a fucking hellcat," Der swore behind me, rubbing his cheek, "with a really thick fucking skull."

I fought to get out of Sam's grip, and once again a hard slap across my arse had me howling in pain, even with a gag in my mouth. "Stop it. Or I *will* bleed you now and leave you here to die."

My head slumped against his back as I heard him speak

harshly to the others. My eyes smarted with unshed tears, and I fought hard to hold them back. I had to accept it. I was alone. I had no one coming to help me. My body jerked as my stupid brain caught up to my predicament. I was only a clairvoyant, but these demons were convinced that I was a witch.

Witch or not, I knew one thing for certain. I *could* summon the dead. Closing my eyes, I fought for inner calm.

I was zen.

I was so *not* zen.

I was freaking furious, and all my fury was currently directed towards the demon that carried me like I was a bag of bloody oats.

Breathe. I had to calm down and concentrate.

I'd never summoned the dead before whilst hanging upside down over a demon's shoulder. I'd never tried to summon vengeful spirits before either. This was a bad idea. I made rash decisions when I was angry. I needed a time out.

No. What I needed was to show this stuck-up prick what and who he was dealing with.

I was Star Elizabeth Archer, and I was going to make them, *him*, regret the day he ever thought he could mess with me. Closing my eyes, I forced myself to concentrate.

CHAPTER 7

THERE'S A SCENE IN *LORD OF THE RINGS* WHERE THE DEAD SWARM the battleground and basically wipe out the enemy. In the book, it's described beautifully; in the movie, it's absolutely epic to see it on the big screen, and as you watch it, you're internally crowing with glee at all the bad guys getting their comeuppance.

What I summoned was nothing like that scene of long-awaited retribution and liberation for the dead.

No. I summoned…well…I summoned demons. Dead ones.

Hound started to whine and look around as he sensed them in the night a lot sooner than the demon Guard I was in the company of.

Suddenly Sam stilled and dropped me to my feet as he peered down at me. "What have you done?" he asked me softly right before the first swarm hit. And swarm was the best way to describe them.

Terror clawed at my throat as hell was unleashed on the six demons. I literally unleashed hell. Creatures of the night swamped them. They burst out of the earth, appearing suddenly from the shadows, and dropped from the sky like ravenous birds. All shapes, all sizes, all manner of the dead. The six Guards fought them, but how do you kill what's already dead?

Der called out in the language they spoke amongst them-selves, and I heard the answering grunts and shouts. Hound wasn't fighting; instead, his red eyes watched me, and I felt so guilty under the judgement that the hellhound was looking at me with.

"You don't understand," I whispered to the hound.

Suddenly Zel was in front of me, and his fury had me turning and running away from him. A hand grabbed my long blonde hair, and I was jerked backwards before he turned me and grabbed my throat. My feet were dangling off the ground as he lifted me, and I met angry blue eyes. "Make it *stop*."

"Go to hell," I bit out as I struggled futilely.

"Fucking witch," Zel growled as he turned to his companions. They were all fighting, but I saw Der was limping, and I felt a pang of guilt. *"Nis pustuali zut prohivere sa!"*

I saw Sam look at us before he barked a command. Suddenly Chaz was in front of me, and for the first time, I felt fear of this demon. His hand raised, and he brushed my forehead. *"Samnim pytherissum."*

I went limp in Zel's grip as Chaz's sleeping spell rendered me unconscious.

I WAS LYING on wet grass, and I was sore. I was also insanely hot, and as I peeked between half-closed lids, I saw the giant paw of Hound. *I'm sleeping beside a hellhound.* If I wasn't scared of the wrath of six demons, I may have laughed.

"She's awake."

Sighing, I sat up and looked at the demons glaring at me. Four pairs of eyes scrutinised my every movement as I rose to my feet. They were around a small fire, and not one of them looked friendly. Well, I did set an army of dead demons on them. I trudged forward reluctantly. "Still got my arm, I see." Nothing. Yeah, lighthearted humour was perhaps not the way to go. "Where are they?"

"Do you mean your dead army?" Pen asked me casually. Of the four in front of me, he looked least pissed off.

"Um, yeah. And Chaz?" I looked around and back at the four. "And...Sam?"

"We thought it best not to have Sam here when you woke," Der grumbled as he rubbed his leg.

I nodded as I pursed my lips together. *Shit, he was going to kill me.* "And Chaz?"

"Why did you do it?" Ros asked me as he stirred the fire.

"I was defending myself."

"From?" Pen asked as he leaned forward.

"You!" My cry was unnaturally loud in the silence of the night. "My God! You abduct me, you're all demons, I was buried alive, monsters with shark's teeth tried to *eat* me, and then your fucking dickhead leader tries to gag me and threatens to kill me." My arms flung in the air in distress. "I mean *come on*, what the hell did you think I was going to do when he spoke to me like that?"

They stared back at me impassively. Zel's eyes were narrowed in anger, but the other three didn't look as pissed off. Or maybe I was delusional?

"You had a tantrum?" Pen asked doubtfully after a moment.

"No, I didn't have a *tantrum*," I snapped defensively even as I realised that I did. I had a big old cry baby tantrum. *Fuck.*

"She had a tantrum." Ros nodded as he glanced at the others. "Shit, girl, next time just ask for a hug or something." He stood and walked over to Hound, who instantly snarled at him. "She *sleeps* beside it, and it won't let me anywhere near it," he muttered as he crouched down in front of the hellhound. "Witch, come tame this beast, it's hurt."

"Hurt?" I spun and hurried over to Hound. "Where are you hurt?" I asked it as I checked his legs and back. The hellhound growled at me, and I swatted his nose. "Stop that, you're just being grumpy," I muttered as I lifted his foreleg. I saw the three claw marks oozing blood. "Oh no!" I cried softly. "Ros." I held Hound's leg as Ros inched closer to inspect.

"Okay, I have a salve," he said after he inspected it. "You're going to have to put it on him, witch."

"Star," I corrected softly.

"Star's what your friends call you," Ros snorted. "You summoned an army of the dead to kill me; witch is fine."

"Well, you threatened to kill me first," I mumbled as I stroked Hound's leg. The hellhound fixed disdainful red eyes on me. "Don't you start," I warned it.

Minutes later, a tin was thrust in my face. "A thin coat is all he needs."

I nodded to acknowledge the instruction, and then I gently and very, *very* carefully applied the salve to the hellhound's leg. Hound watched me the whole time through narrowed eyes, and once or twice his fangs bared in protest. I have never been so nervous in my whole life. When I was finished, I was covered in a thin layer of sweat.

Hound stood and tested his leg. With a condescending snort, he turned his back on me and walked off into the darkness.

"You're welcome," I huffed at his retreating back as I twisted the lid back on the salve. Turning back to the others, I faltered when I met Sam's baleful glare. "Oh goody, you're back," I snarked even as my stomach dropped in fear.

"Did she say anything?" Sam asked the others as his gaze held mine.

"Had a tantrum," Ros answered as he dug through a pack. I had no idea where the pack came from.

"A tantrum?" Sam asked evenly, and Zel snorted in contempt. "You had a *tantrum?*"

"I did *not* have a tantrum." *You totally did,* I corrected myself.

"She is merely a child," Zel bit out angrily. "She cannot do this."

"Do what? What do you even *need* me for?"

"We need to move," Sam said as he turned to the others. "Chaz is scouting ahead; Ros, go east." Sam looked to the sky. "Night is almost over, we need to be quick."

"Do you burn in the daylight?" I asked stupidly, and five pairs of eyes stared at me. "Sometimes, I'm as surprised as you are with the things I say," I rushed out defensively.

"And you wonder why we wanted to gag you," Zel muttered as he bent to pick up a pack.

"I say stupid things, okay, so hang me." I backed up a step at the speed at which Zel's head snapped up in interest. "Not *literally*, arsehole. I mean, sometimes I say things without thinking and I know that, so okay, I know you don't burn in the daylight, but what about the things chasing us? Do they? Is that why there was a fog when they attacked me?"

"Nothing is chasing *us*," Pen reminded me wryly with a gleam in his brown eyes.

"Har de har har, comedian. Honestly, my sides are splitting at your wit."

"Sarcasm is the lowest form of wit," Der chimed in.

"Whoever says that is a snowflake," I scoffed. "Sarcasm kicks arse, and those that don't get it are too stupid to understand it."

"You done?" Sam asked me as he materialised beside me. I gulped at his huge presence towering over me, especially with Hound coming up behind him. I nodded as I shut my mouth. "Well, thank fuck for that." Bending, he put me over his shoulder.

"Why can't I ride Hound?" The hellhound looked at me as if he wanted to eat me for the suggestion, a low warning rumble sounding loud in his chest. "Or you can let me ride piggyback?" I averted my eyes from the growling demon dog and fixed my stare on Sam's back.

"You tried to kill me and my Guard. You travel like this, or you don't travel at all." Sam's hand rested across the back of my thighs. "Choose."

They would totally drop me here to die, I had no doubt.

"Fine." I tried to move, but he held me tight. "It's just all the blood rushes to my head," I muttered.

"So that's your excuse?" Sam asked quietly as he turned us and we began to travel. I ignored him as I was jostled gently in rhythm with his stride.

"Why is it called travelling? Why isn't it just called walking?"

"She never shuts up," Zel protested. "Did we drop the gag?"

"You're a complete dick, you know that, don't you?" I snapped as I tried to rise to glare at wherever he was, but Sam's arm tightened on my body, restricting my movement.

"I need eyes north," Sam said, his voice low. "Go, get some peace."

I heard the grunt, and I fumed internally. "You mean me? Peace from me?"

"I do."

"You sought *me* out," I reminded him. "I was minding my own business, in my home, in my own country, doing nothing wrong. *You* came for *me*."

"Mm-hmm."

"Did you just *humour* me?"

"Are you part harpy?" Der asked curiously.

"Harpies exist?" I asked fearfully, trying to look up into the sky.

"She knows nothing," Pen said to Sam quietly. "This will not be easy."

"I know," Sam answered. "We need to go back to her source."

"What source?" I asked. No one answered. "Sam? Pen? What source?"

"We should have kept the gag," Der mumbled, and I heard the answering murmurs of agreement.

I snapped my mouth shut before I asked the next question. Arseholes. They were all arseholes. Sometime later, I was almost sleeping when I was moved off of Sam's shoulder. He caught his arms around me and held me to his chest. "What's wrong?" I asked as I looked around cautiously.

"Dead arm." He shifted me in his arms and kept walking. "Go back to sleep."

"I'm awake now," I said quietly as I looked up at him, taking in his sombre profile.

Dark green eyes flicked to mine, and his mouth hooked up, showing the dimple. "I was afraid of that."

I smiled despite myself. "Dick." I looked around and saw it was just me, Sam and Pen. "Where are the others?"

"Scouting and watching our backs."

I laid my head against his chest. "I can walk if you're tired."

"Look at the trees," Sam instructed me.

I did and my fingers clenched into fists. The trees were moving rapidly past us. I looked at Sam's feet, but they looked to be normal. "How?"

"Demon," Sam answered easily.

"Are you moving that fast?" I asked, ignoring his standard answer of deflection.

"*Or* are we standing still and the world is moving too fast?" Pen asked me with a twinkle in his eye, and I saw Sam shoot him a look of amusement.

"The world is always moving," I answered as I stared at our surroundings. "How fast are we moving?"

"Speed is relative."

"Relative to what?" I asked incredulously. "This is so odd. Yet oddly amazing." I watched the scenery blur past us, and after a while, I felt almost seasick.

"Your powers have been bound," Pen said suddenly. "Who and when?"

"I really think you need to let this go," I told him, my head resting against Sam's chest again. "My powers, as you call them, are not bound. I'm a clairvoyant."

"Clairvoyancy is having inner sight," Pen mused. "But you have more than that. You summon the dead."

"I haven't summoned them like that before."

"Your summoning tonight was your first?" Sam glanced down at me in question.

"Um, no." I rubbed my eyes. "If you come to me for a reading." I saw their looks of confusion and explained. "A spiritual reading to know your future or talk to a loved one, I can usually channel the dead person to pass on a message or assurance. I give peace."

"To who?" Pen grunted. "You summon a soul from a slumber, you give them no peace."

Hurt welled inside me. "I don't force them."

"Those dead you summoned tonight were not at peace," Sam corrected me. "You took them from their eternal rest on a whim."

"It was hardly a *whim*, Sam." I tried to move in his arms, but he held me tight. "I'm hardly a grave robber."

"That's exactly what you are," Pen mused. "I don't dispute that there may be some restless spirits waiting, but the majority of the ones you summon, they are at rest."

"No." My whisper was choked as tears welled in my eyes. "The dead are always waiting around for me, do you know how many times *I* send them away? I don't call *all* of them."

"You're a necromancer," Sam said bluntly. "You wield their souls and spirits for your own use and not theirs."

"No." I shook my head. Were they trying to scare me? "I help them move on."

"A soul leaves a body before the body is even cold," Pen told me. "Do you know what reapers are?"

"Yes." I nodded. I knew the term, but I didn't believe they existed.

"A reaper knows the moment a soul is being set free. They collect them, and they move them beyond the veil." Pen glanced at me to ensure I was listening. "A reaper doesn't miss collecting a soul."

"I've seen the dead all my life," I argued. "*All* my life. Your reapers miss some."

"No," Sam's quiet voice interrupted me again. "You're seeing their...*reflection* almost. Their imprint is still within your world, held in their loved ones and their friends' memories. What you see is a *shadow* of what once was." He frowned as he thought about it. "When you call to that imprint, your pull is so strong, you are bringing them back *through* the veil."

"And disturbing their eternal rest," Pen added. "You use their souls for your own goals, your own gain. Necromancer is what you are, witch." Pen looked at me speculatively. "More too, but more *what*, I don't know yet, but I know you're going to have to learn fast."

"I didn't know I was disturbing them, I thought they were restless," I told them both. "Are you sure it's me that's calling them?" I looked up at Sam pleadingly, ready for him to tell me they were lying as some form of punishment.

He frowned as he looked down at me, and I saw a flash of pity in his eyes before he curtly nodded. "You may not know you've been doing it, you may be unaware of the fact you're pulling them to you, but you are. Another sign your powers are bound." Sam looked to Pen who nodded in agreement. "You'll understand when you are free of your bonds," Sam told me quietly.

If he thought he was comforting me with that last comment, he was wrong. I closed my eyes in despair and let the tears fall. I thought back to yesterday when all I had to worry about was the fact that my weekend was going to be dull, but instead my world was suddenly demons, harpies, Scavengers and reapers, and despite it all, it seemed I was the biggest monster of them all.

CHAPTER 8

WE TRAVELLED FOR A WHILE LONGER. I WASN'T SURE FOR HOW long, because it seemed that time and speed were "relative" as Pen had suggested. Sam carried me easily, and I think I maybe dropped off and slept in his arms, because when I felt myself being laid down, I was a bit reluctant to let go of him as sleep was still a heavy blanket clinging to me.

"Where are we?" I asked tiredly as I went to sit up. Sam's hand pushed me gently back onto the bed, and I turned my head into a soft pillow. "A hotel?" My eyes were already closing again.

"Sleep more, witch, you'll need your energy," was his soft reply, and I felt the brush against my forehead as either he or Chaz cast the sleeping spell.

When I woke the second time, I was in my bed at home. I know that wasn't where I had been when Sam put me down, I would've recognised my own pillows anywhere and my bed. Daylight streamed through my closed bedroom curtains, and I took a moment before I swung my legs over the bed to go face them. I had no doubt they were still here—they wouldn't leave me without the blood or the spell. When I was on my feet, I looked down at myself in surprise. I was in my flannel pyjama bottoms and my long-sleeved, tartan teddy, grey pyjama top. The pyjama top did not match the bottoms, but they were both mine and they were clean.

The problem I had was not the fact that I was in mismatched jammies, it was *who* had put me in the pyjamas.

They wouldn't. *He* wouldn't. I fumed silently for a moment.

He so bloody would.

I crossed the floor, and taking a deep breath before I opened it, I prepared to do battle. My cottage was a two bed, one-level, stone-built cottage with a slate roof. I had two reception rooms, basically a living room and a small dining room, and a separate kitchen. It was traditionally a one bed cottage but had an extension with a second bedroom with an en suite shower room added on about thirty years ago. The extension was older than me, but it served its purpose, and Dad had upgraded the bathroom about ten years ago. The main bathroom was small, with a three-piece suite and a shower over the bath. I hesitated at the door to the bathroom because I could hear a low baritone singing over the sound of the shower running.

The thought of a naked demon showering in my bathroom made me hesitate for all the wrong reasons. I wasn't aghast that someone was taking liberties with my hot running water, I was considering *which* naked demon was in my bathroom, and my imagination was too busy trying to force images of a naked Sam into my brain.

Sam singing? No, it didn't make sense in my head, and I stopped lingering outside my own bathroom door like a complete perv. My kitchen was at the back of the cottage, and I headed to it on quiet feet. I heard the low murmurings and contemplated eavesdropping, but they went silent, and Ros's head stuck out the kitchen door suddenly as he looked at me.

"You're awake," he said as he ran his eyes over me, and I saw his eyebrows rise in surprise as he took in my attire. Ros was not the one who changed my clothes.

"Have I been asleep long?" I asked him calmly. I felt well-rested, and it wasn't like when they had used the spell on me before; I actually felt like I had enjoyed a good sleep.

"Come in," Ros answered instead as he held the door open for me. It wasn't lost on me that he was inviting me into my own kitchen. For a cottage, Gran had a good-sized kitchen, and there was room for a kitchen table, which four demons were currently sitting around whilst Pen sat easily up on the kitchen counter beside the kettle.

"Making yourselves at home?" I asked as I avoided Sam's watchful gaze. Chaz was missing; it made sense that he would be the nice singer. A sudden image of Chaz in the shower made me flush, and I kept my head down as I made my way to the kettle.

"There's no coffee pot," Zel told me grumpily. "I knew you would be one of the weird ones who didn't drink coffee."

"Morning to you too, sunshine," I said as I reached the cupboard above the kettle and pulled out my instant coffee jar. I filled the kettle, and in the adjacent cupboard, I considered my mug collection, hoping I had seven. I could just make it, but I wasn't sure who should receive the unicorn farting rainbow mug. *Was I brave enough?*

There was silence as I went about the simple routine of making coffee, and I could feel all of them watching me. My kettle just made seven mugs of coffee, and I put the milk in its container on the table. "Excuse the crystal jug," I muttered self-consciously. I heard a snort of amusement and knew at least one of them got my sarcasm.

"You made coffee from powder?" Zel asked dubiously, and for that insult to my americano instant coffee, I awarded him with the unicorn mug.

His look was worth it, and I smiled pleasantly as he sniffed the coffee. "If you don't like it, put milk in it."

"I haven't had it this way before," Der said as he took a cautious sip. He hesitated and then made a grimace as he reached for the milk. "Maybe try this."

Sam drank his wordlessly, black. Obviously. His green eyes fixed on me as he drank, and I wondered if he knew how unnerving it was.

"You okay?" I asked as I stared into the hallway over his shoulder.

"Where were you when your powers were bound?" he asked me.

"I wasn't anywhere, my powers haven't been bound, simply because I have no powers." I took a drink of my own coffee and winced as it burnt my tongue. I cast a quick glance at the almost empty cups of the others and couldn't fathom how they were drinking it.

"We could torture her?" Zel asked as he glared at his mug like it was personally offending him.

"You mean make her drink this?" Pen asked as he set his coffee aside. "I've drunk better in hell."

"No one's asking you to stay here," I reminded him as I stood with my back to the sink, facing the room, but my head was down as I stared at my coffee. I heard Zel snort, and I looked up ready to growl at him when Sam caught my attention. He always caught my attention, why was that?

"Your powers have been bound." His stare was hard, and his face was set in that "no nonsense" mask he wore so well. "When you recklessly went out into the fog and were attacked, the bonds that tie them cracked. You shone like a beacon of light in the fog. When you pulled the dead to you in a fit of ill temper, you broke them more. You need to return to the source of where they were bound so we can break them completely."

"I can't help you," I told him defiantly. I was *not* taking six demons to my mum and dad's house to ask dad if he did something *other* than tell me to close my eyes when I saw dead people. My Dad would have them arrested and me back living at home before I would be able to finish the sentence. My dad was just under six foot, broad and an ex-policeman. You did not mess with my dad, and you definitely didn't mess with his daughter.

"Leave us," Sam said quietly, and with a sigh I placed my mug on the counter and started to walk out of my kitchen. I heard him give a long sigh. "Not *you*," he growled. I looked at him quickly and realised Ros was grinning as he stood up, as was Der. Pen patted my shoulder as he passed me with a low chuckle.

I stood awkwardly as they filed out of the kitchen, and I realised Zel wasn't moving. I flicked my eyes to Sam in question, but he was only looking at me.

"He gets to stay?" I asked. I had a bad feeling about this.

"Where else would I be?" Zel asked as he leaned back in his seat and stretched out his arms. I watched the muscles flex, and a tingle of fear ran down my back.

"Sam?" I asked, and I didn't care how much pleading was in my tone.

Sam's eyes narrowed slightly before he looked to Zel. "Brother."

Zel's head snapped to Sam in surprise. "Really?"

"Brief Chaz," Sam said as he continued to hold my look, his mouth tightening with displeasure when I failed to hide my obvious relief.

Zel stood stiffly, and his glare was deadly. Well, I wasn't on his Christmas card list anyway, but the slamming of the kitchen door still made me flinch.

"I don't think he's a fan," I said as I crossed my arms over my chest. I went back to my spot at the sink.

"Sit."

"I'm okay here." I was too nervous. I had no reason to be nervous. This was *my* house.

The chair scraped back over the vinyl floor, and then I was scooped up in his arms and carried to the table. Which was quite frankly overkill. He took two steps and he was at the sink, another two steps back and he was at the table.

"Was that necessary?" I mumbled as he plopped me down on a chair.

"You're obstinate."

"*I'm obstinate?*" I asked him in surprise. "Are you kidding? Have you *met* you?"

"You also deflect when you're uncomfortable." Sam's steady green-eyed perusal was unnerving.

"No, I don't." I glared at the tabletop.

"And you avoid eye contact when you don't like what you're hearing."

My head lifted, and I glared at him. Cocky bastard. "Anything else?" I snapped.

"You snore."

"I beg your pardon?" *The complete audacity!*

"You asked." Sam shrugged as he finished the coffee in the mug. I noticed it wasn't the one I gave him.

"Are you just drinking everyone's coffee?" I asked as I looked around the table.

"It tastes like tar, but I'm thirsty."

"There's water in the tap."

"The water has too many pollutants." Sam held his hand up when I went to speak. "We're not used to it; it's fine for you, but you're human."

"I used the water to make the coffee," I told him stupidly.

"Boiled water gets rid of the impurities."

I stood and went to the fridge and retrieved two bottles of spring water. Wordlessly, I handed him one, and he took it almost cautiously. Twisting the cap off, I watched him sniff the water, and then with a careful look towards me, he took a drink. I saw his surprise register, and then he tilted his head back and drank more of it down.

"Better?" I asked him quietly as I opened my own.

"The plastic taste is unwelcome, but the water is better." Sam crushed the now empty bottle between his strong fingers.

"You're welcome," I snarked at him.

"Deflecting again."

Remembering his earlier comments, I rubbed my hands over my face in exasperation. "What am I possibly deflecting about? *Water* and your lack of manners?"

"You've slept for twelve hours," Sam told me.

And I was the one who deflected. Sure. "You're a complete hypocrite." I shook my head as I took another drink, and then I realised what he said. "*Twelve* hours?"

"Yes." He nodded as he looked out the kitchen window. "You summoned a demon army, it exhausted you."

"I didn't mean to," I muttered defensively.

"You are untaught." Sam considered me as he spoke. "Your power is bound, it may be that your skill is also bound."

"My skill?" I asked curiously. "My *skill* is being a clairvoyant."

He frowned at me, and I noticed that when he frowned, he looked even more attractive. How was that possible? "We already had this discussion."

"No, you and Pen had a discussion. I fell asleep, bored."

"You fell asleep, crying," Sam scolded me. "If you can take us to where your powers were bound, I can lift the binding. It is not here. We thought it may be."

"I don't think I can help you."

Sam moved in his chair and then handed me the weathered parchment. "Read it."

"Do I have to touch it, it looks...*wrinkly?*" I asked as I shied away from the offending spell. It was unfortunate that as I spoke, that's when Chaz walked into the kitchen. He stopped dead with a surprised look and then turned and walked right back out again. "He really is forming an unfortunate opinion about me," I said as I bit my lip to stop from laughing.

Sam's mouth curled up in an almost smile in agreement as he reluctantly gave a soft chuckle. "Yes, you need to touch it." His eyes danced with amusement. "It's skin, not human, before you ask me."

I reached out hesitantly. The vibe coming off the spell was not a good one. My fingers brushed the edge, and I cried out at the pain I felt from the contact even as they curled around it and tugged the parchment out of Sam's hand. I studied the script on the parchment, and the words moved as I read, making it impossible to decipher what it said. My head tilted to the side as I held it up in front of me, trying to chase the changing letters as they raced across the page.

"Stop it," I muttered as I attempted to catch a word I recognised. In frustration, I pressed the parchment onto the table and tried to focus. The whispering was putting me off—when did the others come into the room? "Quiet!" I snapped as I tried to concentrate. The whispering trailed off, and I nodded in thanks. "I just need to catch a word…" I murmured as I tried to concentrate. "Is this in Latin?" I asked Sam as I realised that the words were no longer moving.

"An earlier form of it," he answered me quietly.

"Pie…ther…iss…um?" I sounded the word out before I got it. "Pytherissum?" I cried out and leapt back as the words rushed off the paper and swirled in front of me in an almost cloud-like formation of script. "Sam…" I asked as I watched warily. The words stopped moving and suddenly fell onto the parchment.

"Oh my God," I murmured as I picked it up. It was in English.

"You can read it?" Sam asked me knowingly.

I was scared to take my eyes off of it in case it went crazy again. "It changed to English." I ran my finger under the words as I read it. "It doesn't make sense though."

"Read it to me," he said softly.

I tried. I really did, but the words wouldn't come. "It won't let me." I looked up at him in confusion. "Sam?"

He was watching me, and his gaze dropped to the spelled parchment. "Nothing at all?"

I looked back down and gave a frustrated cry when I saw the

words were all jumbled and racing across the parchment again. "Ugh, they moved!"

"Moved?" Sam leaned forward and looked down at the spelled paper.

"Can't you see them?" I asked as I pointed. I reached onto it as if I could almost catch one of the words. "And they're back to the foreign language." I desperately searched for the word I had spoken and found it again. "Pytherissum!" I called out, and once again the words swooped up into a jumbled ball in front of me. "Can you see the words?" I asked Sam quietly.

"On the hide?" he asked me just as quietly.

"No," I answered, pointing cautiously, "dancing about like something out of a Winnie-the-Pooh film."

"Like a *what*?"

"Shut up and focus," I said instead of trying to explain the very best bear in the whole world to a demon. One impossible task at a time. "Do you see the words dancing about in front of me at my *eye level*?"

"No."

"Well, shit, this is interesting," I said just as a huge bang shook my cottage.

CHAPTER 9

I JUMPED TO MY FEET A MOMENT AFTER SAM DID. HE LOOKED AT me before he slowly reached forward and picked up the parchment. "You need to stay with me," he told me carefully as my eyes followed the parchment as he folded it and then tucked it away in his tunic. "Do not stray from my side, witch, I need you to stick beside me." He glanced at the walls as the cottage shook again. "I cannot carry you this time, you *must* stay close."

"Okay." I looked at him as he reached out his hand to motion me forward. "Or, you know, you could go out there, and I could just stay in here. Out of your way."

Sam looked at me, and a small smile hovered around his lips. "You come outside with me, where I can keep an eye on you." The others came through the door into the kitchen. They had their weapons out and ready, with everyone except Chaz having their hood drawn over their head. "Where *we* can keep an eye on you."

"I'm hardly a flight risk," I muttered as I watched them. Zel was already at the window, looking out as Ros stood beside him as he went about tightening his weapons on his body.

"They could be here for you," Chaz told me as he stepped up beside me, his hand running lightly over my shoulder in a gesture of comfort.

"What is it?" I asked Chaz quietly. "What's out there?"

"Stay close to me," Sam barked with a hard look at Chaz.

"I have her," he told Sam.

Sam looked at him for a long moment, and my head swivelled between the two of them as I tried to understand their unspoken communication. Chaz dropped his gaze first, and I noticed Pen let out a small sigh. I looked at him in question, and he also looked away from me. What was going on?

"Guys?" I asked as I looked at all of them. Only Zel would look at me, and his look was one of scorn.

"They've surrounded the house," Der told them. "Who's carrying the witch?"

"The witch can walk," I snapped at him. Hound padded into the kitchen and looked at everyone gathered and then at me. With a look of contempt for us all, he walked out through the kitchen door into the garden.

"Did everyone else know that the hellhound can walk through the solid doors?" I asked curiously. I wasn't going to lie, it was some totally freaky shit to witness it.

Zel grinned at me and then followed Hound.

Without opening the door.

"Are you *freaking* kidding me?" I asked in disbelief. I heard one of them chuckle, and before Der could follow Zel, Sam opened the door wide.

"Witch, with me," he ordered.

I was so close to denying him, but Chaz placed a hand on the small of my back and gave me a gentle nudge. With a rueful look over my shoulder to Chaz, I walked forward to Sam. He was frowning at me, and I fought the urge to stick my tongue out at him.

"What does pytherissum mean?" I asked him as I drew up beside him.

Sam glanced at me once, his eyes already taking on a faint green glow, and he flashed his teeth at me before he turned away. "*Witch.*"

Of course it did, I thought to myself as I followed the demons out of my kitchen and into the back garden. My feet wouldn't move me any further though. I stopped dead two steps from my kitchen door and stared into the fields beyond the cottage.

I felt a hand brush against mine, but my eyes would not be

moved from the sight before me. The ringing in my ears was so loud I startled when Sam suddenly appeared in front of me.

"I don't have time for your panic attack," he told me crossly.

My eyes blinked rapidly as I looked at him, trying to focus on him whilst also trying to look over his shoulder and see what awaited us beyond my simple low-level stone dyke. "Sam?"

"Okay, you can hear me." He looked almost relieved. "Did I tell you to stay with me?"

"Huh?" I tore my eyes off of the fields and looked at him in confusion. "Are you serious? We're still in my garden! Can you *see* them?" I demanded as I pointed past him.

Sam glanced behind him. "You're being hysterical."

My mouth hung open. I was being hysterical? I was being *hysterical?* My mouth closed with a snap, and pulling my arm back, I punched him solidly on the upper arm. He didn't even move. "Of course I'm *hysterical,* you stupid flipping ridiculous *demon.* There is an *army* of fucking Scavengers in the fields behind my home. An army, Sam."

"I know." He shook his head, looking at me with a frown. "I told you to stay with me, I didn't say loiter behind me and gape into the field like a goldfish, did I?"

My eyes closed for a moment as I counted futilely to ten. When I opened them, he was looking at me with even more impatience, if that was possible. "I'm going with Chaz," I declared as I marched past him.

I was scooped up off my feet and deposited behind Sam with a grunt. "You stay behind me, little witch, or I'll give you to Zel."

My eyes snapped to Zel, who turned his head and met my worried stare. He grinned at me, and I was suddenly perfectly okay to press closer into Sam. "That was mean," I mumbled as I slipped my hand into his leather strappings that kept his weapons in place.

"You have to be cruel to be kind," Sam said quietly.

"What's the plan?" I asked as I looked into the surrounding fields. "Can you protect yourself if you have to worry about me?" I let go of him as I pulled my blonde hair back into a ponytail. I looked down at myself in despair. "I'm in my jammies for Christ's sake."

"He doesn't care what you're wearing." Sam nodded towards the field. "Neither do they."

"Did you change me?" I asked, realising I should have asked him earlier.

Sam glanced at me before he started walking forward. "Is that a problem?"

"Yes?"

"You don't sound too sure, little witch," he said with a smirk.

"I *am* sure," I told him with an irritated sigh. "But you're right," I added begrudgingly. "There is a time and a place for that particular conversation."

Sam stopped and looked down at me. "I'm right? Did you just say that *I* am right?"

"Shut up."

"Der?"

"Heard." Der grinned at me.

"Ros?" Sam called to the blond demon while he watched me with what I would describe on anyone else's face as *glee*; on Sam it was amusement...maybe. Even then, I could be pushing it.

"Heard," Ros said with a laugh in his voice. I narrowed my eyes at the back of the Viking demon, who faced the field with two curved blades in his hands.

"Pen?"

"Okay fine!" I yelled. "Fine! I get it, they *all* heard me say you were right, fine." I glared at all of them before looking back to the dangerously dark demon in front of me. "Happy now?"

He gave me his cocky smirk and turned back to the army in front of us. "Wouldn't say I was *happy*, more...vindicated."

"Vindicated?" I shook my head. "Only I would get a demon with a superiority complex."

Sam snorted as he listened to my mumblings. "Quiet now and listen," he instructed me as he became serious again. "You must stay within arm's reach of me at all times." He drew his own two swords, and I had no idea where they came from. He reached behind him to his empty back, and then they were in his hands. "You are safer when beside me, they cannot touch you. If they touch you, I may not get you back. Do you understand?"

"Back from where?" I asked fearfully.

"Don't worry about things you cannot change or what may be, worry only about what is in front of you."

"There are hundreds of Scavengers in front of me, Sam," I said quietly. "I'm already worried."

He turned to consider me again. "If you know where your powers were bound, now would be the best time to tell me."

My look must have conveyed my thoughts to him, as he turned again with a huff of annoyance.

"What are they waiting for?" I asked curiously as I noticed the Scavengers weren't advancing, they were just standing there.

"We need to leave this ground before they can move," Chaz told me quietly.

"They can't come into the garden?" I asked hopefully.

"No," Sam confirmed.

"Then why are we going *out*?" I looked between the two of them. "If they cannot come *in*, why would we leave?"

"Your wards are fading," Chaz explained. "The longer *we* stay in here, the more they drain."

"Then leave." It was out before I could stop myself. "Leave me here. I'm safe here."

"How selfish of you," Zel griped.

"I never asked the six of you to come to me," I bit out viciously. "You invaded my home. Remember?" I took a step back from Sam. "I still don't know why." My gaze travelled over the Scavengers. "How do I know I'm not better off with them?"

"She's an idiot," Zel said loudly, seemingly aimed at no one.

"Go back to hell," I snarled at him.

"Enough." Sam scowled at me. "We're here now, we're going nowhere without you. As soon as I unbind you, you do the spell, we leave."

"You leave me as soon as I do the spell?" I asked as I chewed my lip, my mind was racing.

"Yes."

"Even though I can't read the jumbled script?"

"You will," he answered with a confidence that I wasn't feeling.

I looked to the Scavengers again and then at the six demons on my lawn. I closed my eyes as my foot tapped in agitation as I considered the possibilities.

"Why are you twitching?" Der asked me.

"I'm thinking."

"Looks painful for you," Zel said snidely. "Can we go fight now? This is taking too long."

"What are you thinking?" Chaz asked me softly.

I opened my eyes and looked into his bright blue eyes and smiled at his quiet but obvious concern. "I'm trying to remember."

"Who bound you?" Sam asked as he gave me his full attention.

"Yes."

"And?"

"I think," I started reluctantly, "that it may have been my dad."

"Why?" Chaz asked me as he glanced at Sam.

"When I was little, I used to see the dead and talk to the dead, but one day, Dad asked me to close my eyes and think happy thoughts so that when I opened my eyes, they would be gone."

"What does little mean?" Ros asked Der in a whisper which we all heard. "She's *little* now?"

"Younger! I mean when I was younger," I told him as I rubbed my eyes. "Maybe I did this to myself?" I looked up at Sam. "Is it possible?"

"Pen?" Sam asked as he considered me.

"Possible but unlikely," Pen told us. "Closing your eyes and wishing what's in front of you will go away is not the same as removing yourself from your powers."

"You think your father bound you?" Sam asked me quietly.

"No." I sighed loudly. "No, Dad doesn't like what I do on the side, but he wouldn't do this." I looked back to the fields. "If we go out the front door, will they know?"

"As soon as we take a step off this land, they will try to overwhelm us," Zel told me.

"And we can't stay?" I asked again. Four of them shook their heads. "And you can't leave without me?"

"Is it just your own voice you like to listen to?" Zel grumped as he turned back from me. "You're merely repeating what we have already told you."

"I'm *thinking*."

"You make too much noise *thinking*." Zel's head rolled on his shoulders as he spoke.

"I have a van," I ploughed on before anyone could interrupt me. "If we were to go out front, would you go in the van and would we be able to leave them behind?"

"Go where?" Sam asked as he turned his full attention on me.

"I think my mum might know more than I do."

"I thought it was your dad?" Pen questioned me.

"Dad wouldn't know how, my mum would." I licked my lips. "I need to talk to my mum."

"Three can stay, three can go," Der said, looking at Sam.

"You can't fight them with only three of you," I protested as I looked at them all.

"Chaz, Zel, with me," Sam said sharply. He nodded to Der and headed back towards the kitchen, leaving me staring after him.

"Move, witch," Zel growled as he passed me.

"Why can't he stay?" I whispered furiously to Chaz as we followed the others into the cottage. I turned back to Pen, Der and Ros. "You'll be okay?" I looked past them to the throng beyond the wall.

"Don't get soft on us," Ros said to me with a wink. "We're keeping your pet hound though."

Hound growled low in his throat as he turned his attention to the blond demon.

"Be careful, of yourselves *and* Hound." I hastened into the cottage when I heard Sam demand where I was. "I'm here! I need to change." I quickly walked past him, and he caught my arm.

"Why?"

"Because grown women don't go traversing over the country-side with their pyjamas on."

"More delays," Zel complained as he looked forlornly out of the window.

"You can go play with the shark mouth demons, I'm perfectly fine with you staying behind."

"Enough," Sam cut off Zel's angry retort. "Watch the others. Chaz, you too. I'll take this one to change."

"*This one* can manage to take her clothes off just fine," I yelled over my shoulder as I hurried to my bedroom, closing the door firmly behind me.

Five minutes later, I was in jeans, a thick long-sleeved T-shirt and a simple black hoodie over it. I grabbed my black padded jacket and was putting it on even as I opened the door to find Sam standing in the hallway.

"Scared I climbed out the window?" I asked him as I sorted my hood.

"Scared you wouldn't." His smirk made me laugh as he called out to Chaz and Zel, and the four of us gathered around my front door.

"When we leave, you stay with me, get to the van, then drive like hell is chasing you," Sam told me seriously.

"I know." I nodded. Then I looked at the three demons with suspicion. "Wait, aren't *you* hell?"

"Semantics." Zel grabbed my arm and flung the door open. "Be ready to run!" he told me firmly as he pushed me out of the cottage and I braced myself for all hell to break loose.

I ran across the grass to the beat-up minivan, and it was only when I was in it that I realised that the front of the cottage was clear of Scavengers. The doors slamming told me the three demons were in the van with me, and my foot pressed down on the accelerator.

Just as quickly, my foot slammed on the brake, and even as we all lurched forward, I stared in open-mouthed shock at what stood in front of the minivan.

Ruairidh.

CHAPTER 10

"Witch?" Sam growled.

"Don't witch me," I grumbled as I took off my seat belt, and when Sam's hand caught mine, I looked at him in question. "What? I can't not go out to him."

"We do not have time for this," he said to me as he glanced once at Ruairidh.

"Make time," I snapped as I wrenched my arm free and jumped out of my van. I covered the small space between Ruairidh and me and fell gratefully into his hug. "Hey," I said as he squeezed me.

"Hey, I know you're busy with your guy, but I just wanted to check in. I didn't think he would still be here." Ruairidh looked towards the van and back at me as he rubbed the back of his neck. "Not like you to, well, you know," he finished off with a shrug.

"Not like me to what? Have a guy in my house? My bed?" It really wasn't like me, I never brought a guy home, but the fact that Ruairidh was just putting that out there when said guy was in my van, in earshot, irritated me.

"Jesus, Star, sex is supposed to loosen you up, not make you more agitated."

"Oh my God, shut up, he can hear you!" I protested.

Ruairidh looked past me into the van, and I saw the moment he realised my new "sleeping partner" wasn't alone. "You having a party?"

"What?" The horn sounding made me jump, and I turned to glare at the demon who honked at me. It was no surprise to see that it was Zel who glared back at me. I did not have time for this, they were right. I could hear the sounds of fighting drifting over from behind the house. I had no idea how I was going to explain that to Ruairidh if we stayed here any longer.

"You're acting weird, are you okay?" Ruairidh suddenly pulled me into his arms and bent to whisper in my ear. "Were you forced?"

"What? No!" I stepped back and shoved my hands in my pockets. "Look, I need to talk to you, but I need to go first, can I catch you later?"

"You're leaving me?" Ruairidh's eyebrows rose in surprise.

"I'll catch you later, yeah?" I started walking backwards to the van. "I'll call you at home?"

"Star?" His attention kept flitting between me and the occupants of the van.

"Later, I'll catch you later." I smiled with what I hoped was a convincing smile.

Hastily, I was back in the van, and although I told them to look normal, the three demons still cast dark looks to my best friend as we drove past him.

"We're stuffed if he goes into the cottage," I told them as I drove away, even as I watched the side mirrors to ensure Ruairidh merely walked away.

"He won't see anything," Chaz assured me as I drove.

"You sure? Is it over?" I asked as I almost turned to look at him, and Zel and Sam both shouted at me to watch the road. "Oh, cool your tits, I know these roads like the back of my hand." I turned to face the front and promptly swerved to avoid the sheep straying along the side of the verge. "Okay, fine, that was an unlucky coincidence."

"Just look ahead," Sam told me quietly. "I'll watch the boy."

"He's hardly a boy," I defended my best friend. "He's only three months older than me."

"And that would be what age?" Zel asked.

"I'm almost twenty-five." I sat straighter in my seat and tried very hard to ignore the unimpressed huff from the demon. "Okay, what's the plan when we get to my mum and dad's? You cannot come in, so what do I need to ask?"

"Why can't we come in?" Sam was looking straight ahead, but I almost felt the side eye he was giving me.

"Because you're three demons."

"Only you know we're demons," Zel stated.

"My mum is going to know," I wailed loudly. "You stood and gave me my bloody family tree. You think my mum won't know there is something inhuman in her front living room?"

"We can disguise ourselves," Chaz spoke to the other two, but I knew he was trying to make me feel better.

"No way," I told them adamantly. "I don't care how good you think you are, my mum will know, and even if she won't, my dad will take one look at the three of you and have you out of the house and me in a convent."

"Why?" Sam asked even as his lips twitched in amusement.

"Because you *look* dangerous!" I looked at him and noted his smirk. "Seriously, dude, you're like, what? Six four? Zel's almost as tall and has those scars and everything that stick out, and Chaz doesn't blend either."

"I thought your world had healed itself of its discrimination and hate?" Zel bit out tersely.

"It's not because of the colour of your skin," I explained as I felt a pang of regret at my harsh words. "It's your scars, they add to your whole danger vibe. I mean, personally speaking, if you tried smiling now and again, you maybe wouldn't look like you were going to sacrifice my first-born child to the new moon."

"I do *not* sacrifice children."

"Okay."

"Their mothers though?" His smile blinded me. "Well, they're fair game."

Sam chuckled, and I saw even Chaz hide his smile. "Yeah, you can't come into my parents' home. You say shit like that in front of my dad, you'll be locked up before nightfall."

"We're not mythical creatures of folklore that need to be invited in," Sam said to me, his voice still rich with amusement. "We can enter should we want."

"And I'm telling you right now, you're *not* going into my parents' home." I glared at him as my frustration bubbled. "Are you hard of hearing?"

"One may be better than three," Chaz suggested. The quiet calm of his voice soothed me, and I noted that Sam held his stare for a long moment before he nodded curtly.

"Yeah?" I asked hopefully as I looked to Sam for confirmation.

"Fine."

"Then Chaz will come in with me." I looked to the demon in the rear-view mirror. "That okay?"

"Of course." Chaz smiled at me, and I returned it with one of my own.

"Cool."

I pointedly ignored the low growl that emitted from Sam and the disgruntled look of Zel's, who sat sullenly looking out of the window as we drove the remaining way to Inverness in silence.

When we got to my mum and dad's street, I pulled over. "Where are you going when we're inside?" I asked Sam as I checked my hair in the visor mirror. It was tied back in a messy bun, and as I scrutinised it to see if mum would know I hadn't washed it, I felt his hard stare.

"We won't be seen."

"Are you invisible?" I snarked at him.

"Do I *look* invisible to you?" His look was condescending.

"Oh forget it." I scowled at him. "Get out." His eyebrows rose, and I looked over my shoulder to Zel. "Both of you, out. I can't drive up with you in the van. Go scare small children and their mothers."

Both of them exited, and I watched as they walked along the pavement. How the hell did they think they would blend? I said as much to Chaz, who snorted out a laugh, and then I realised he was never going to blend either. "Crap, you can't go in like that."

"I have an undershirt under this tunic," he said as he pulled the tunic over his head. It looked for all intents and purposes like a long-sleeved white T-shirt. I should have averted my eyes from the strip of bronze skin that he revealed as he pulled the tunic off, but I didn't. Chaz cleared his throat, and I hastily looked out the window. "There's nothing I can do about the leathers," he said apologetically.

"I can fix that." I turned fully in my seat to look at him in the back of the van. "That overnight bag, the one with the brown trim." I pointed and Chaz followed the line of my finger. "Ruairidh leaves his shit at mine all the time, so there's jeans in there that he left last time that I was going to return before all… this." I eyed the demon critically. "I think you may beat him on leg length though, you're going to have to tuck them in your boots and hope no one notices."

Chaz held up a pair of faded black skinny jeans and looked from them to me. "Star?"

"I didn't say they were nice, but they beat leather trousers in the north of Scotland in October." I sighed loudly. "It isn't Halloween yet," I added defensively.

"No peeking this time," Chaz said with a small smile as he started to unbutton his trousers, and I turned hastily away, my own grin wide on my face.

I heard him huffing and puffing, and I felt bad for him. "They too tight?"

"They're buttoned," he grumbled, "just don't ask me to sit down."

"Can I look?" I asked tentatively.

"No." His tone was sharp and actually made me jump a little.

"Star, these are…*indecent.*"

"Huh?" I turned in the seat, and my mouth dropped open. The jeans were snug across his thighs, and as I thought, they were too short on his leg, but the boots would hide that. What the boots wouldn't hide was the "appendage" clearly outlined in his trousers. "Whoa."

"Star!" Chaz protested, grabbing his tunic and holding it in front of him.

"Holy shit, Chaz, what the hell?" I started to laugh as his face turned scarlet. "Does your T-shirt even cover that?"

"You're a cruel woman," Chaz grumbled as he opened the back of the van and jumped out. He pulled his boots on, and then he stood as he pulled in vain at his undershirt.

"Can you tuck it?" I asked as I got out and fixed my hoody.

"Tuck it?" Chaz looked at me with wide eyes. "*Where?*"

"I dunno, slip it, um, under? Or something." I shrugged as I watched his eyes get wider. "Oh my Lord, I didn't say cut it *off*! Stop looking like I just suggested castration."

"I'm going to make this easy for you. I can't tuck it, hide it, slip it under, or whatever ludicrous thing you are going to mention next. At the moment, all I can do is shove it down and hope for the best."

I bit my lip to stop from laughing as I turned my head away from him, but my laughter couldn't be quelled, and I started to giggle. "I'm sorry."

"He has no other clothes?" Chaz asked as he rummaged through the bag. He pulled out an old hoodie and held it up to his chest. "Why is this man so puny?"

"He isn't *puny*," I defended my best friend. "He just isn't a demon." I walked up to Chaz and looked down. "How about you tie it around your waist?"

"I don't understand."

Taking the hoodie off of him, I pulled it around his waist and tried to tie a loose knot. The arm of the hoodie draped down his thigh and, if anything, brought attention to what we were trying to hide. "Shit." I stood back and looked at it, I mean the problem, I considered the problem.

"Why are you still out here?"

I jumped when Sam spoke and turned to face him and Zel. Both were wearing T-shirts, fashionable navy padded jackets and nice straight-legged jeans. Zel had acquired a hoodie and had it pulled up over his head. I narrowed my eyes at them. "How?" I asked as I gestured to their clothes.

"What the fuck are you wearing?" Zel barked out a laugh as he looked at Chaz and then bent over laughing at his friend's humiliation.

Sam spoke to Chaz in that language I didn't know, and Chaz's face flared with embarrassment as Zel laughed harder.

"Stop it!" I chastised both of them. "You're being cruel."

"You waste time out here," Sam said to me as he sobered. "Come, witch, let's meet the parents."

"I'm going with Chaz," I resisted stubbornly, but my gaze flicked to Chaz's groin again, and I looked away. "Did you at least bring him clothes?" I asked as Sam took my arm and started to walk down the street.

"He will be properly attired when we return," Sam said solemnly even as his lips twitched.

"Poor guy," I said as I looked over my shoulder and saw that Zel was still laughing and Chaz was hurriedly pulling his tunic back over his head. "Although maybe I should say poor woman."

"Woman?" Sam glanced at me curiously.

"Well, he's packing quite a punch down there, know what I mean?" He looked at me, his face blank, and I felt my own cheeks flush. "I'm just saying, you know." I shrugged.

"Saying what?"

"Ow."

"Ow?" Sam was definitely trying not to laugh at me. "You're so young and clueless," he chuckled as we walked together.

"Shut up," I muttered as I pulled him to a stop at the gate. "Mum and dad's house. And ooh goody, they're both home." My sarcasm was lost on him as he considered the semi-detached house.

"This is good, we want them both here." Sam nodded in agreement, and I fought the eye roll when he glanced down at me. "Make this believable."

"Make what believable?" I asked him in confusion. A couple walking their dog across the street caught his attention, and with a frown, he looked down at me again. His large hand enclosed around mine. "Sam?"

"Holding hands will relax them, yes?"

I looked up at the dark-haired demon and wondered what on earth I could say. "Um, sure. I guess?" No. My dad wasn't going to fall for this at all.

"Come, let's get this over with." Sam led me down the garden path and knocked hard on the front door.

"It's my house, Sam, I can go in," I hissed at him.

"Would you bring your beau in with you, unannounced?" he asked me as we waited.

"Okay, you cannot say *beau*." My whisper was low and fierce. "They'll think you're a male escort."

"I *am* a male escort," Sam said in bemusement just as my dad opened the door.

"Star?" Dad asked me even as he took in Sam and our joined hands. "What's going on?"

"Hi, Dad," I greeted with so much fake enthusiasm it took my dad's attention off of the hulking demon beside me. "Surprise!" I added lamely.

This was going to go horribly, horribly wrong. I could feel it in my bones before I even took one step inside the house.

CHAPTER 11

WE SAT IN THE LIVING ROOM, SAM AND I ON THE SOFA, WITH DAD watching us while Mum made us tea. Sam sat effortlessly, his hands resting on his thighs, my hand still tangled with his, and every time I tried to wiggle free, he didn't relinquish his grip.

"You're not working today?" my dad asked me. This was the third time he had asked me, and I forced the smile.

"Yeah, this morning I was in the office, like I said, then Sam met me for lunch, and now we're here."

"Where'd you go for lunch?" Dad asked me casually as he eyeballed Sam.

"The Mustard Place," Sam answered easily. "Isn't that what it's called, pumpkin?"

Pumpkin? I nodded in agreement because I knew I wouldn't be able to speak. Dad's eyes narrowed infinitesimally as he watched him, and I felt my palms get sweatier.

"Here we go," Mum said joyfully as she walked into the living room with a tray overladen with the teapot, teacups and a plate of shortbread.

"Wow, Mum, you brought out Gran's china." This was terrible, she was genuinely excited that I brought a guy home.

"Well, if I don't use them, then they just sit there, taking up space." She beamed at Sam, who smiled back. His smile was so dazzling and easy I gaped at him. "Biscuit?" Mum offered him.

"They're cookies," I muttered. "We call them biscuits here."

"You're American?" Dad asked sharply.

"No," Sam answered as he reached forward and picked up a piece of shortbread. "Thank you, Mrs Archer," he added with another smile.

My dad's eyes were so narrow now I was sure they were

going to close. "Where are you from, Sam? How do you know Star? When did you meet?"

"Whoa, Dad, let's ease off on the interrogation, eh?" I forced a laugh. "Sam's Italian." What was I even saying? "Do you know he can speak Latin?"

"Can he speak Italian?" my dad asked me shrewdly.

"*Ciao, mi chiamo Sam, come stai oggi? Hai una bella casa. Sai parlare italiano?*" Sam met my dad's look steadily.

"Oh my." My mum beamed at him. "Such a beautiful language, what did you say?"

"You have a beautiful home, Mrs Archer," Sam said as he smiled at her again.

"Oh, well." My mum *giggled*. "Thank you."

"Okay, anyway," I cut her off and gave Sam the side eye. "Um, we were just passing by and wanted to say hello." I took my teacup off Mum with a murmured thanks.

"Sam, do you take milk?" Mum asked sweetly. He declined, and when his massive hand reached out to take the tiny delicate cup off my mum, I feared for the china.

I sat in silence as Sam ate his shortbread, his eyes roaming over the furniture as my mum asked him less aggressive questions than my dad did. My dad sipped his tea and watched him the whole time.

I picked up my teacup and took a sip just as my dad asked, "So why did I hear you tell Star that you were a male escort?"

I sprayed my tea everywhere when Dad spoke, and all three of them looked at me in disbelief. "Sorry," I murmured as I dabbed my chin with a napkin and then looked at the napkin and then at Mum. "Napkins?"

"You didn't need to go to any extra measures for me," Sam said to Mum as he rubbed my back gently. "Are you okay?" His look to me was hard and held a warning, and I wanted to stick my tongue out at him.

"I'm fine." I nodded.

"It's a little joke between my pumpkin and me." Sam turned to my dad with a smile.

"Care to share?" Dad asked me as he drank his own tea.

No. I have no answer. "Um, well, you can see *Sam*," I stammered as I waved my hand up and down in front of him. "I mean, he looks like he should be on a Chippendales stage or something, and the fact I met him *here*, in Inverness, ya know." I bit my lip to hide the fact my bottom lip was wobbling.

"Uh-huh." Dad placed his cup down and sat back again. "You're an accountant?" he asked Sam.

"No."

Dad's shoulders pushed back as he straightened in his chair. "Care to elaborate?"

"I'm in logistics," Sam answered as he took a hold of my hand again.

"Logistics?" Dad asked dryly. His gaze flicked to mine for a moment.

"Yes. I deal with the overall process really, managing resources, how they are acquired, stored, and of course, how they're transported to their final destination."

"And what do you *handle*?" Dad quizzed him.

"People, their business, their assets."

"Really?" Dad nodded. "When I was in the police force, we called that human trafficking."

"Okay, so I think the Spanish Inquisition is about done, yeah?" I hastily stood, tugging Sam with me as I shot an exasperated look at my dad. "Sam has this ridiculous desire to see my bedroom. I told him I had no posters of boy bands or anything on my wall, and he doesn't believe me." I pulled him to his feet as I headed to the door. "Won't be a minute. Dad, maybe we could be more friendly when we come down, hmm?"

I heard him mutter *not bloody likely*, and I sighed as I heard my mum admonish him. I pulled Sam up the stairs, and when we got to my bedroom, I firmly closed the door.

"Logistics?" I asked in disbelief.

"It isn't a lie. I deliver people or things to where they need to be." Sam was looking around my pink and cream bedroom, his attention on the double bed.

"And am I one of your *resources*?" I snapped angrily, "That you *transport*?"

"Why are you being sensitive?" he asked me as he studied me.

"Forget it." I sighed as I closed my eyes tiredly. "Did you get what you needed?"

"I told you that your mother wouldn't know," Sam said to me smugly as he opened my wardrobe.

"What are you doing?" I crossed the room to him, shoving the wardrobe closed hurriedly.

"I need to check everything."

"Just ask, don't be snooping," I whispered furiously. My eyes widened when he lay down on the bed. "What are you doing *now*?"

"How long did you sleep here? In this room?"

"Since I was six until I left for uni."

"It holds onto your presence." He nodded thoughtfully. "Lot of emotions still cling to these walls, these things." He picked up and examined my little blue bear I had owned since I was an hour old, and then rose from the bed, dropping Blue Ted behind him. "Interesting."

"Okay." I rubbed my hands on my jeans. "Can you stop the Mystic Meg shit?"

Sam flashed a smile at me as he opened my dresser. "I don't know who she is?"

"Forget it." I snatched my underwear from his hands. "Seriously?"

"You were not bound here, but you have been here since you were bound."

"Cryptic much?" I was so out of my depth and confused that I jumped a mile high when the door opened and my dad looked at both of us with a frown.

"You okay, Star?"

"Yes, you startled me," I answered him honestly.

"Door should be open when you have a boy in the room, you know that," Dad said gruffly as he turned away.

"I'm almost twenty-five, Dad," I protested, given the circumstances, probably irrationally.

I looked over at Sam, and he waggled his eyebrows, which caused me to snort, easing some of my tension. I followed my dad out of the room as I wondered idly on what planet he was on if he considered Sam a boy.

"So, Sam." My mum smiled at him as we went back into the living room. "Have you lived in Inverness long?"

Sam sat down on the sofa, bringing me down with him. "Not long," he answered as he leaned over and picked up another piece of shortbread.

"What brings you to the north then?"

"Director's orders," Sam said vaguely. "Star is such an unusual name for your daughter, I'd be interested in knowing the story behind it."

Mum laughed as she smiled fondly at my dad. "Well, you may have noticed that Roy's a bit stern." She ignored my dad's harrumph and carried on happily. "My mother, God rest her soul, was always tinkering with herbs and things, and well, they didn't exactly gel when we got married."

"Jean, is this detail necessary?" my dad grumped from his chair.

"Hush now, I'm talking to the boy," Mum chided.

Boy? Did she know he was probably older than they both were combined?

"Now, my mother was a firm believer in the"—Mum flushed a little—"well, the *unknown* for want of a better word. She was always talking about spirits and not upsetting the elements or the balance." Mum rubbed the back of her neck as she spoke. She seemed almost apologetic. "Mum was always going to fortune-tellers, and then they would say to her that she didn't need to be there, she could read her own destiny."

"Gran was always looking at tea leaves," I remembered with a fond smile.

"Never saw anything other than mush." My mum shared a smile with me. "But the spiritual plane, as she called it, was important to her, so Roy being the amazing man he is"—the dead stare my dad was giving her was contrary to her words—"when we had Star, he asked my mum what we should call her."

"So your grandmother named you?" Sam asked me with a speculative look in his eye.

"Yeah, I guess." I looked at Dad. "I didn't know you did that," I said to him. He gave a noncommittal shrug and shared a grin with my mum. "It must have killed you that she called me Star," I added with a light laugh.

"You grew on me," he joked lightly, the first time he had eased since Sam entered the house.

"Yay me," I teased him.

"And I'm guessing Elizabeth was the name you picked for your daughter," Sam asked him casually.

"Beth is a nice name," my dad replied, the stiffness coming back to his voice.

"And you, Mrs Archer?" Sam turned to my mum again after watching my dad for a moment longer. "Do you not believe in the *spiritual* plane?"

"I think there's something," Mum said with a nod. "My

mother took me all over Scotland when I was younger, always telling me stories about pagan rituals and beliefs."

"Pagan?" Sam asked sharply.

Mum never noticed and carried on, oblivious. "Oh yes, she was a firm believer in Druids and believed they were still active, especially in the north of Scotland and the islands. She moved us to Slate when I was just wee, seven or eight, I think." My mum smiled fondly in remembrance. "She was convinced the High-lands were still wild and held onto the *rawness* of Scotland."

"Druids," Sam mused. "That makes more sense."

"It does?" my dad asked.

"Druids are very powerful, well, so legend says." He glanced at me. "Did she ever meet a Druid?"

"No." My mum rolled her eyes. Then she seemed to think about it. "Well..."

"Well?" Sam leaned forward slightly, and I squeezed his hand in warning, he was showing too much interest in a bizarre story. I needed to stop him before Dad cut him off.

"Well, there was the old man, Hamish MacDonald."

"Wow." I forced a jovial laugh. "You can't get a more Scottish name than Hamish MacDonald."

Sam frowned at me even as my mum looked at me quizzically. "Mrs Archer, please continue."

"Hamish was old," my mum told him, enjoying the attention, I realised, but also because my mum could tell a great story. "He lived in an old cottage about five miles from Slate. He had no electric, no gas, the cottage still had a tin roof. Can you imagine?"

"Rustic." Sam smiled, but I saw the look in his eyes: Mum could have described Sam's dream home, by the looks of it.

"Rustic is definitely the term!" Mum laughed. "I was in the cottage once, and I had to go outside to get warm!" She shook her head in fond remembrance. "We were there for hours, he was brewing nettles, ugh the smell. I can still smell it now."

"Why?" I asked. I was completely caught in the story.

"Nettles can be medicinal," Sam murmured. "Did your mother buy many lotions from him?"

"You know what, she did," Mum told him. "None of them worked. In fact, once, I had a rash from one of his lotions that I had to be put on antibiotics. We didn't go back after that, but I was older then, so that made sense." She gave a slight huff as she thought about it. "I completely forgot about that," she spoke more to herself than us.

"You reacted badly to it?" Sam glanced at me. "What age were you?"

"Oh, I can't remember." She looked at Dad and then at me in thought. "You know, it wasn't long after I met Roy."

"And there it is." Sam's eyes gleamed in triumph.

"What do you mean?" Mum asked him curiously.

"I'm also a believer in the unknown," Sam confided with a sly smile to Mum. "In fact, when I met Star, I was hooked the moment she told me her name." He threw a smile my way as he continued to feed bullshit to my mum. "I think Hamish was a Druid, and whatever the lotion was that he made for you, reacted badly."

"Or you shouldn't be putting boiled weeds on your body," my dad reprimanded gruffly.

"You were pregnant at the time?" Sam asked boldly, completely unperturbed by Dad's comment.

"Sam!" I protested loudly. "That is *not* cool."

Sam ignored me as he leaned forward and caught Mum's hand in his. She was completely enthralled. "You were pregnant, and the lotion reacted to Star, not to you, didn't it? You didn't get antibiotics." He was completely focused on my mum, and I think I was the only one to notice that he struggled over the phrase *antibiotics*.

I stared at him wordlessly and looked at my dad, who was also watching the exchange, but he didn't look shocked, he looked furious. "Sam." I nudged him.

"Jean, were you pregnant?"

My mum nodded slightly, and Sam stood swiftly. "I have what I need," he told me as he headed to the living room door.

"Sam!" I called after him helplessly. He looked at me and then at my parents. With a sigh, he flicked his hand and muttered his strange language, and then he walked out.

"Star?" My mum looked startled to see me. "Why are you standing?" She looked at the tray and my dad. "Have you been here long?"

Goddamn demon.

CHAPTER 12

"I DON'T KNOW WHY YOU'RE STILL BEING CHILDISH," SAM TOLD ME as we drove back to Slate.

"I told you, do *not* speak to me." I was internally fuming, and when I saw Zel roll his eyes, I lost my temper. "You *left* me in the house with my mum and dad and wiped their memories! You left me with my mum and dad, who had no clue why I was in the house or that I had been having tea and shortbread with them and a demon!"

"You shouldn't drive if you are excitable," Sam commented.

"I swear to God, demon, I will mutilate your corpse." I glared at the road in front of me and tried to pretend I was alone.

"He sent Chaz in," Zel muttered.

"I sent Chaz in," Sam told me with what looked like a grateful look to Zel.

"You sent Chaz in?" My glare shifted from the road to him. *"You sent Chaz in?"*

"Why is she repeating our words?" Zel murmured to Chaz.

"You sent another demon into my home to wipe my mum and dad's memories when you had been in the house and you could have done it, if it *had* to be done at *all*!" I was very conscious of the fact that I was shouting.

"I do not know what you are protesting, woman!" Sam grumbled. "Is it that *I* didn't wipe them or that Chaz did?"

"You're a complete moron," I seethed.

"I do not know what a moron is." Sam took a deep breath, and I saw his fists clench on his lap. "They are not hurt, we got what we needed, and I think you protest just for the sake of speaking."

He had my full attention again, and I ignored Zel's grumblings about driving us off the road. "You think I'm *overreacting?*" I asked him incredulously.

"You should be happy we know what we're dealing with." Sam turned his attention out the passenger side window. "A Druid bound you when you were still in the womb, probably unintentionally. We need to find his bones."

"*I am not digging up Hamish MacDonald.*" My screech pierced my own eardrums.

"Let us all be silent for a moment," Chaz spoke softly. "Tensions are high, and maybe we could have dealt with things better." He ignored Sam's irritated look. "The others are at your village drinking establishment, with your friend Ruairidh. Let us go there and plan the next step."

I said nothing as the van descended once more into a tense silence. It wasn't until I was on the back country roads heading to Slate that my brain registered what Chaz had said. "Wait, what?"

Chaz's eyes snapped open when I spoke, and Zel turned his attention from the dark road to me. "What is it, Star?" Chaz asked me.

"Ruairidh is *drinking* with Ros, Der and Pen?"

"Yes, for some time now," Chaz answered with an easy smile.

"How do you know?" I asked him as my eyes narrowed. "I swear to God, if you say telepathy, I'm getting out."

The three of them exchanged what I could only describe as an awkward look. That was it, I had enough. I swerved to the verge, and then I was out of the van, marching away from them.

"Witch!" I heard Sam shout after me.

He could go back to hell. They all could.

"Star."

I walked on hurriedly, trying to ignore Chaz as he caught up to me. "Star, please wait."

"Why are you the only one who is nice to me?" I demanded.

"We lack in our manners, it is true." Chaz nodded beside me. "It is very dark to be walking on these roads, Star."

"I'm not getting back in the van until someone tells me everything." I shoved my hands in my jacket pockets as we walked. Of course it was freaking freezing, and I was regretting my rash decision already.

"I will deal with her, brother."

"Oh fuck off," I barked at Sam as Chaz hesitated and then left us.

"You have very strong language for a woman," Sam said with a slight smile.

"Do women not swear in hell?" I snapped peevishly at him, trying my best to ignore his playful grin.

"You always surprise me when you swear," he carried on. "You are so delicate, it feels wrong when you do it."

"I'm hardly a porcelain doll."

"I don't know what that is," he told me as he put his hands in his navy jacket. "Are you angry that I did not wipe their memories? Or is it more?"

"Yes."

I could see his mouth hook in his signature smirk. "Yes to both, the memories or the more?"

"All of it," I cried. "I'm so confused. I'm angry. I don't know what the fuck is going on, and you tell me nothing."

"We are demons. You are required to do a spell, and I need your blood to do it."

"You're useless," I muttered. "Give me Chaz back, he would make more sense."

"My brother is not for you." Sam gave me a heated look, and I swear to the holy angels, my jaw dropped.

"Are you jealous?"

"You're impossible," Sam groaned. "The spell was cast by one of your ancestors, on one of my...lords. Only one of your blood-line can cast the spell."

He seemed to hesitate over the terminology, and I turned to him, as he had my full attention now. "Lords?" My head tilted as I considered him. "Or master?"

"I have no master, witch," Sam scoffed as we walked on. I was aware that the van was following. I didn't want to have a hissy fit about the fact Zel was driving my van, but it was irritating me.

"If you have no master, then why are you following orders?" I asked him shrewdly.

"It's an exchange. Of sorts."

"Huh." I stopped on the dark road and looked over my shoulder. I knew that demon had driven my van. "I didn't say he could drive."

"You left it in the middle of the road, it was hardly safe."

"Why did you leave them like that?" I asked quietly. "What was the point of the charade if you could have spelled Mum anyway?"

"She would not have remembered had we not allowed it to be a natural recollection." Sam looked over his shoulder at the van too. "If I had tried to erase them, I could have damaged them, I am not...subtle...with my ministrations." Sam held his hands up to me. "I have a heavy hand."

"Chaz is more delicate?" I squinted at him in the brightness of the headlights. "Is that what you're saying to me?"

"Something like that." Sam turned his head to hide his amusement, and I fought my own smile at Sam admitting he wasn't good at everything.

"What does the spell do?"

"Lifts a curse," Sam answered as he looked back at me.

"If it's a curse, there must be a reason why they were cursed."

"It's not for us to decide whether they deserved it or not." Sam's stare was back to being cool as he looked at me.

"Who is it?"

"You wouldn't know them."

"Ha. Ha ha," I deadpanned. "You're hilarious."

"We can talk more with the others, I could make us travel, but if you prefer, I think you may want your van back from Zel, he is likely to crash it." Sam looked to the van.

"Is he not a good driver?" I asked worriedly as we both turned back to the van.

"I think this is his first time," Sam answered as he started to walk back to the others, ignoring my squawk of alarm, and then he looked back at me with a wicked grin. "But I think he would crash it anyway," he said with a laugh.

"Why?" I was almost jogging back to the van now.

"He just doesn't like you."

"You're all dicks," I grumbled as I pulled open the driver's door. "You." I scowled at Zel. "Out."

As I got back in the van, ignoring Zel's shit-eating grin, I sorted my jacket as I put my seat belt on. "Are you telepathic?" I asked softly.

"Yes," Chaz answered.

Placing my hand down beside my thigh so they couldn't see it, I crossed my fingers. "Can you read my thoughts?"

"No."

"Now answer honestly." I held Chaz's stare. "Chaz, don't lie to me."

"Not all the time," Sam said calmly.

"You complete fucking wankers." I shook my head angrily as I started the van. "I mean it. Fucking wankers."

We drove the rest of the way in silence. As I fumed internally, I thought of the complete carnage Sam had left when he walked out of my mum and dad's house. Mum and Dad had been staring at me and each other in confusion. Mum kept looking at the four teacups and back at me. I hadn't been able to say anything at all, too stunned that Sam had just walked out and left me to handle the situation.

As I was trying to explain that I had been there having lunch with them, Chaz had walked in, completely calm and assured. Dad had yelled for us to run while he dealt with the intruder, and Chaz had simply done his sleep mojo trick on him. Dad had dropped like a stone into his armchair, while Mum picked up the teapot, ready to launch herself at the demon, who stood over a foot taller than her.

Chaz had whispered something, and it had taken all my reflexive skills, which weren't much, to catch the teapot from smashing to the floor as Mum too fell backwards.

Five minutes later, I had tidied away the tray, the china and the shortbread as Chaz *wiped* my mum and dad. Even the term *wiped* freaked me out. *They* freaked me out. All of them, one of them, none of them. I couldn't breathe right when I was with them. I had moments of normality, like this afternoon with Chaz and Ruairidh's jeans, and then they brought me back, screaming, to reality. The reality was that they were demons. They had scary powers, and they fought with flaming weapons, not a euphemism, actual weapons of flame.

I was so in over my head that I was no longer drowning, I was merely bobbing along the rapid rivers of madness, face down, waiting to go under and never resurface. I felt the tear drip onto the back of my hand, and I hastily wiped it away. I could feel Sam's stare, heavy with unspoken words. Judgement more like. "I don't want to talk to you," I said quietly.

Sam didn't answer, he merely turned his head and looked out into the darkness. A light rain started to fall, and my mind was genuinely taken off my inner turmoil as I had to concentrate on the road.

When we reached Slate, Zel was out of the van before I had even stopped. He still had his new clothes on, and I had been momentarily distracted by Chaz earlier when he had come into my parents' house with dark jeans, a normal black T-shirt and a simple zipped hoodie. He was slower to leave the van, and I saw Sam look at him once before Sam left the van too.

"Your jeans are better," I joked lightly.

"They are." Chaz smiled softly. Reaching forward, he tugged my bun and detangled my hair from the hair bobble. "Can I borrow?"

I frowned as I turned in the seat and watched him gather his long brown hair. Within moments, he had a fashionable man bun. "Holy shit, Chaz, you look like that guy on the internet, what's his name…Brock something…Hurn!" I shouted as it came to me. "No, I don't think that's it, but anyway you look hot, I mean not hot, just um…like him." *Kill me now.*

"I don't know if that's a compliment." He smiled teasingly. "But I'll take it as one."

"Chaz, witch, now," Sam barked brusquely.

Rolling my eyes at Chaz, I got out of the van. Sam cast his eye over us both once before he turned and entered Abby's. Zel grinned at me with malicious glee before he followed his master like the lapdog he was.

"I don't like Zel," I confided in Chaz as we walked together.

"I think he knows." Chaz chuckled. "He is a good brother, you should be nicer to him."

"Why? He is nothing but horrible to me." I fluffed my hair up just before we entered the village pub. "Can I swap him out for Ros? Or Der?"

"Not Pen?" Chaz teased as he held the door open for me.

"No, he sees too much," I said, surprised at my own insight.

Chaz rumbled with laughter as he followed inside. "He does indeed."

The usual silence met my entrance. The fact that six demons were in their precious pub was irrelevant. The fact that their local *witch* was in it, scandalous. I tossed my hair over my shoulder as I made my way to the bar.

"Star." Abby looked at the men before her like she had won the lottery and then realised she only got five numbers instead of six, and I was the prize for runner up. "You're back."

"Still stating the obvious, I see," I quipped as I plopped my arse onto a bar stool. "Cider and blackcurrant."

"Pint?"

"Absolutely, I'll take a shot of McCallan to wash it down." My smile bared my teeth, and she turned away from me. I looked to the table where Ruairidh was playing cards with Pen, Der and Ros. I shook my head, I wasn't even going there. My stare caught and held Sam's, who stood beside me and was not hiding his amusement at my obvious level of pissed-offedness.

"A pint of beer and a whisky chaser?" he asked with a grin.

"Cider, I don't like beer."

"Fair enough." He shook his head with a slight chuckle as he picked up his own pint and walked over to the table his fellow demons were at.

"You sitting at the bar then?" Abby asked me with a pout.

"Nope, I'm currently floating high above it, pissing on your parade."

"Jesus, you're such a bitch, Star." She went to pour my whisky, and I stuck my tongue out at her.

"I think I'll be over there," Chaz murmured as he too left me.

Typical. Six demons and a witch walk into a bar...I snorted as I took a drink. If there was a punchline, I knew the joke would be on me.

"Your whisky," Abby snarked as she placed it in front of me.

I nodded and downed it, slamming the shot off the bar. "Again."

"Hey, Starbar, what's going on?" Ruairidh was beside me. "You know you're a useless drunk."

"Yip, I'm not good at anything, am I?" I said as I nodded to Abby as she placed the refilled glass in front of me, and I downed the next shot.

"Your boyfriend isn't saying much," Ruairidh said with a glance over his shoulder before he leaned on the bar.

"Shocking." I took a hearty swallow of my cider and black-currant.

"You're in a mood, huh?" Ruairidh asked me.

"Nope. I'm just dandy."

"Oh." He nodded as he looked at Abby. "Make it doubles, Abs."

"Doubles?" I asked him curiously.

"You said *dandy*." Ruairidh grinned at me. "That means you're fucking pissed as hell; I'm buckling in for the ride."

Despite myself, I laughed and flung my arms around my best friend. "I missed you," I whispered into his neck as he engulfed me in his familiar hug.

"You saw me yesterday and earlier today," Ruairidh laughed as he stood back, and I saw him cast a guilty look to Abby.

The look soured my mood. "I'm gonna go sit with"—I looked at the demons—"them."

I stood and made my way slowly over to the others. An old timer mumbled as I passed him, and in retaliation I hissed at him. Superstitious arseholes, all of them.

"Your natural likeability is overflowing, it seems," Zel wise-cracked.

"Blow me."

"We need a moment," Ruairidh said as he came over. He bent slightly and took my arm. "Come."

Before I could protest, I was pulled to my feet and dragged behind my best friend into the darkness, outside.

CHAPTER 13

"Out with it," Ruairidh ordered as he let go of me, and the two of us stood outside the pub in the rain.

"It's always raining lately," I deflected.

"As you often tell me, it's winter in Scotland."

"Wiseass."

Ruairidh looked at me and shoved his hands in his jeans pockets. "Is it me and Abby?"

I'd been staring at the road to the cemetery, remembering how this shitshow had started. My head whipped back to him. "What?"

"Are you pissed about me hooking up with Abby?"

"You're hooking up with Abby?" I asked incredulously. "For real?"

"You didn't know?" Ruairidh flushed. "Oh, um, well, yeah."

"She hates me."

"You don't like her either."

"Are you kidding me?" I stared at him in wonder. "Why must you always sleep with the women who hate me?" I couldn't believe this. "She has *always* been a bitch to me."

"Why don't you ask yourself *why* they hate you?" Ruairidh said in exasperation.

Arsehole. "This is what you brought me out here for?" I demanded.

"No." He sighed. "Kind of. Well…"

"Well what?" I snapped.

"The guy."

"The guy? What guy?" He was sleeping with Abby, this was horrible. He knew how much I detested her and she me.

"*Your* guy. The guy with the friends who are all inside the pub, the guy who was making you scream yesterday when I walked in on you and him going at it in bed."

I had so many questions, like what did he see, was Sam as amazing looking naked as he was dressed, but I didn't think this was the time or how I could ask what he looked like naked when I was supposed to have been naked with him. Yeah, that conversation would only be awkward. "Why would this be about the guy? And his name is Sam."

"Where the hell did he come from?" Ruairidh asked me irritably. "You've never mentioned him."

"Dating site."

"What?" Ruairidh stared at me.

I wet my lips and nodded. "Yeah, singles dot match or something like that."

"*You* met someone who looks like *him* on a dating site?" Ruairidh looked sceptical.

"Yeah, all the cool kids are doing it."

"Cool kids don't say *cool kids*," he mocked me.

Enough was enough. "Really? Maybe they just sleep with their best friend's arch enemies. It's so hard to keep up when the knives are so deep in your back." I went back into the pub.

When I sat down, there were three shots of whisky beside a fresh pint of cider and blackcurrant. I took a drink of my half-finished cider. "Who am I to thank for my drinks?"

"We thought you may need it," Chaz said with a gentle pat on my hand.

"You could hear?" I asked as I stared at my hands. My peripheral vision registered Ruairidh walking back into the pub and heading to the bar.

"We guessed," Der offered.

So they could hear. Fantastic. "I thought you guys were playing cards and strategizing." My unspoken plea was answered, and they picked up their game of cards again.

After a while, I had drunk my three whisky shots and was almost finished with my second cider. I had a lovely buzz on with a strong undercurrent of vengeful bitch happening.

Sam leaned into me and dipped his head, his mouth level at my ear. "Just so you know, I do look just as good as you imagined naked."

Holy shit, was I daydreaming about Sam naked? No. I met his mocking stare with irritation. "You eavesdropped on my mind."

"You were practically screaming." He shrugged as he sat back.

I looked up at the table. Der and Ros were now playing darts. Pen was deep in conversation with Chaz, and Zel was playing pool with one of the local farmers. "When did they leave us?"

"Well, you've been moping into your drink for so long we didn't think now was the time to talk to you about what we need, so they moved on."

"Like Ruairidh," I snorted as I drank more alcohol.

"I don't see the attraction you have for him," Sam said easily as he drank his beer. "He's pale, he's not loyal, which makes him a shit friend."

"You know nothing about him!" I whispered fiercely.

Sam huffed out a derisive snort. "I know enough."

"Like what. What do *you* know?" I challenged him. Sam met my stare and looked over the bar with a slight shake of his head. "As I thought, *nothing*."

"He plays you for a fool, and you let him," Sam bit out. "Look at him, drooling over that bar woman, yet every few minutes he looks to see if you are watching. When you're not, he stands there hardly speaking. When he thinks you are watching, he leans over to her, whispers in her ear, touches her. He's so obvious he's pathetic."

I looked at Sam before my eyes flicked to Ruairidh. "Obvious about what?"

Sam ignored me. "He watches us all the time to see if we're

talking. And you sit and mourn over a lover you don't even want."

"What are you talking about?" I demanded quietly. "Are you saying he's jealous? Of you?"

"You are as ignorant as you are stupid."

"Wow." I took another drink. "You're a dick." I stood up, ignoring the sway of my body as the alcohol took effect. "I'm going to the ladies', feel free to not be here when I return."

I ignored everyone as I headed to the bathroom. I didn't know what Sam was trying to say. Ruairidh was *trying* to make me jealous? I was making him jealous? My head was swimming. When I came out of the toilets, Chaz was going into the men's.

"Demons pee?" I blurted. *Ooops.* Chaz gave an embarrassed laugh and nodded, his hand on the door to go in. "Well, it is a python you're packing, you best go drain that snake."

Holy shit, did I say that out loud?

Chaz looked embarrassed *for* me, but he said nothing and simply went into the toilets. Turning, I came face to face with Sam. "Oh."

"Oh." He grimaced as he looked me over.

"You heard?"

"Unfortunately," he answered as he leaned against the wall as he watched me carefully.

"Not my best pick-up line," I laughed carelessly. *Pick-up line? What was I saying?*

"Do you mean flirtations?"

I giggled. "Flirtations, that's kinda cute."

Sam didn't seem to appreciate being called cute. Very suddenly, I was against the wall with a whole lot of demon caging me in. "You are so young, but not *that* young." His finger traced my jawline as he watched me, his eyes taking on a low green glow. "Your red-headed useless friend is not for you." When I went to protest, his finger pressed against my lips. "He only wants you now because he has an image imprinted on his brain of me fucking you hard from behind, while you scream in pleasure." His finger pressed harder against my lips, stopping my words. "He has kept you dangling for years. Even if you were meant for him, the way he has treated you is poor. Have more respect for yourself, you're not a potholder."

I jerked my head to the side and glared at Sam. "*Place*holder, stupid demon. You mean *placeholder*."

Sam didn't look bothered by my interruption. "My brother, Chaz? Actually, none of my brothers are for you. Leave Chaz alone, you confuse his loyalties with your *flirtations*, and you disrupt our mission."

"I'm hardly a femme fatale." My hands came up to pull his arms away from the wall. I needed away from him. He was so close. "Flirting is harmless."

"Not for you," Sam growled, and his eyes glowed brighter.

"Why are you such a dick to me?" I asked him softly as I looked up at him. "What did I ever do to you?"

"We will find the Druid's remains in the morning. You should sober up now so you are ready for the day. You have drunk enough."

"You're *such* a prick."

Chaz stepped out of the toilets, looking between the two of us with uncertainty. "Are you okay?"

"I'm peachy," I said as I beamed at him, deciding to ignore every single word Sam had just said to me. He really was hot. He smiled easily at me, and as he passed, I made to follow him. I heard the long-suffering sigh before I registered it properly.

Sam tugged me back and smoothly turned me to face him. His look made me lose my smile, and as I went to question him, he glowered. "He is not what you want."

"Look, I think I know—"

His mouth covered mine. His tongue parted my lips and then

was stroking mine as my hands tangled in his hair. *He felt so good.* I was pressed against the wall, and using the wall for support, I basically climbed up his body to wrap my legs around him, even as his hands dug into my bum, pulling me closer.

Dear Lord and all his heavenly angels, where the hell did this guy learn to kiss? I was lost.

Lost in his touch, lost in his kiss, lost in *him*.

His lips left mine, and I mewled in protest but soon was gasping as he kissed down my throat, his tongue and teeth nibbling on my neck. Sam's hand moved up and snaked under my shirt, his calloused fingers amazingly rough against my soft, sensitive skin. I felt my shirt get pushed up, and I didn't even care I was in the back of a pub, between the toilets, making out with a demon, who was now licking and sucking at my nipple.

Sam let out a low groan, and suddenly we were moving. I was in a stall, perched on a toilet cistern as my hands greedily unbuttoned Sam's jeans. As I reached in past his fly, I felt a shiver of fear as my fingers brushed against his dick. *Were all demons hung like horses?* Stroking him, I was aware of Sam growling at me to lift my arse as he pulled my own jeans down.

Pushing my underwear to the side, his hand was between my legs, and I almost combusted as he stroked me skilfully. His mouth was covering mine, and I relished the way he kissed me, strong and confident, like his touch. I was on the brink of a huge orgasm. Then his hand tangled in my hair, and I clenched around him, riding his hand with wild abandon as his mouth captured my cries of pleasure.

I felt him withdraw from me and opened my eyes to see him licking his fingers with a wicked gleam in his eyes. With a grin, I moved off the cistern and sat on the toilet lid, the wooden seat lid cold on the back of my legs. Without a word, I reached forward and took him into my mouth, my tongue lapping at his crown before moving down to lick and taste more of him before I closed my lips around him. Sam's hands buried in my hair as I worked his dick, needing both hands to wrap around it and keep it steady. God, he was huge. He hit the back of my throat, and I knew I had barely any of him in. My hand dropped to cup his balls, and I heard him groan in appreciation. Picking up my pace, I worked him hard, and soon he was thrusting into my mouth with more speed, his hands tightening in my hair. I heard a whispered warning, and then he was coming in my mouth with a low groan. I looked up at him to see his head tilted back, his eyes closed as he enjoyed his release. My head dropped against his abs as he slipped free of my mouth and we both caught our breath.

We stayed like that for a moment or more before reality crashed in and bitch-slapped me back to the present. I had just given a demon a blow job in the men's toilet in Abby's bar.

What the fuck was I doing?

I looked up at Sam, who had stepped back and was buttoning himself back up. "As I was saying, we go to the Druid's in the morning, so you need to go home and sleep it off."

"What?" I shook my head to clear it a little.

Sam dipped his head to kiss me full on the lips, regardless of where my mouth had just been. "As I said, those outside are not for you." He pulled back and straightened. "And now they know it as well as you do." He tugged me to my feet. "Now go home to bed before I finish what we started and you get no sleep at all." His smug smirk made me want to physically harm him.

My only saving grace was that the pub had a back door, and I had no problem slipping out of it and walking the long road back to my cottage in the dark. I felt kind of shitty, but I refused to cry. What had I expected? Regardless of whether human or demon, the males in my life were complete wankers.

IN THE MORNING, I was reluctant to get out of bed. I knew they were in my cottage, I had a hellhound lying across my bedroom doorway. My head ached and I felt sick. Cider and blackcurrant was bad. Whisky was good, cider was bad and *always* gave me a hangover. But if I didn't drink the cider, then I was usually wasted after a few whiskies. I groaned as I remembered Sam from last night.

My thighs clenched as I thought about him in the toilets. I pulled my pillow over my face as I screamed into it in frustration. Images of him kissing me, touching me, pleasuring me swam in my head. I could still taste his kisses and feel his lips moving over mine. I felt my cheeks flood with shame as I thought about what came next. Sitting on a toilet, in *Abby's* bar of all places, giving a demon head. I fleetingly felt a twinge of excitement as I remembered how *manly* he was. Why my jaw wasn't broken was a credit to the whisky, I think.

I could never *ever* look at him again. With the pillow still over my face, and both hands curled into the sides of it, I contemplated my options.

I had always wanted to go to Norway. Especially in winter. All that snow and hot tubs sounded amazing. However, to leave the country, I needed my passport, and it was in the drawer in my desk in the living room. Running away was off the table.

I could pretend I didn't remember? I mean, I drank a lot of whisky in a short time on an empty stomach, and the whole village knew I was a terrible drunk. I immediately dismissed this. That wasn't fair to Sam, I had been aware of what I was doing. True, it may not have been a situation I would have found myself in if I was completely sober, but to blame alcohol for my actions? No, that made me out to be a liar. Plus, I wasn't one hundred percent sure I wouldn't have done the same sober, he was the walking definition of sex, and to say I wasn't attracted to him would be a lie.

So…I would just own up to being a desperate, emotional female who made bad decisions when she had been drinking whisky. Something told me he may already know that.

I threw the pillow away from me, and it was caught by the very demon I was hoping to never see again. I half sat up in shock and then lay back down again, pulling the duvet over my head. *I was not ready for this.*

"Morning." Sam's voice was full of amusement, and I felt him get closer to the bed. "How's your head?"

"Sore," I answered truthfully.

"How you feeling?"

"Mortified," I whispered under the duvet.

"You have nothing to be ashamed about," he said gruffly, and I felt the bed dip as he sat on it. He tugged the duvet off of me, and I looked up at his devastatingly handsome face with that bloody smirk and hated myself some more because all I wanted to do was kiss him again. "You enjoy sex, there is no shame in it."

"So, it was just sex for you?" I asked quietly.

"Sex is natural." Sam shrugged. "Humans put too much weight on the *act* itself. It's good you're freer in your thinking."

"Did you just say I was *easy*?" I don't care that I was thinking like that about myself, *he* wasn't getting to call me easy.

"Easy, loose, they're just words." Sam stood looking very pleased with himself and handed me back the pillow. "Now, we need to go find the Druid's remains. Your red-haired friend will be here soon, try to be convincing."

"Convincing about what?" I yelled after him as he left the room. "Sam! *Sam.* Bloody useless demon." I threw the duvet off, ignoring the fact my hair was unbrushed and my pj bottoms had holes in them and that my pj top had a Care Bear motif. They were comfy. I thought about changing, but deciding they'd seen me in worse, I rushed to the kitchen to find them all in it, *including* Ruairidh.

"Ah, here she is," Sam said as he placed his cup down and crossed the kitchen to meet me. He was wearing jeans again and a navy chunky cable knit sweater. I looked them all over—they looked like they fell off the local Woollen Mills catalogue. I didn't want to know what they had done to secure the clothes. "You oversleep? I knew I wore you out," Sam told me with a gleam in his eye.

Ruairidh coughed lightly in embarrassment, and I was ready to disclose everything when Sam kissed me. In the kitchen. In my cottage. In front of everyone.

Dissatisfied with the lack of my response, he deepened the kiss. I felt myself relax into him, and soon I was wrapped in his embrace, kissing him back with perhaps too much enthusiasm for someone who had yet to brush their teeth. I felt my feet lift from the floor, and we were moving, but Sam still had my full attention as his hand cupped my bottom. He pulled back from me and looked down at me.

"Not feeling *that* bad about last night after all." A smile played around his lips. "Get ready, we leave in twenty." He stood back, and I felt the chill as he did so.

"What?" My eyes blinked rapidly as I tried to figure out what had just happened and why I was back in my bedroom.

"The Druid, witch. Get ready. You're wasting time."

"What was *that*?" I asked as I pointed to the door.

Sam looked over his shoulder and back at me blankly. "What was what?"

"In the kitchen!" I exclaimed as my hands flung up into the air, betraying my exasperation.

"A reminder that his days of dangling his dick in front of you like a carrot are over." Sam's grin was full of menace. "He missed his chance, I won't."

"Excuse me?"

"You're excused," Sam said as he turned to the door. "Eighteen minutes, don't be any longer, I have no problem coming in and getting you."

He closed the door behind him, and I stood in my bedroom in confusion. My head hurt. My lips were swollen, and all I could taste was Sam. My fingers traced over my lips as I tried to catch up with what was happening.

His head popped back around the door. "Oh, and don't forget to brush your teeth. Morning after bar breath? Not a fan. Go, get moving, I don't have all day to wait for you."

Please, God, kill me now.

"YOU'RE VERY QUIET, STAR," CHAZ SAID TO ME AS WE WALKED OVER the uneven ground in a hidden nook of land at the edge of the Cairngorms National Park.

"Am I?" I avoided looking at him directly as I answered. I had managed to avoid eye contact with them all, which considering there were six of them, seven if you included Ruairidh, who we left in the van, was actually a great achievement. "Cider doesn't agree with me."

"And they say that whisky is the devil's water." Chaz's tone was light, and I loved him in that moment for not throwing my wanton abandonment with Sam in my face.

"Do you know the devil?" I asked suddenly. "Oh my God, is one of *you* the devil?" I don't know why my eyes instantly sought out Zel, but his look of contempt made me flush scarlet.

"It depends what you term as a devil," Pen said from his side of the area of ground we were currently combing through. "Devil to some could mean any being of hell; to others, it could be someone or something with wicked intent; or to others, a red-skinned, black-horned, pointed-tail, forked-tongue monster." He looked at the others and then me. "But then taking *that* further, what is a monster? A figment of the imagination? A horror? A bad thing? Language is open to so much interpretation."

"Um, that's a lot," I admitted. "And more than I was actually going for, but now my head's thinking about it all, and I'm actu-ally fascinated to talk about this more." Pen looked genuinely pleased at this, and I returned his smile shyly. "But, I actually meant Satan, or Lucifer. Or whatever you call him..." I trailed off as I felt them all give me their attention.

"Are you asking if he is real?" Sam asked me with amusement. "Or are you asking if one of *us* is him?"

"Both?" I answered hesitantly.

Der started to laugh, and Ros joined in. "You're so much more fun when you're sober," Der said with a twinkle in his eye. "Terribly moody when you're drunk."

"Not that Sam was complaining," Ros said in a low voice meant for all to hear.

I grimaced as I heard their chuckles and saw that even Sam had a small smile as he started to search again. My eyes met Chaz's, and he gave me a sad smile, and I remembered avoiding eye contact was key to getting through today.

"We are not the devil. Not as you know him," Pen continued as if the others had not spoken.

"So you *could* be devils because you are demons, but you are not Satan?" I nodded in understanding.

"Exactly." Pen beamed at me. "Sam told us you struggled with the spell?" he asked me casually.

"Yes." I stopped looking around me. We were looking for a Druid's buried bones. It was ludicrous, we had no idea where or when he died and a general vicinity from my mum and Ruairidh's recollection of old tales of the eccentric Hamish, who sometimes wandered through Slate when I was younger. I had no memory of him at all, but Ruairidh was more popular with the village, and old men told old tales in the pub on a cold winter's night.

Ruairidh had accompanied us out to the wilds, as I was calling them, but we had left him in the van. Sam's hands hadn't been shy as they caressed my arse on the way out of the van, and despite my glare and shove, he had still dropped his arm around my shoulders as we left Ruairidh behind. When we were out of sight, he had told the others to spread out and start searching for a marker. Apparently, the Druid wouldn't have "returned to the earth" without some form of marker showing. When I quickly realised they didn't mean a gravestone, I shuffled through the weeds, the dead thistle bushes and the long grass on the pretence that I knew what I was looking for.

"The words moved," I said with sudden remembrance. "Just before the Scavengers came." I looked up at Pen, Der and Ros. "Oh my God, I'm a terrible person!" The three of them looked confused, whereas Zel nodded in agreement. I ignored him. "I didn't even ask how you got away from them!" I looked the three of them over. "I mean, obviously you are fine, you're here." I shoved my jacket sleeve up, baring my arm. "And this is *still* here, so why aren't they?"

"This isn't the time for this conversation," Sam said as he pulled my jacket back down.

I looked up at him as the others resumed their search. "The highest bidder," I murmured.

"Hmm, what's that?" Sam asked me distractedly.

"You said Scavengers worked for the highest bidder." I pulled his arm to get his attention. "You paid them off?"

Sam looked down at me and then over at the others, who were all steadfastly not paying attention to us. "It's complicated."

"Is it?" I asked him quietly. I searched his face for any clues, but his face was impassive and his eyes impenetrable. "Did you help me?"

His deep green eyes met mine, and his mouth hooked up in that sexy smirk he sometimes wore. "You're helping me, I prefer it to go as smoothly as possible."

"How did you even—" I stopped when I suddenly considered I may not *want* to know how he did it. "Is this one of those things that if I don't know, it won't hurt me?"

"Something like that." His voice was rich with humour, and he cast an amused glance my way. "You letting go?" His eyes dropped to his arm where my fingers were still curled into his jacket.

"Sorry," I mumbled as I pulled my hand back and looked up at him in surprise when he easily laced our fingers together. "What are you doing?" I cast a look at the others, who were all searching and either not paying attention to us or pretending they didn't see us.

"I'm trying something," he told me with a sly smile, and I was going to ask more questions when he called for Pen. The blond demon came over to us easily, his eyes dropping to our joined hands, and his grin was wide.

"You think it would work?" Pen asked Sam, and Sam shrugged slightly. Pen nodded thoughtfully. "I mean, it could?"

"Could what? What would work? Oi, fill me in." I poked Sam's ribs to get his attention.

"Thought Sam did that last night?" Zel mumbled to Der, who snort laughed and dropped his head when he met my baleful glare.

"You know what, Zel? I don't like you either, so why don't you take your bad attitude, your bad hair and your bad *manners* and fuck off somewhere where I don't need to look at you?"

"What's wrong with my hair?" Zel demanded as his hand ran through his short dark hair.

"Nothing, brother," Ros eased him.

Zel opened his mouth to retaliate, but Sam raised his hand, and his mouth snapped shut. "Both of you squabble like children," he admonished us both.

"He eats children, more like," I mumbled as I pulled away from Sam and shoved my hands in my pockets.

"I do *not* eat children," Zel looked outraged, and if looks could kill, I would already be dead.

"What, no comeback about eating their mothers?" I asked crassly.

"Could you stop?" Sam asked me quietly.

"No." I looked away from his reproachful stare.

"Witch," Sam's low voice held a warning, and I rolled my eyes.

"I'm back to witch?" I demanded furiously.

"You were *always* witch," Sam looked at me with confusion.

"Really?" I knew my voice was too loud. I knew it, and I didn't care that I was causing a scene. "Even after…" I looked at the others, who were all fixated on anything but me, well, except Zel, *he* was grinning wildly. "Forget it."

"Did you think you were *special*?" Zel mocked me.

"Go fuck yourself," I bit out savagely.

"Enough!" Chaz cut off Zel's response. "This is not productive, and it is not why we are here." He looked at all of us. "Can we please hurry this up?"

Sam nodded curtly and moved over to Zel. The two of them soon had their heads bent close together. With a sigh, I looked at Pen. "What were we going to try anyway?"

"Nothing, we can come visit it another time." He gave me a speculative look before he rejoined the others.

Perfect. I had alienated them all. With a disgruntled huff, I turned away from them and continued to canvas the ground, looking for who knew what. I had asked them as we drove here why Hamish MacDonald's bones would be so far from where he allegedly lived. Pen had told me that Druids rarely had a fixed abode, they roamed rather than settled. The cottage my mum remembered visiting with my gran was most likely not where the Druid resided while he was alive. Ruairidh had confirmed this when he had been asked. All tales of Hamish were that he was rather nomadic in his lifestyle, but this stretch of country, a few hundred meters away from the A9 road, was a favourite walking route for him, allegedly.

How on earth were we supposed to find a dead man's bones in this wilderness? I sighed. Glancing over my shoulder, I looked towards the six demons, who now seemed to be huddled together. My eyes narrowed, as they were no doubt conspiring without me. It seemed to be their thing.

Where are you, Hamish? I closed my eyes, hoping for a premonition or at least an itch on my elbow. I felt the familiar tingle and opened my eyes. A striking man stood in front of me. Thick dark brown hair, full beard, he was broad-shouldered and solid looking, although he wasn't too much taller than me.

"You seek to disturb what shouldn't be disturbed, girl," he spoke to me.

"Hamish?"

He nodded, and his gaze flickered past me over my shoulder. "Their aid will not save you."

"Save me?" I kept my focus on the ghost of the Druid. "They're not here to save me."

"No, they are not." He looked back at me, and I took a step back.

"I need to know if you bound my…powers." I still hesitated over the word *powers*, convinced I was nothing more than a mediocre clairvoyant.

"You were born wrong," he answered instead.

"Um, I don't even know what to say to that," I muttered as I folded my arms across my chest as I rocked back on my feet.

"You came out the wrong way," he continued.

"Yeah, I think you said," I said sharply.

"Feet first."

Oh. "Ohh, you mean I was a breach birth!" I exclaimed in relief.

"Yes, that is the word they used." He nodded as he thought about it. I knew that sometimes spirits who came back or loitered too long, lost familiarity with words, places or time. It was a huge thing to realise you were dead. As shocks to the system went, that was a big one.

"Because I was breach, you think that interfered with my powers?" I asked curiously. It sounded far-fetched to me.

"You took your mother's energy," Hamish continued.

"Well, she always said I was difficult," I mumbled self-consciously.

"From conception to the last moments of gestation," he said confidently.

"Gestation?" *Eeew*. "You mean pregnancy? Please tell me you didn't refer to my mum's pregnancy as *gestation*."

"You took her natural gift, absorbed it like it was your own." He looked at me with profound disappointment. "You fed off her."

And now I was going to be sick. "Look, I don't give a flying monkey's if you're long dead and forgetful, but you have to stop being so disgusting. I did not *feed* off my mother."

"But you did." Hamish looked at me in perplexity. "You took the food from her body as all babes do, and you also consumed her gift until there was nothing left for her."

I shook my head in denial. "No. My mum never had the gift." I shook my head again. "You're wrong."

"We tried to stop it, I made a salve for her to rub into her skin, to slow you down, without harm." He looked to the sky as if seeing it for the first time. "Old magic, blood magic."

"Blood magic," I whispered in shock. "No, that's…so wrong."

"She was desperate. Her gift was strong, but it could not stop you."

I felt the wind on my wet cheeks, and I knew I was crying. "I didn't mean it," I whispered futilely.

"You were a babe, too much power." He shook his head. "We had to contain it."

"What did you do?" I asked in despair.

"Blood spell."

My eyes closed against his words. I didn't know much about

witchcraft, believing myself to be a poor psychic, but even I knew a blood spell couldn't be broken. "You cursed me."

"Bound you for eternity."

"My gran would not have agreed to this?"

"Foolish woman, used much of her power on the cottage she lived in. Placing wards, wards against dark magic, but you are not just dark magic." His look turned from confused spirit to cold malevolence.

"How do I break it?"

He laughed, and as he did so, I felt the cold shiver of fear at his laughter. "You can't. Your demon scum cannot either. You are bound, and you are *useless* to them *and* their prince."

"You knew they would come looking for me," I realised. "You didn't do this for my mum, you did this for *your* master." His laugh carried on the wind, and I realised it was now howling around us as rain slashed from the sky. "You evil old bastard," I muttered as thunder crashed above us. "Go! I send you back."

"I don't want to go," he told me as he advanced. An eerie red glow appeared in his eyes as he got closer. "They can't save you, girl, and I've been sleeping for too long."

"I don't need them to save me," I whispered as I reached for the part inside me that I pulled upon when I was doing a reading. What had always felt like a tranquil pool inside me surged up in a wave to greet me. Grabbing onto it, I thrust it out of me and cast him back to the grave. Wherever his may be.

His scream died the moment that the wind did, and suddenly the rain too stopped. I stood with my head bowed as my mind raced, thinking over what he had revealed. I wasn't only *bound*, I was bound with no hope of recovery.

"Are you hurt?" Sam asked quietly beside me.

"No." I thought about it. "Yes? Maybe."

"It is to be expected." Chaz's voice was gentle and soothing as always. Unthinkingly, I reached out and took his hand. He squeezed mine in comfort, but let me go quickly.

"Did you hear everything?" I asked as I clasped my hands in front of me, trying to shield my hurt.

"He was very clear," Der said bitterly. "Old Druid had a soul of blackness." I looked up curiously, but he looked too pissed off to question.

"This changes nothing," Sam said with confidence beside me. "The binding is already breaking, you can see the spell, and you now know you can use it. We just need to find the old one's bones."

I looked up at him in bewilderment. "Why do we need his bones? We got what we needed, didn't we?"

"He cast a blood spell on you," Pen told me as he resumed his search. "Stains your soul, blood spells."

"I just let his soul go," I reminded him.

"Your body encapsulates your bones and your soul, human," Zel explained. "Blood spells stain the soul, and strong ones? Well, they stain the bones as well."

"Find his bones, crush his bones, break your binding," Ros told me with a conspirator's wink.

"So..." I looked around at the six demons. "Did you know this already?"

"Suspected," Sam grunted out as he walked away from me.

"A heads-up would have been appreciated!" I called after him and chose to ignore his amused chuckle. "Bloody demon," I muttered as I started searching again too. I didn't walk carefully. I more or less trampled the vegetation underfoot, mumbling about Druids, demons and secrets being bad things for everyone while I carried out my search. My foot went right down the hole in the ground, and I pitched forward onto my hands and knees with a startled cry.

"Fucking useless bloody stupid bastard rabbit holes, nothing but dirty rats with fur coats, diseased good-for-nothing-but-the-pot fluffy dickhead bunnies."

"The woman's propensity for bad language is truly remarkable," Pen murmured. I heard several grunts of agreement.

However, my sharp retort died on my tongue as I stared at the skull two inches from my nose. "Sam?" I called out. "I think I found Hamish."

CHAPTER 15

I HAD INDEED FOUND HAMISH. PEN HAD STOPPED ME FROM touching the bones just as my fingers almost brushed the smooth skull. Instead, he and Der had gathered the remains in a cloth bag, and then Zel and Ros burned the ground while Chaz examined every inch, it seemed, of the surrounding area. Sam stood to the side, overseeing everything, but his eyes kept flicking back to mine, and his hard scrutiny was making me nervous.

After a long walk back to the road, I was not in the least surprised to find Ruairidh stretched out on the back seats, fast asleep.

"Why do you even have a van?" Zel asked me as he glared at Ruairidh's sleeping form.

"Oh, it was my gran's," I said with a fond smile. "Gran couldn't drive, but she used to make people drive her around the Highlands to do readings. She would do tarot readings and stuff in the van."

"Explains a lot," Der said with a thoughtful nod.

"It does?" I asked curiously. I got in the van even as Ros unceremoniously sat on top of Ruairidh. "Seriously?" I snapped peevishly.

Ruairidh jerked awake and struggled to sit up. His protests were smothered with the laughter of the others, and within moments I was grinning at their antics. "You're pains in the arse, you know that, don't you," I snickered as I started the engine. "I think I need a hot bath to get rid of the chill in my bones tonight," I said to no one in particular as we started the journey back.

"So, did you find anything?" Ruairidh asked as he looked at us all. "Why couldn't I come?"

"Someone had to stay with the van," I fed him the same bullshit lie that I had told him when we got here. Sam didn't care what I had told him, as long as he didn't follow.

"But did you find anything useful?" Ruairidh asked again.

"We found Hamish's bones," I told him, ignoring Sam's sharp glance.

"Oh." Ruairidh looked at the others in the car. "Um, that good?"

"Very much so," Pen murmured as he leaned his head back.

"You need them for a reading?" Ruairidh was digging, and I wasn't sure how to explain this to him. How do you tell someone they're in a van with six demons? Ruairidh never doubted my ability to see spirits, but he also never *saw*, and I feared that this was maybe not the time to test his "seeing is believing" attitude.

Ruairidh looked over the demons speculatively, his stare resting on Sam for too long, and then he met my stare dead on in the rear-view mirror. "Star's seen dead people for years. She turned it off, but it came screaming back when she left here," Ruairidh said.

I knew exactly where he was going with this. "They don't need to know this," I said with a meaningful glance at him in the rear-view mirror.

"She left?" Sam asked as he turned slightly in his seat and looked over his shoulder to Ruairidh. "Where did you go?" he asked me.

"Not far," I answered him with a fake smile and clenched teeth.

"St Andrews is pretty far from Slate, Star. Especially when you could have gone to Inverness to study." Ruairidh shook his head at me in amusement.

"St Andrews?" Pen perked up in the back. "The town?"

"Yes." Ruairidh darted a quick glance to Sam and dipped his head. "She went there for university."

"A long way to go for education." Chaz was looking at me curiously.

"Not really," I objected slightly. "It's only three hours away."

I saw Ruairidh glance at Sam again, and I caught his eye. Ruairidh looked away hurriedly. "It was my fault," he admitted as he pretended to look at his hands. My eyes narrowed as I watched him.

"And why was that?" Sam asked him, his eyes fixed on me.

"I upset Star, so she wanted to put distance between us." Ruairidh was still playing coy, and my temper was rising.

"Ruairidh, enough," I warned him.

"And what did you *do*?" Sam asked, turning his hard stare to my best friend.

"Well, I kinda slept with her nemesis." Ruairidh tried to laugh it off, ignoring my disgusted shake of my head.

"The bar wench?" Der asked, his head moving between us both, trying to put the pieces together.

"Did you say *wench*?" I asked him incredulously.

"Abby?" Ruairidh laughed guiltily. Oh good, he was realising he looked like a dick with this story. "Err. No. Bonnie."

"Who's Bonnie?" Zel asked as he looked my way with a gleam in his eye.

"She was kinda a bitch to Star in school. On our last day, she and her friend Steven chucked buckets of red paint over Star and chanted *Carrie*." He saw their blank stares. "You know, from the Stephen King book?"

"Fun times," I grumbled as I felt my cheeks heat.

"You had sex with this vile thing? Did you know she was like that before you slept with her?" Chaz's eyes were wide.

I pursed my lips together and thought the less they knew, the better. I realised that Ruairidh finally knew it too and was grateful he shut up.

"You slept with her *after* she humiliated your best friend," Sam said in the quiet of the van. I could feel his heavy stare, and I absolutely refused to make eye contact with him.

"Well," Ruairidh said and then opted for humour. "She gave me a blowie. I mean, it's hard to think straight in that situation, you know?"

Oh Rue, you complete arsehole.

"I mean, *you* know that, don't you?" Ruairidh said as he leaned forward and nudged Sam's shoulder. The speed with which Sam's hand wrapped around Ruairidh's wrist made my mouth drop.

"No, I *don't* know." His grin was full of danger. "By keeping my dick out of women who would try to cause a friend harm, physically and emotionally, I find is what helps me *think* straight."

"Sam, stop." My voice was hushed in the van. "Please. It was a long time ago."

"And you *still* defend him," he spat out in contempt. "He is not worth your loyalty."

"Enough." I kept my voice steady. I looked over into those perfect forest green eyes and tried a smile. "It's not a problem."

Sam held the look for longer than was probably necessary given I was actually driving a vehicle. He gave a curt nod and looked out the window into the darkening sky. I surprised us both when I reached over and took his hand. Wordlessly, he laced his fingers through mine, and we drove in silence.

"What happened in St Andrews?" Ros asked after a while when we were almost back at Slate.

"My gran died," I answered. "Her spirit came to me in the old cathedral."

"Just hers?" Pen asked shrewdly.

"No," I huffed in remembrance. "It was a busy day."

"The first break," Pen murmured to the others.

"Significant too," Chaz said as he nodded thoughtfully. "The loss would warrant a forceful break."

"The cathedral is a ruin now," Zel told Sam. "Although it is still consecrated ground."

"You think that's the place?" Sam asked, and Zel, as well as Pen, nodded. "You may be right," Sam mused.

"Let me guess," I said dryly. "Tomorrow we go to St Andrews?"

"How did you know?" Ros teased with a grin.

"Clairvoyant, remember?" Thankfully, my less than witty sarcasm broke the tension in the van as they laughed at my poor joke. Ruairidh was sitting in silence, but since he had decided to describe one of my worst experiences followed by a day of loss, I opted not to make him feel better. Let him stew a little bit longer.

The general consensus was that they would return to the pub. I wasn't sure if they were prone to Abby's beer or gleaning information from the locals, but not having six demons in my cottage tonight meant I could get that nice long bubble bath.

They called goodbye as they piled out of the van, and I sat and looked at Sam. "Um?"

"Witch?" Sam's eyes twinkled with amusement.

"Demon," I answered with an eye roll.

Sam leaned forward, his hand slipping behind my neck as he pulled me closer, his lips close to mine. "Tell me to go into the bar," he said against my lips.

"Or?"

"Or you take me to your bed, and I fuck you all night long." His tongue licked my bottom lip in a soft caress, and I pushed forward slightly to catch his kiss, but he moved back slightly. "Your choice," he said as he watched me with narrowed eyes.

"All night?" I whispered as I reached out and pulled him closer.

"You won't sleep," he promised as his other hand curled around my waist.

"I don't know if that's a promise or a threat," I sighed as I unclipped my seat belt and very easily, and slightly alarmed at my lack of care, I manoeuvred over the centre console and fit myself into Sam's lap. My hands travelled over his chest and curled up into his hair as I looked down at him in the dimly lit van. "Tell me, demon, what do you think I should do?" My words were muted against his lips before I captured them with my own. He let me kiss him for a moment, maybe more, before his hand was slipping to my jaw, angling my head the way he wanted, as he kissed me passionately. My hand slipped past his collar and down his back, trailing over the taught muscles of his back.

I felt a rush of cold air before his warm hand was sliding up my back. He'd unzipped my jacket and worked his hand under my jumper. Sam's hands dropped to my hips, and he ground me down on him. I felt his hardened length as it rubbed against the apex of my thighs. I remembered his size vividly from the previous night, and I felt apprehensive at the thought of it anywhere near my nether regions. But when he did it again, the friction was so good, I lost my inhibitions about size and moved my hips slowly over him.

"I need to fuck you, witch," Sam groaned as his nose skimmed my jaw before his lips were on my neck, causing me to pant.

I was seconds from agreeing when a loud bang made me jump. Opening my eyes, I saw Ruairidh standing in front of the pub. His look of condemnation felt like it burned me as he turned to go back inside. I pushed myself away from Sam's hold and clumsily climbed back to the driver's side.

"You should join your friends," I said hoarsely, avoiding his harsh glare.

"You should choose what *you* want," Sam bit out before he got out of the van. "Trust me, it's not him," he added before he slammed the door behind him.

I drove home with my feelings in turmoil. I didn't even like the demon. No, I did like the demon. Kind of. He was sexy. To be fair, Zel was sexy, he just killed your libido because he was an obvious psychopath. They were *all* sexy. Sam was just…more. My groan was low and tortured in the van. So much more. He was *so* much *more*. He made my heart race, but then so did Zel and possibly Der. Only that was possibly fear.

Sam made my heart race with excitement, he made my tummy flip with butterflies when he gave me that long sexy smirk. His kisses left me breathless, his touch made me erupt in pleasure. I had absolutely no idea why I was driving *away* from him.

Ruairidh.

Ugh, he didn't even fucking *want* me. He had never wanted me, why was I turning down a perfectly good demon…wait, what? A perfectly good demon? I bit my lip. Was that my problem? Because Sam was a demon? I didn't even know what *kind* of demons there were. Could you Google demons? I snort laughed at my own stupidity in the van as I parked at my cottage.

Hound stood in front of the house like a vigilant watchdog.

"Hey, Hound," I greeted as I rubbed his head as I passed him. "You look surly. Miss me?" The hellhound looked at me with what I could only describe as scorn. "You know the looks you give me, Hound, are almost human."

Hound walked away from me in disgust.

"I need a bath," I told my empty house. "I need a bath and no thinking." Armed with a plan, I ran the bath while I stripped out of my muddy clothes. I was going to need a clothing allowance if we continued on like this, I joked inwardly as I pulled on my fluffy bathrobe. In the kitchen, I made a roast beef and cucumber sandwich, which I ate while I waited for the bath to cool a little. I liked scorching hot baths, no cold water was added, but I was conscious of how cold my body was, and I didn't want to make myself sick because I didn't allow my body to warm to room temperature first.

Food finished, I locked the bathroom door and sank into the depths of my bath. I let out a long sigh and closed my eyes. That was it, perfection, better than a man *or* a demon. Okay, so that's a lie, but it was still a good bath.

They had been right, my powers had been bound. As I lay in the soothing bathwater, I contemplated what powers I had. I could see the dead, and personally speaking, I thought that made me pretty powerful already. I had premonitions of things that were going to happen, but that wasn't often and vague at best. Gran had seen auras, but I never understood the colours she described or the meanings. I was guessing I wasn't going to have that ability. When I did my readings at home now, I used a crystal ball and stones as props. I had never seen anything in a crystal ball except my upside-down reflection. The stones, although I knew people read them well, were simply stones to me.

Mum had crystals in the house, she was always telling me about the healing power of rose quartz or giving me chunks of amethyst to hold and take home. The only thing I liked about amethyst was the colour. I had a jade bowl that she had given me a few years ago for purity. I hadn't been too clear on what I was keeping pure; if it was my virtue, that ship sailed.

"I'm the worst witch ever," I muttered in the quiet of the bathroom. "I seriously know nothing about witchcraft."

Was it preposterous to consider a Google search? I got out of my bath and went in search of my laptop. Forty minutes later, I had no idea what I had just read. Gran was Wiccan? I looked at the depictions of the horned god and the goddess and frowned. My gran was a tad off on the normal scale, but she still believed in God. *The* God. The one upstairs. According to this site, Wicca was a form of paganism, and there was no mention of baby Jesus. I read on as it went on to describe how Wicca was associated with witchcraft, so to be a Wiccan you had to be a witch? No. That wasn't what they were saying. You *could* be a witch and believe in Wicca, *or* you could just be a horned-god-worshiping pagan.

I shut the laptop. That was far too confusing, and I was fairly certain that if my gran had ever burnt sage it was because she had cooked smoked haddock the night before. I snorted at my own scepticism and mentally apologised to all the sage burners in the world.

It was official. I sucked at being a witch. I looked at Hound. He was laid out over the floor, taking up every inch of space. So I wasn't that bad a witch, I could see hellhounds after all.

Tiredly, I made myself a cup of lemon and ginger tea and then headed to bed. I was tired. I had an emotional day, and I still had Sam to deal with. I felt a pang of regret as I climbed into bed that I was sleeping alone. He would be much more fun than reading about quartz, herbs and paganism. As I finished my tea, I wondered idly if paganism was an alert on internet security sites. Smiling at my own active imagination, I switched the light off. It was possible I would know all the answers to my problems tomorrow.

CHAPTER 16

I WOKE UP TO THE SOUND OF MOVEMENT IN MY COTTAGE. I WASN'T alarmed that they had come back to my cottage after they had been drinking; I genuinely didn't think they had anywhere else to go. Well, not on this plane anyway. What I *was* alarmed about was that I woke wrapped up in the arms of a male. In the dark, I wasn't entirely sure who was in bed with me, and I may have called myself easy only yesterday morning, but that didn't mean I was *actually* free about who I slept with.

"Sam?"

"Hmm," he answered.

Thank you, Jesus. "Why are you in my bed?"

"Trying to sleep," Sam said as he pulled me closer.

I assessed the situation. He was on his back, his arm curled around me, with my head on his…chest? I felt with my fingers, yes, that was definitely a chest. My leg was over his, my lower body pressed in *tight* to his thigh. Wonderful. I had dry humped him in my sleep, I just knew it.

"I didn't know demons slept," I confessed, and even I frowned at the stupidity.

"Don't need much," he answered with a sigh as he moved in the bed, taking me with him. "*Some* would be nice though."

Hint received loud and clear. "Will I leave?"

"No."

My smile was small in the darkness, but I knew he felt it against his skin, as his hand tightened on my arm. "Okay." I closed my eyes again, and feeling an odd sense of contentment, I fell back asleep. When I woke again, I was alone, and the disappointment at being so surprised me.

Getting up, I went into the en suite, noting the damp towel, the wet shower cubicle and the open bottle of shower gel. Shaking my head in rueful acceptance that my life was officially upside down, I took care of my morning routine and emerged out of my own shower sometime later. Tying my hair up in a towel, I went back into my bedroom to find Sam stretched out in the chair with a mug in his hand.

"Morning," I said with a blush. I knew I was blushing, but it felt oddly intimate waking up beside him in the middle of the night. I was also weirdly shy, and I knew I was avoiding eye contact, but I couldn't help it.

"Zel got you a coffee maker," Sam greeted me as he raised his cup. "This is better."

"He didn't need to do that," I replied. "Let me guess, he also got a coffee grinder?"

Sam's mouth spread into a smile. "He's particular about his coffee."

"You mean the scary demon is a coffee snob," I mused as I undid my towel from my head and shook my wet hair out. "There's a sentence you don't expect to say."

"Zel is not…friendly." Sam sounded like he was struggling for the right words.

"No shit, Sherlock," I agreed as I brushed out my long blonde hair.

"He brought this to your house," Sam carried on as he seemed to focus on my hair.

I stopped brushing my hair in surprise. "What are you saying, he got *me* a *gift*?"

Sam reluctantly nodded. "I heard Pen say it was baby steps and that you would appreciate the term."

I snort laughed as I resumed brushing. "Okay, I'll thank Zel for the gift."

"He would like that, although…" Sam hesitated. "He may not *show* it."

I rolled my eyes as I got out my hairdryer. "It's fine, Sam, I'm willing to take baby steps with him too."

He crossed the room and stood almost hesitantly behind me, his attention flicking between my hair and the hairbrush. Curiously, I held out the brush to him, and he gently took the brush from me and began to brush my hair. "In my…culture, brushing a female's hair is considered a great compliment for the male."

I looked at him in the mirror as he stood behind me, and I picked up my hairdryer. "You brush, I dry." I had no idea why my mouth was dry, but I felt strangely exposed and vulnerable to him. Once Sam realised what the hairdryer was for, he took it off me, and for the next few minutes, he dried and brushed my hair.

"There," he said as he stood back and appraised his handiwork. "Done."

As I would had I been in an *actual* salon, I had kept my eyes cast downward; I hadn't once looked in the mirror, and as I looked at my hair, I wondered briefly what the cost of this would have been in the hair salon. Sam had magic hands, which was probably true, but man, that demon could style and blow dry hair.

"Wow, it's…" I turned my head. "It's amazing." I saw him turn his head, and I whirled on him. "Oh my goodness! Demon, are you *blushing*?"

Instead of answering, Sam kissed me. His mouth moved over mine hungrily, and his hands deftly untied my bathrobe. I was naked underneath, and I didn't care as his hands travelled over my body in soft exploration. Strong hands cupped under my bottom and lifted me onto the dresser. Sam's knee parted my thighs, and he stepped between my legs as he continued to kiss me hard.

My hands went to pull his cable knit sweater off him, but he stilled my hands. "You gave me a gift, let me return it," he murmured against my skin as he knelt on my bedroom floor, and his mouth moved over my core.

Holy shit fuck demon balls.

Sam kissed me *down there* like he kissed my mouth. I was a quivering mess of sensation. His tongue worked in rhythm with his fingers, and oh holy gumdrops, his fingers felt good. My hands were in his hair, and my legs wrapped around his head. I almost choked when he lifted me from the dresser whilst his mouth still moved over me relentlessly.

The bed dipped as we both landed on it with a thump, and my entire lower body raised itself off the bed to meet the thrust of his fingers. There was slight discomfort at his roughness, but the pleasure of his mouth overrode it.

"Sam," I moaned as I pulled him into me more. "I'm so close, don't stop," I begged him. His tongue rolled over my nub, and then he sucked it gently, just before he bit it hard, and despite the shot of pain, my body felt like it fragmented as I reached the point of no return.

"I knew you would taste good," he told me as he kissed his way up my spent body before kissing me deeply again. "Fuck, the things I want to do to this tight little body," he growled against my mouth. My hands were on his belt, undoing it as my hand hastily slipped inside and pulled him out. I stroked his hard length, relieved that my memory of his dick had been distorted with alcohol. Sam groaned as his own fingers returned to caressing me. Our breathing was loud in the room, but I didn't care as I picked up my pace, pulling him to my centre.

"Do it," I urged. My legs were still parted, and he was between them, hot and hard and so ready. "I want it."

"Not today," he groaned as he took control of my hand, his grip tightening on my hand painfully as he used my hand to stroke his length. "Tighter," he commanded with a stern tone of voice as his speed picked up and my fingers gripped around him.

His head dipped down so his chin was on his chest as he watched our hands work him hard. With a grunt of satisfaction, his head fell back as he spilled his release on my stomach.

He dropped my hand before he fell down beside me. Sam's teeth bit into my neck, and I flinched even as his tongue soothed the bite. "You're late, get dressed, they are waiting." He lifted himself off of me, but he seemed hesitant. "Fuck," he groaned as he dipped his hand back in between my legs and thrust two fingers roughly inside me. I cried out at his touch, which caused him to close his eyes. "Soon," he promised as he backed away from me and turned on his heel and left me in the bedroom.

It took me a few minutes before I was able to get up and make my way to the bathroom to clean up. I came back out and sat on the edge of my bed, with my head in my hands as I tried to figure out what was happening to me. I was falling for a demon? I couldn't be. He was a *demon*. Bad. Demons were bad. Wicked. My tummy flipped as I thought of his *wicked* tongue. Good Lord, I could get too used to that. I hadn't told him I had never had *anyone* do that to me. I'd heard about it, read about it, but neither of my sexual partners had ever reciprocated in the oral sex department. I didn't like the pain bit of it, but I couldn't deny the end result.

If I knew that had been what I was missing out on, I would have been insistent. As I stood on shaky legs, I realised they probably weren't as aggressive as Sam. *Was anyone?* I had to concentrate, this was not the time to lose my head over a man.

Not a man.

Male?

Demon.

With a groan, I stood. I didn't need this to distract me. What I needed was to get dressed. It was a long drive to St Andrews. My legs clenched as I thought about being with Sam in the small confines of my van.

You'll be with five other demons.

I grinned at the wicked thoughts my brain just turned to, but as much as I wished my life may turn into a reverse harem novel, I knew a certain tall, dark, and green-eyed demon would never share. In all honesty, I didn't want to be shared. I wanted him. My lady parts throbbed with agreement, and I opted for a quick cool shower to calm my libido down and wash all evidence of my morning off my skin.

Longer than it should have taken me, I was eventually dressed in black jeans, a long black oversized hooded jumper and my black biker boots. I'd never been on a bike in my life, but they had solid grips and looked badass.

When I got to the kitchen, only Zel and Der were there. "Hey," I greeted.

"You're late," Zel grumbled with a dark look.

"Morning to you too," I said with a forced smile. I noticed the coffee maker and frowned. The pot was empty. "No coffee for me?"

"There was," Zel said with a shrug as he leaned back in the kitchen chair. "But you took too long."

My eyes narrowed as I watched him. "If I had been in this kitchen when the coffee brewed, you still wouldn't give me any, would you?"

"Sounds like you *got* what you needed earlier." Zel's look spoke volumes.

"You're such a hateful dick," I hissed at him. "Where is Sam?"

"He and Ros are patrolling the perimeter," Der replied as he stroked his beard while he watched me. "You should be careful," he told me. "It is a dangerous game you play."

"Game?" I looked between the two of them. "What game?"

Zel pushed the chair back as he stood abruptly. He walked towards me, his face twisted in a sneer, and when he reached me, he dropped his head to my ear. "I can smell him on you, and it *disgusts* me." He shouldered past me, and I looked after him as I rubbed my shoulder.

"Wow," I mumbled as I tried to hide the hurt. "Haters gonna hate, right?" I tried for joking, but my voice was flatter than a pancake.

Der stood and picked up his two axes. "You should be careful, he will react badly."

"Badly? Who will? React to what?"

Der's look was almost, *almost* pity. "You are not skilled enough to play this game, witch," he said sadly. He left through the back kitchen door, and I stared after him in confusion.

"What the fuck was that?" I demanded of the empty kitchen.

"Morning," the voice greeted me from behind.

I turned to Chaz, and I smiled. "Hi, it's nice to see a friendly face," I said to him.

A fleeting look of hurt flickered over Chaz's face before he schooled his features. "Have they explained what's happening today?"

"Road trip?" I quipped as I again tried to lighten the mood, but Chaz also looked disappointed in me.

"Come, Star, let's get this over with." Chaz walked back out of the kitchen, and I followed. The demons were acting very strange in this cottage this morning. As I left the cottage and turned back to lock the door, I heard the roar, and I jumped, dropping my keys in fear.

Turning swiftly, my jaw dropped as I saw Sam being held back by Ros, Zel and Der. His eyes were glowing bright green, and the snarl on his mouth couldn't possibly be directed at me. It wasn't, I realised. He was focused on Chaz, and I took a step towards him in confusion.

"Sam?"

"Let me go, brothers," Sam snarled as he shoved them off of him, but even though he seemed to have shaken the demons off of him, Zel and Der were immediately on him again. Ros pushed Sam back, and I couldn't hear the whispered words.

"No!" Sam roared as he surged forward again. "I will *skin* him for this."

"What did you do?" I asked Chaz fearfully. The long-haired demon was watching the struggle, looking as confused as I was.

"Pen?" I turned to the brown-eyed demon, who was watching Chaz with suspicion. "What the actual fuck is happening?"

"Shut your mouth, whore," Zel snapped at me.

"Excuse me?" I shouted back at him. "Sam?" I demanded.

It seemed my voice was enough to settle the dark-haired demon. "I am calm," he told the others as his gaze fixed on me. They each looked at him and then each other, then as one, they stepped back.

How they fell for his shit was beyond me, because he sped past them, and suddenly I was pressed against the wall of my cottage with a hand wrapped around my throat, my feet off of the ground and something sharp and *pointy* pressing through my coat and jumper right against my rib cage.

"Sam?" I tried to plead as I searched his eyes. They glowed so brightly I wasn't sure he could actually see me.

"Brother," Pen murmured. "We still need her."

"Do we?" Sam snarled as he gripped my jaw and twisted my head. He looked at my neck and then bent his head low. He inhaled, and with a disgusted grunt, he dropped me to the ground. "She has to be alive?" he asked Pen quietly. "Because right now, I don't want to hear her breathing."

It was the quiet of his voice that scared me more. "Sam?" I pleaded.

"Silence, witch." His hate-filled stare glared down at me. "You speak only when I allow it."

"Fuck you." I rose unsteadily to my feet, the tears falling rapidly. "I don't know who the fuck you think you are, but you can go back to hell!" I rubbed my neck where he had grabbed me, even as a sob escaped me.

"Brother," Chaz began, but whatever he was going to say was cut off with the look Sam gave him. Chaz's hands rose in a placatory manner. "*Brother*," he said again. "I would *not*."

Sam was breathing heavily as he looked between the two of us, and with a reluctant nod, he accepted Chaz's words.

"Would not what?" I demanded. "What does he mean? Would not *what*?" Sam refused to look at me, so I turned to Pen, who also turned his head. I looked to the one male who hated me enough to be honest, and I sobbed out loud when I saw the malice on Zel's face. "Zel?"

"Whore?"

My eyes closed in despair before I opened them and looked at them all. "What is going on? What's happened?"

"Your act of innocence can stop," Sam snarled as he spat on the ground beside me. "Gag her and bind her," he snapped at Der and Ros as he walked to the van. "I don't want to hear her lies."

As the two demons advanced on me, my scream tore from me, and as I lifted my hands in the air, the wind and rain swirled around us. Six demons looked at me, some in shock, some in hate, all six of them with weapons drawn.

"Witch," Sam growled in warning.

"Fuck you," I yelled at him over the wind. "Fuck you all. Bastards, all of you. Stay the fuck away from me." *Hound, I need you.* The hellhound appeared before me, and his head lowered in warning to the demons. Any other moment in time, I would have fainted with shock that the hellhound obeyed me, but as I locked eyes with Sam, my anger was ruling my emotions. "Protect me, Hound," I ordered the hellhound, and I heard his snort. Two more appeared, forming a protective barrier around me. Even over the wind and rain, I heard the shocked intake of breaths from the demons. "You come close to me and they attack."

You can attack, can't you, Hound?

One glowing red eye met mine, and I almost apologised, because my relief was real.

"Witch, *stop* this, now," Sam ordered, stepping forward.

"Stop?" My hand flew up in the air, and lightning crashed above us. "Like you stopped when you choked me?" More lightning. "Like you stopped when *he* called me whore?" Another crash above me. "Like you stopped when you were going to *stab* me, you fucking prick demon?" Tears streamed down my face as I glared at all of them. "How dare you, how *dare* you." I choked on a sob, and I angrily wiped at my face. "After this morning? And last night? I hate you so much," my voice cracked on another sob. "Do your own spell. You get nothing from me again."

"Star?" Chaz's voice was as always calm and cool, even as he held two long knives in his hands. His eyes flicked to Sam quickly before he sheathed his knives. "Star." He took a step forward, and three hellhounds growled. "Okay, okay." His hands rose in the same placatory gesture he'd used with Sam. "Star, what happened this morning?"

Lightning sounded again, and I stared up at the sky in wonder. *Was I really doing this?*

"Star," Chaz prodded, bringing my attention back to him. "*Who* were you with this morning?"

"What?" I looked at Sam in confusion, although he refused to look at me. "*What?*" The wind picked up again. "What, *now* you can't even look at me?" I yelled at Sam.

"No, I can't *look at you*," he snarled. "Not when I can smell it on you."

"Smell what?"

"His seed," Zel growled at me, the loathing in his eyes tangible.

"You fucking demons have no boundaries." I tossed my hair over my shoulder. "His *seed*? Seriously, that's why you're all acting like fucking animals right now? Because he came on my stomach?"

Sam growled low in his throat and took a step towards me in anger, regardless of the three hellhounds in front of me.

"Star!" Pen shouted to get my attention, and I looked at him reflexively. "*Who* were you with this morning?"

Thunder and lightning boomed above me as I looked at Sam, and his green eyes glowed in anger. "You!" I choked. The lump in my throat was making it difficult to speak. "I was with *you*."

Sam straightened in shock. I heard more sharp gasps and dropped my head into my hands as my tears overwhelmed me.

"Hello, brothers," the new voice and demon walked from behind my van. Thick black hair hung low over his forehead, almost in his eyes it was so long, and it curled around his ears. His straight roman nose sat over sensual lips. Cold blue eyes watched me in amusement. "She tastes like a peach," he told them casually. "Such power, I'm eager to tap into that—and all the other things she offers so...*freely*."

"Who the fuck are you?" I asked hoarsely as I looked between the newcomer and Sam. Sam's entire body was rigid as he stared at the newcomer with scorn; he was clearly no longer listening to me. It would be untrue to say they were identical, but in the pouring rain with my heart shattering around me, I couldn't tell them apart.

I couldn't tell them apart.

"Oh God, no." My hands flew to my lips as my eyes met Sam's, and I saw the flash of realisation in them. "Hound!" I called as I backed away from the demons. "Take me away from here, now."

The hellhound crouched in front of me, and I clumsily clambered onto his back. The storm chased us as we sped away from the cottage, chased me or followed me, I no longer cared. I needed away from them all. My arms hugged tightly around

Hound's neck as he carried me away from my cottage and the cluster fuck that I left behind me.

The taunting voice of the demon rang in my ears, reminding me of what I had shared with him this morning, shared something so intimate, only I shared it with the *wrong* demon.

CHAPTER 17

MY MUM CAME HOME TO FIND ME CURLED UP ON MY OLD BED IN my room, in tears. "Star? Baby? Star, baby, what's wrong?" she asked as she gathered me in her arms.

"It's all my fault, Mum," I sobbed into her embrace. "I let him use me, and I liked it, and Sam knows, and he'll never talk to me again."

"Who's Sam?" my mum asked me as she stroked my hair. "Who used you? Talk to me, sweetheart," she soothed me gently.

"And I took your powers! I fed off of you in the womb, and I stole your powers," I wailed even as I sobbed harder.

"Who told you that?" Mum asked me as she rocked me gently. I felt her kiss on my head. "Who fed you such rubbish?"

"Rubbish?" I looked up at her, at my mum whose dark blue eyes had a lighter ring of blue around the pupil, like a beacon of light. I had her eye colour, only in reverse. I had the lighter blue eyes with a dark circle of blue around my pupil. "Why is it rubbish?" I sniffled as I rubbed my nose. "Am I not the same thing as a stupid vampire?"

"What?" My mum giggled as she produced a tissue from her pocket and wiped my eyes. "Why are you a vampire, you silly girl?"

"I fed off you."

"Babies do that in the womb, my sweet baby," she said as she stroked my hair again. "That's how they grow," she teased me gently.

"But the Druid told me I took all your powers. I *ate* them." I had hiccups, and my mum pinched me so hard on my side that I gasped. She grinned at me when my hiccups stopped.

"What Druid? You should stay away from Druids, that's dark magic," she told me as she stood to open the bedroom window.

"I spoke to Hamish MacDonald," I admitted as I sat up and blew my nose.

"What!" Mum gasped at me. "Why?"

"I have six…" I hesitated. Oh well, in for a penny, in for a pound. "Demons. I have six demons who need me to break a curse on one of their lords."

"Star, no." My mum looked horrified. "Two *threes*? Are you daft, girl?"

"I know, I know." I nodded as I sighed. "They scared the shit out of me too when they turned up."

"Turned up? Where are they now? Oh my Lord above, Star, what are you involved in?" My mum had her hands clasped under her chin as she looked at me. "Downstairs, come on, you make tea, I'll get Gran's leaves."

"Mum," I protested as I followed her down the stairs. "I can't call Gran to read tea leaves," I muttered, plus Gran was rubbish at reading the leaves.

My mum stopped at the foot of the stairs and looked over her shoulder at me. "I don't need your gran to read leaves, Star. Been reading the leaves all my days."

"But I ate your powers!" I said as I hurried after her.

"That twisted old bastard speaks as much shit now as he shovelled when he was alive." Mum rolled her eyes at me. "Do you think every woman before us got their powers taken when they were pregnant?" Mum scoffed. "Do you think *every* woman before us had a baby girl?" She frowned at me as she switched the kettle on. "Didn't we send you to university?" her tone was teasing, but the message was clear, I was being dumb.

"I didn't suck you dry?" I whispered as I crossed the kitchen and wrapped my arms around her.

"No. I almost bled to death because you decided to come out

feet first, like you were ready to walk, but no." She cupped my face with her smaller hand. "You have such an active imagination, but you know when the spirits are lying."

"Did you bind my powers?" I asked as I took a seat.

"I did." Mum filled the pot with tea leaves. "And when you tell me why you have two threes in your house, I'll tell you why I did."

"They came for me on Friday." I retold my story to Mum, and she listened as she brewed the tea.

"So which one is Sam?"

"Their leader, I think." I felt myself redden and couldn't meet her eye.

"Good looking?"

"Amazing looking." I dropped my head into my hands.

"Mm-hmm." She stirred the pot. "You sleep with him?"

My head snapped up, and I looked at her in shock. "Mum!"

"What, I can't ask if you slept with a demon?" she scoffed as she poured the tea. It looked like black tar.

"You used the liquorice mix?" I asked in trepidation.

"Best results, you know to put honey into it," she admonished me.

"It's like cough syrup," I muttered as I stood and went to get the honey.

"So, did you do the *deed* with him?" Mum persisted as she stirred the tea.

"No, Mum, thanks for the air quotes though." I sighed and my face twisted in a scowl. "Stuff, but not the *deed* itself." I mimicked her use of air quotes, and she smiled briefly.

"Okay." She nodded as she pursed her lips together, and I knew the lecture was coming. "You *just* met this demon."

"I don't think they do demon date nights," I snarked.

"Just straight to sex then?" she quipped with sarcasm even as she shook her head. "They're so slippery, you have to be careful when you deal with them."

"I haven't had to deal with them before."

"Well, falling into bed isn't the way." Her look was stern, reprimand delivered. "Drink your tea."

I took a drink of the tea and failed to hide my grimace as I swallowed it down. God, it was vile. "I didn't *fall into bed* with him."

"Did you sleep together, in the same bed? In the same space?"

"Yes." *Had I?* Was it actually Sam who had been in my bed? "I think so." I felt dirty.

"You *think* so?" Mum stopped stirring in her honey. "Explain."

So I had to tell her about this morning, and by the time I was finished, her mouth was hanging open, and my face was burning with embarrassment.

"You couldn't tell the difference?" she asked me for the third time.

"Seems not."

"How?" Mum shook her head as she stood. "How could you not know?"

"He kissed kind of the same. He was a bit rougher, but I thought that was…you know"—I shrugged—"passion."

My mum blinked at me and then sat down across from me, a determined look in her eye. "Star, how many men have you had sex with?"

"Mum!"

"Don't mum me, tell me right now."

"Two. And stuff with Sam. And I suppose the one this morning."

My mum exhaled loudly. "You're so innocent."

"Most mums would be proud," I grumbled as I gulped my tea. "Jesus, this stuff is disgusting."

"Shut up and drink it," my mum ordered as she rubbed her forehead. "Demons are possessive."

"I know, I've met Sam." I sighed as I looked at my teacup. "I'm done." I showed her my cup.

"Drink it *all*," she instructed with a glower. "I cannot believe I have to ask this." Mum looked tortured. "Did you...swallow, with the demon?"

"Fucking hell, Mum!"

"Don't swear like that."

"I think my swearing is the least of my problems at the moment," I protested as I stared at her in disbelief. "Did you just ask me that?"

"Yes, you see"—she took a deep breath—"if he spilled his *essence*, then you are more or less marked as his until he no longer claims you."

I felt my face pale, and Sam's words from the toilets came back: *now they know it as well as you do.* "He marked me?"

"Basically." My mum finally looked uncomfortable. "Only if you take the essence *into* your body though."

"What do you mean?"

"Oh my God, Star, pick a hole and use your imagination," Mum snapped.

"Oh." I bent my head in mortification at her crudeness. "Shit."

"And the one from this morning, did he...give you anything?" Her stare was hard and unyielding.

"No, not like that."

She breathed a sigh of relief. "The others reacted?"

"Yes, Zel called me a whore."

"Bastard," Mum muttered.

"Sam thought it was Chaz, he was going to kill him."

My mum was staring at me, her face white. "Sam? Chaz? Zel?" My mum's face was so pale I thought she was going to faint.

"Star, no. No, no, no." She shook her head even as she stood and paced in the kitchen. "*No*, this cannot be."

"Mum?"

"Give me the cup," she demanded, almost snatching it out of my hands. She stared into the tea leaves and then crossed to the window over the sink for a better look. "No," her whispered denial was loud in the kitchen.

"Mum?"

Her head snapped from looking at me to the doorway. "I did not welcome you, demon," she snarled as Sam walked into the room.

"She led me in the other day, which I am sure she has told you," Sam spoke calmly.

I was on my feet as I watched the two of them warily. He was so big and broad, and my mum was…my *mum*. I crossed the space and stood in front of my mum protectively.

"You don't need to protect me from demons." My mum's sneer and tone made me look at her in concern.

Zel appeared behind Sam, and Sam moved further into the kitchen to allow Zel and Pen in. I glanced between them all, and I faltered when I saw my mum dip her head to Pen in greeting.

"What's going on?" I asked almost inaudibly.

"You stepped in shit, and I don't know how I can get you out of it," Mum said grimly. With a tired sigh, she took her seat at the table. "You joining me or going to stand there and call my daughter more names?"

"Did she tell you why?" Sam asked darkly as he looked at me, and I almost started crying again at the look of loathing in his eye.

"My daughter is mostly untaught," my mum bit out. "She sees spirits, she makes a little extra money from pulling souls and telling fortunes."

"You knew I pulled souls?" I asked as I tore my eyes away from Sam.

"What do you think necromancy is?" Mum looked at me with a fond smile. "I have Black Sea tea or juniper and lavender," she told them as she stood again. "We have a lot to discuss."

Pen opted for the juniper one, while Zel and Sam both took the black tea. I sat and stared at the tabletop.

"Where's Chaz?" I asked softly.

Sam snorted in answer, and Zel ignored me. Pen looked at them both and then at me. "We thought it best to keep them separated for a while."

"Sam and Chaz?" I asked in confusion.

"No, I mean—"

"Why didn't you react to me when I was here two days ago," Sam asked my mum, cutting Pen off.

"I take a draught," Mum replied as she made two separate teapots. "I've run out."

"Now is not the time to drown us out, Jean," Pen murmured quietly as he accepted his teapot and teacup.

"How do you know my mum?"

Mum huffed dryly as she spooned the tea leaves into the bigger pot. With a shrewd look between Zel and Sam, she added another spoonful. When she was done, she sat back at the table and wordlessly handed her own teacup to Pen. He glanced at it before he handed it back to her.

"I always feel like I'm playing catch up," I grumbled as I looked around the table.

"I know Penemue because he is the very personification of *what* he is." Mum poured Sam's and Zel's tea. She whispered in their strange language, and then with an almost geisha-like bow, she handed them both their teacups.

"Penemue?" I tried again. "Pen-nee-mue?"

"Correct." He raised his teacup in salute before he sipped the almost clear tea.

"Isn't juniper and lavender basically just some form of flavoured gin?" I mused, and my mum gave a light laugh.

"Always so blunt," she chuckled. "And curious unfortunately."

"So." I looked around the table. "Who's filling me in?"

"You cannot hide it from her," Mum told them quietly. "Her power will unleash since you are hell-bent on breaking it free."

"She was bound in front of the arch at St Andrews?" Pen asked.

"No." Mum looked away from them all. "Dunnottar."

Zel's hiss was loud. "Dangerous and stupid."

"She was too strong, they would have come for her."

"What are you?" I asked, my voice firm. "You're the personification of *what*?"

"They are Watchers." Mum topped her cup up. She actually liked the hideous tea.

"Okay, and what do they watch?" I looked at them all cluelessly.

"You. People." Pen smiled.

"I don't understand the reference," I confessed.

"We have always Watched," Zel told me. His vibrant blue eyes met mine with less scorn. "We Watched, and eventually we wanted."

"Wanted what?"

"What humans have, what humans disregard and take for granted," Pen said wistfully.

"So, you were allowed to…Watch?" I was not keeping up.

"We rebelled," Sam said as I met his steady gaze.

"You rebelled, and you fell so far." My mum's look to Pen was full of sadness.

"Fell?" I had a horrific thought forming, and I was ready to bolt.

"We Watched, we coveted, we rebelled, we fell." Zel ticked the items off on his fingers. "We were free." His smile was savage.

My eyes were closed as I tried to control my emotion. "Heaven?" I said as I opened my eyes and met Sam's glowing green eyes. "You *fell* from heaven?"

"We did."

"You were *angels*?" I demanded as my heart thumped heavily in my chest. Zel nodded, and now I knew why he was such an egotistical arsehole. "And who led the rebellion?"

"Samyaza was the leader of the first twenty," Zel answered proudly.

"But you, witch…" Sam's mocking smirk appeared. "*You* can call me Sam."

CHAPTER 18

THEY HAD BEEN ANGELS. I LOOKED AT THE THREE OF THEM AND AT my mum and then back to the three of them. They had been *angels*.

"Do you have wings?" I blurted.

"Not as you think of them," Pen told me quietly.

"You're an *angel*?" I said incredulously, looking at Sam.

"Demon." He drank his tea. "All demon."

"I think I'm having a stroke." All the weirdness in my life, I dealt with it, no problem. This? This was beyond my comprehension.

"Dramatic," Zel snorted as he too drank his tea.

"Shut up."

"What age was she when you bound her?" Sam asked my mum almost pleasantly.

"Five."

"And the Druid's lotion?" he spoke on, ignoring her obvious hostility.

Mum looked at him and then at me in disapproval. "I told you this when you were here last?"

"You did." Sam didn't flinch under my mum's hard look.

"I reacted to it when I was pregnant, but I thought it was *me*. When Star was born, the spirits were so thick it was difficult to breathe. My mother was able to dispel them, but all through her infant years, Star was surrounded." Mum shook her head slightly as she recalled. "When she went to kindergarten, she started passing on their messages, she scared the children." Mum ran her hand through her hair. "My husband taught her not to see them. But she is a stubborn, wilful child, and she was soon talking to them again. She would leave in the night. We'd find her in a graveyard, a church, Christ, sometimes even at the side of the road." Mum's tone was heavy with her former worry. "She was in so much danger. They surrounded her wherever she went, I had no choice."

"Who bound her?" Pen asked.

"Hamish and my mother."

"We have his bones," Zel informed her. "Your mother?"

"My gran was cremated."

Zel tipped his head back and sighed. "Every fucking step we gain, we fall back two."

"Who did the blood spell?" Sam asked.

"Blood spell?" Mum asked warily. "Blood magic is dark magic, my mother did not practice dark magic."

"The Druid then," Pen said to Sam quietly.

Zel stood abruptly. "We go to the old battleground."

"Battleground?" I asked as I watched Pen stand too. Sam remained seated.

"So much blood has been spilled on the ground at Dunnottar, Viking raids, Scottish battles, killing of soldiers, treason. It's soil is heavy with the stain of evil and hatred." Zel looked almost saddened as he thought about it. "A dangerous, *dangerous* place to bind a child." His look to my mum was full of judgement.

"We work with what we are given," my mum answered him softly, not in the least bit intimidated by him. "Nowhere else close by would hold her power."

"Go, tell the others, there's a change in plan," Sam said as he looked at Zel, whose gaze flicked to mine once, and with a nod of acknowledgement to Sam, he left.

Pen offered my mum his hand and smiled. "It's been so long." He gestured to the teacups. "Will we?"

My mum actually blushed. The two of them gathered the cups and went out to the back garden. I went to the window to watch them, curious to see the exchange. Mum always burned the leaves after a reading, and I assumed that Pen went with her to ensure she did. I noticed he didn't hand her Sam's cup.

Sam. He was still seated at the table, silent and unmoving. I was going to have to address this sooner or later.

"I thought he was you." I continued to watch my mum dispose of the tea leaves as she spoke to Pen. "He looked like you, and I was…" I inhaled deeply. "After sleeping beside you, I was, I dunno, *shy*." I turned to him to see him watching me closely. "It *was* you I slept beside?" Sam nodded slightly. "Well, thank fuck for that." My laugh was harsh before I felt overwhelming sadness. "I'm sorry, I should have known," I whispered dejectedly.

"You should have." He stood swiftly.

"What happens now?" I asked quietly as I watched him with building unease.

Sam's look was heavy with scorn. "Now? We go to Dunnottar, we break your bind, you do the spell and you bleed." His grin was vicious.

"Be careful, your savageness is showing," I muttered. "You stay pissed off then?"

"I'm indifferent."

I barked out a laugh. "You're not even in the same general region of indifference. You're full of shit."

He moved so quickly my back hit the sink with a thud. "No," he hissed in anger. "I'm not *indifferent*." His head bowed as he leaned forward, and he inhaled deeply. "I can smell his spilled seed on you, and it fills me with a rage I struggle to contain." His finger trailed along my jaw before his hand circled my throat as he drew his head back to look at me. "The scent of betrayal makes me ill. *You* make me ill." He stepped back from me. "The sooner this is done, the sooner I am free of you."

"Sam." My fingers caught his arm, and he looked at me before dropping to look where my hand curled around his arm. I dropped my hand when his eyes glowed softly.

"Do not touch me again, witch." Sam took a step away from me. "Once you are unbound, the spell will be easy." He strode out of the kitchen as Mum and Pen came back into the kitchen.

"You okay?" Mum asked me as I hurriedly wiped my eyes.

"Yeah, all good," I lied as I rubbed my hands over my jeans. "So." I looked at Pen. "Angels, huh? Kept that quiet."

Pen smiled despite himself, and after a brief farewell with my mum, he gave me a few moments in the kitchen alone with her. She opened her arms, and I hugged her tightly.

"It's all gone to shit," I whispered in despair.

"I don't think this was ever a good situation for you," Mum said with light humour. "His ego is wounded, he will come around."

"I don't think so, Mum."

"Trust me." She let me go as she reached up and smoothed my hair. "You call to him, he will forgive you."

"What a mess."

"Yes," she agreed as she collected the teapots. "Ugh," she groaned. "And I have to tell your dad."

"Do you? I mean really?"

"Lies have consequences," Mum chided me slightly.

"I'm currently living through one now," I snarked and immediately regretted it when I saw her face fall. "Sorry, Zel brings out my inner bitch."

Mum's smile made me smile in return. "He is full of right-eousness, still has too much angel than demon," Mum remarked. "You must be careful. They will not tell you all that you need to know, you *must* be clever, Star. Your emotions cannot rule your head."

Well, there was no danger of that. "I'll be good, and it will be over and done with in a jiffy."

Mum groaned as she dropped her head in her hands. "Stubborn, obstinate, *wilful* child," she berated me. "They want to unbind your powers, to lift a curse, on a *prince of hell*. Do you *really* think you can walk away unscathed?"

A prince of hell? I shifted on my feet. "They didn't say he was royalty."

"God above, Star. Open your ears and *listen* to what they are *not* telling you," Mum fretted as she tipped out leaves from the teapots. "I cannot stop them, I am not that strong." She wiped her hands on the tea towel. "*You* are, you must be careful." She looked over my shoulder quickly. "Do you have allies amongst them?"

I nodded slowly. "I think Chaz is a friend."

"Chazaquel is more of a lover not a fighter." Mum worried her lip as she thought about it. "Penemue is the same, both more scholars than warriors. You need a fighter on your side."

She looked so worried that I knew I had to assure her. "I do." I grinned at her dubious look. "I have a strong fighter who likes me," I promised. I didn't think it was necessary to mention that it was a hellhound. No need to kill her outright with fright.

"Promise me you will be careful?"

"I promise." I hugged her tightly.

"And stop kissing demons," she chastised me as she squeezed me back. "You need to find a real man."

"Ruairidh?" I teased as I put my coat on.

"Good God, no, your father will kill you if you end up with that drip, you'd have more success with the demon."

"Dad doesn't like Ruairidh?" I asked in surprise.

"Another conversation for another day." Mum patted my bum as she ushered me to the door. "Be careful, and if you are in danger, you call them forth, Star," she whispered in my ear. "I don't care if it disturbs their rest, you call every soul to you if you need to."

"I will." I gave her a final hug, and then with mounting dread, I headed out to my van.

THE DRIVE from Inverness to the edge of Stonehaven on the northeast coast was, to say the least, tense. And silent. The silence was almost deafening. When Ros tried to make conversation, he was shut down so savagely by Zel that I actually apologised for him getting his head bitten off. When I was told to shut up, I spent the rest of the journey imagining a horrible death for the dark demon.

Dunnottar Castle was situated on the cliffs overlooking the North Sea and was so exposed to the elements I was freezing before I even got out of the van.

"We need tickets," I blurted as they went to leave the van. "To get in."

Sam snorted as he got out, ignoring me, and I looked at Chaz in despair. "We have ways of getting in," he told me gently before he got out too.

I sat a moment longer. They hadn't mentioned the other demon, he was not with us, and I was too scared of the backlash from Sam to ask about him. The window got rapped loudly, and I jumped even as I glared at Zel whose grin showed more teeth than normal.

As I got out, I smelled the chips from the food van and realised I was starving. Ignoring them all, I ordered a coffee and a plate of chips. Ros sniffed them as I sat and opened a sachet of vinegar, sprinkling it over the crispy golden goodness, my mouth watering in anticipation.

"I want some," Ros told me. I handed him my credit card and told him to order everyone a portion. "What do I ask for?" He looked uncertain.

"Fries," I decided. His accent was almost American, I thought. "We call them chips here, but if you order six portions of fries, the girl will know." I pointed to my card with a chip. "Just hold it up against the device she hands you to pay, okay?"

As I finished my coffee, I tried not to show the hurt I felt as they sat at an opposite bench, eating chips and drinking coffee that *I* had bought them. It was like being back at school, forever the outcast. I watched them out of the corner of my eye. Sam didn't eat anything, he did drink his coffee though. As I tried not to watch him, I felt a pang of remorse.

His dark hair blew in the breeze, his mouth twitched in a smile as Der said something that the others laughed at. He never fully smiled, I realised. The demon I had been with smiled freely. That should have been my first warning something was wrong. I also thought of the way Sam had kissed me in the bar and the van, hard but careful. His hands had been the same, rough, but his touch had been gentle. He had never once caused me discomfort when he had his hand between my legs. I bowed my head as I felt the tears well. How had I not known from his touch, how had I not known when he kissed me?

"Witch," Zel called me, and I realised they were all standing, waiting for me.

"Well, it's a step up from *whore*," I muttered as I stood.

We walked down the path to the castle, and I took in the sheer magnificence of the ruin. It must have been spectacular in its day, I realised as I walked down. I looked at the stairs down to the castle and didn't relish coming back up them.

"Wait," Chaz called, looking up at the sky, his hand up in warning. "Wait."

I caught up to them and looked up at the sky as I looked over at Chaz. "What's happening?"

"He reads the clouds," Pen said softly beside me.

"Clouds?" I looked at Chaz again and then at Pen. "I didn't know that was a thing," I admitted.

"Don't know much, do you?" Zel said with derision.

"No, I don't." I glared at him. "But I know a dickhead when I see one," I snapped.

"You seem to know a lot about *dicks*," Zel growled as he returned my glare.

"You know, maybe it's time you fucking *dick*heads, remember *you* need *me*. I don't need any single one of you." I brought myself up short at the realisation. "I don't actually know why I'm here," I realised as I looked at them all. "And I don't want to be here anymore." I turned and walked away, walking back to the van.

I made it to the van and was about to get in when I was turned and pinned against it. I looked up at Sam and met his angry stare with one of my own.

"What?"

"Get back down there."

"No," I answered stubbornly. "You want my help? Well, I no longer *want* to help you."

"Witch," Sam warned.

"Demon."

I glanced around us and fought the eye roll. I really needed to learn to reverse park. If I had done, then I would be seen by all the visitors to the castle, but no, I had to drive into the space front first. The only thing that could see me was the small robin sitting on the hedge. The bird flew off. Of course it did.

"The quicker you are unbound, the quicker we leave," Sam reminded me.

"Maybe I like being bound," I said to him with a careless shrug. "I've been bound since I was five, I don't know any different."

Sam stepped back from me and looked me over. "You're so fucking clueless, it's infuriating." He glared at me. "*You're* infuriating."

"Well, you're a bossy bastard."

Sam rolled his head on his shoulders, as if he were trying to relax, before he looked at me again. "This is not the time or the place to have an exchange of insults."

"Slagging match," I told him reluctantly. "It's called a slagging match."

"It sounds delightful." His tone was dry, and for the first time since everything had gone to shit, he almost looked like himself again.

"I made a mistake," I began and felt a pang of regret as I saw him shut down. "I thought he was you, but when I think about it, I don't know how I could have." I looked away as I felt the familiar tears. "You weren't rough with me before, I should have known." I dipped my head to hide the wetness threatening to run down my cheeks. "I don't want to be here," I whispered into the silence. "Zel *hates* me so much, it feels almost like a physical assault when he looks at me. Chaz looks at me with pity, and the others are too scared to approach me in case they upset *you*. And you"—my head lifted to meet his stare—"detest me and what I did." I tucked my hair behind my ears as I blew on my fingers. "And it's freezing here, and I want to go home, where I'm not hated." I heard him huff in disagreement. "Okay, where I *am* hated, but at least they don't want to actually harm me…that I know of."

"You don't always get what you want," Sam told me coldly. "I however, do." His hand encircled my arm, and he pulled me forward. "You *will* go into that castle, you *will* be unbound, and I promise you, witch, you *will* cast the spell." He began to walk me back to the others. "Then you can return to your sad lonely little life, where I am sure you'll marry that fool you call a friend, and you will die alone after what I am sure will be a long and miserable life with him."

"You're hateful," I gasped as I tried to pull my arm away from him, my mind reeling from his harsh words.

Sam glowered down at me and hissed, "Demon."

"Witch." I pulled away from him and reached for my power. It rushed to meet me, and wildly I called the words that came to me. Sam went flying backwards, and I turned and ran back to my van as I heard the others yelling as they raced towards us.

Hands grabbed me, and I screamed as I was thrown backwards through the air. I landed with a thud on the frozen ground, and I looked up at Sam in shock.

No, not Sam.

Samyaza. The leader of the rebellious angels. His power was wild as it raced around me, his eyes glowed bright green with anger, his twin swords were in his hands as he looked down at me with barely concealed fury.

"You run from me again, witch, and I will cut off your legs so you *never* run again." He looked to the others who had reached us. "Wipe them." He looked at the gathered spectators, some on their phones either recording or calling for aid. His gaze returned to me. "Get up."

"Fuck you."

One large hand reached down and picked me up effortlessly. "Shut your mouth," he growled before he shoved me into Zel's hold. "Keep her contained, and for fuck's sake, keep her quiet."

CHAPTER 19

I WAS SITTING IN A CORNER OF A RUINED CASTLE, SHIVERING. IT had no roof, and the windows were mere open areas of stone, unlikely even to have had shutters, never mind glass. The wind howled overhead, and I watched the demon who stood silently, looking out to the North Sea.

Zel had indeed shut me up. I was gagged, and my hands were tied in front of me. My head rested against the stone as I watched him. The information plaque that was on the opposite wall told me that this was a former bedchamber of the Countess where she entertained her guests. According to the plaque, she also had a private entrance to the chapel, the chapel where the others were now in.

"You're shivering is annoying," he told me with a scowl.

Robbed of being able to snap at him, I simply glared. Zel crossed the stone floor and roughly ripped the gag from my mouth.

"It's freezing."

"I've been colder," was his offhanded reply. When my teeth started chattering, he looked at me as if I was doing it on purpose. "Are you serious?"

"It's October, I'm wearing two layers of clothes, you have me on a *stone* floor. I'm sorry if my dying of hypothermia annoys you."

"You're such a *complete* waste of my time," Zel snarled as he shrugged off his jacket. He threw it at me, and I didn't care about the speed with which I caught it and wrapped myself in it.

"Thanks," I grumbled.

"Shut up."

"Why do you hate me so much?" I asked quietly.

"I don't hate you, I just don't like you." He leaned against the wall, his stare returning to the sea beyond us.

"Okay, well why do you dislike me?"

"You're a witch."

I waited and he said nothing else. "What?" I looked at him in growing disbelief. "You don't like me because I'm a witch?" He shrugged in agreement. "You mean it isn't even *personal*?"

Zel considered it. "You *are* irritating," he mused.

"I can't believe you." I dropped my head onto my knees, as I huddled under his jacket. "So," I asked after a long silence, "what's your name?"

"Did you hit your head?"

"I mean your *full* name. Chazaquel, Penemue, Samyaza." My breath hitched on *his* name. "What are you?"

"Azazel," he said with a mock bow.

"Huh." I squinted at him in the poor light. "Suits you." Zel huffed in reply, but I thought I saw a slight smile. "And the others?"

"Amaros and Gadreel," Sam answered as he walked into the room. He glanced at Zel before he looked at the jacket, and his eyebrow rose in question.

"Chattering teeth are irritating," Zel told him.

"Chaz says a blood moon is in three nights," Sam told him, ignoring me again. "He wants to wait."

Zel glowered at me as if it were my fault there was going to be a lunar eclipse. "Three more nights?" His sigh of discontent was loud.

"Drama queen," I said to him even as I snuggled into his jacket. When I got no response, I looked up and realised he was gone. Sam stood watching me. "What did I do now?"

"We're making camp."

I looked around the stone ruin. "Here?"

"There are caves below."

"Caves?" I struggled to my feet, my bound hands making me clumsy. "In the cliffs?" He nodded, and I looked at him as if he were crazy. "The caves beside the North Sea?"

"Scared of getting wet?"

"Scared of drowning," I answered waspishly.

"Why would we go into caves where we could drown?" His head tilted in question. "Smugglers' caves are exactly that as they keep the goods *dry*."

"Why can't I go home and come back in two days?" I asked indignantly. "My home is warm and dry and *not here*."

"A blood moon isn't always powerful, sometimes the night before has the power, sometimes the night after. It can be temperamental."

"Sounds like a demon I know."

"Sounds like a *witch* I know." His hooded stare met mine, and I felt the butterflies. That he could still cause the fluttering in my tummy confused me. He had flung me through the air. He had choked me. He had made Zel gag and bind me. I refused to be attracted to him.

"You threw me first," he spoke into the night as he looked out over the sea, as Zel had. "You caused the first wound when you allowed another to touch you after I had given you—" He cut himself off.

"After you had given me a part of you," I said quietly as I stepped up to the other window. I refused to say *seed*.

"No matter," Sam said brusquely.

"This rage you have for me is all because of the other demon?" I asked him as I pulled on Zel's jacket. "Even though you know that I made a mistake."

"It's no matter." His voice was hard.

"He looks *so* much like you," I whispered furiously. "Why aren't you mad at *him*?"

"How do you know I am not?" Sam asked me carefully.

"Because you're taking it all out on me!" I wailed. "He knew *exactly* what he was doing!"

"As did you," Sam said coldly as he turned away from me.

"No!" I shouted, uncaring who could hear me. "He knew *exactly* who I was. How many times do I have to tell you this, I thought *he was you.*"

"You thought wrong."

"I *know*," I growled. "But when I called him Sam, he didn't correct me. He did what he did even when I called him another's name."

Sam stopped and half turned back. He looked over his shoulder as he stilled. "You called him Sam?"

"Yes."

"The entire time?"

"*Yes.*"

"Did he tell you his name?" Sam turned back to me.

"No, why don't you ever hear me? This is what I keep telling you, and you won't listen, I *thought he was you.*" My chest was heaving, and I was pretty sure I was out of breath.

Sam bowed his head and cursed in his Latin-that-wasn't-Latin language. When he raised his head, the fiery demon from earlier looked back at me. His eyes glowed green in the darkness. The weird green hue from his eyes illuminated the old granite and was kind of amazing, albeit really, *really* scary. "It changes nothing."

"Okay," I whispered in despair.

"His name is *Yeqon,* and he will pay."

Sam disappeared. He didn't walk out of the room. He vanished. Zel came running into the room, followed by the others.

"What did you do?" Zel prowled towards me angrily.

I recounted my conversation hastily in case the angry demon decided to pick me up and throw me to the rocks below.

"Yeqon knew you thought he was Sam?" Ros asked with a frown. "Ah fuck, he's going to get himself thrown in the pit."

Chaz nodded in agreement. "Who stays with Star?"

"I will," Pen answered, and my mouth dropped when the others all winked out of the room.

"They vanish?" I asked incredulously. "*You* vanish?"

"We call it travelling."

"No." I shook my head in denial. "I've travelled with Sam, I didn't disappear like a goddamn magic bunny in a hat."

"You have a thing against rabbits," Pen said as he studied me. "It's…strange."

"Me not liking rabbits is not strange. It's a preference. Me having an irrational fear of sharks is exactly that, an irrational fear. You being able to vanish in and out of…existence! *That's* what's the strange thing here."

Pen grinned. "You're funny." He held his hand out to me. "Come, there are warmer places we can be."

"My cottage?" I asked with hope as I took the demon's hand.

"Unfortunately no, but I know a nice warm cave with your name all over it."

We winked.

I had no other terminology for it. One minute, I was in the Countess's bedroom, the next I was in a cave. I didn't care. The cave had a roaring fire, and I almost fell over my feet in my haste to get closer. There was also food and blankets.

"This is how you get your clothes. I never know how you get things, but you do this," I said to Pen as I held my hands out to the fire. "You wink."

"Wink?" Pen chuckled lightly. "*Travel.*"

"Why don't you do this when I'm with you, instead of carrying me or using my fuel and my van?"

"Sam didn't want to spook you too much." Pen sat down on a pile of blankets.

"And now he doesn't care if I have a mental breakdown?" I asked quietly.

"It is hard for us, when we—"

"I swear if you say *seed*, I will punch you," I cut Pen off with a glare.

"Do you punch yourself if *you* say it?" he asked me with amusement.

"Good point," I conceded.

"What I *was* going to say, when we *join* with someone, we feel slightly possessive towards them. Sam was not yet finished with you when you decided you were finished with him."

"Finished with me? Such a charmer." I growled as I clenched my teeth. "I *thought* he was Sam."

"Did you?" Pen considered me speculatively. "You don't know Sam's touch?"

"He's only touched me once, and I had a lot of cider and whisky that night," I confessed as I looked away. I thought about it, and I turned away from the fire. "His kiss was different," I admitted softly. "At the time, I wasn't thinking, but now, when I consider it, he was...rougher." I rubbed my head tiredly. "His grip was painful, his fingers almost clumsy in their...ministrations." I looked over at Pen. "Do you want more?" Pen nodded solemnly as he got up and handed me a prepacked sandwich. I opened it realising I was starving. I took a hearty bite and chewed thoughtfully. "It's embarrassing."

"I'm a demon, nothing embarrasses me."

I laughed despite myself. "It's not your embarrassment I was concerned about."

"Keep talking," Pen encouraged me.

"I've never had what he did to me done before." I avoided looking at Pen, my face burning with humiliation. "My previous partners didn't do that. I didn't know it felt like that, I didn't realise it could be sore."

"Sore?" Pen looked confused. "What was he doing?"

"He bit…*it*."

Pen's startled laugh made me want to die, but he quickly sobered. A warm hand covered mine as he sat down beside me. "It's not supposed to be sore," he said softly. "It's supposed to be nothing but pleasure. A little pain some may like, but overall, pleasure is the purpose."

"I mean, I still reacted to the, well, you know. But after I left on Hound, I realised that Sam, he wouldn't hurt me, he has never been anything but what I wanted." I wrapped my arms around myself as I spoke to Pen. "Not before. After it happened, yeah, he now throws me through the air and stuff. I guess I understand his anger, but do I really deserve it? I'm not sure."

"You were tricked," Pen said firmly. "Yeqon can take on some features, he does look similar to Sam," Pen conceded. "His hair is slightly longer, he's not as tall or as broad, but you are slight, all of us are bigger than you." He smiled gently.

"You think I should have been able to tell them apart though, despite your kindness, you think I should have known?"

"Yeqon does not have green eyes," Pen said, and though he was being compassionate, I still heard the condemnation. "And they sure as shit don't glow."

"I never looked at his eyes," I whispered. "After I had slept with Sam, the *actual* Sam, I felt shy." I dropped my chin into my hand as I stared at the fire. "It was sort of intimate. When he was in the room, I was unsure how to react to him. I don't sleep around; it's not normal behaviour for me to sleep with a man." I put my sandwich to the side, my appetite gone. "Then when Sam, no, Yee, the other one," I floundered spectacularly, "he was *so* fixated on drying my hair, it was weird but nice. And so *gentle* for Sam, I didn't look at him, in case it ruined the moment." I gave a disgruntled laugh at my naivety. "Then he kissed me, briefly, and then he was on his knees…well, you don't need a picture drawn."

"He distracted you," Pen mused. "He knew how Sam would react." Pen stood. "He would know you were Sam's, just as he knew that we would all scent another's seed on your skin."

I groaned long and loud. "Ugh, I *cannot* believe I have to ask this, but who did you think it was if you could all *smell* me and know it wasn't Sam?"

Pen laughed. "We are able to change our see—essence," Pen hurriedly corrected himself at my glower. "If we wish for others of our kind to stay away from a female, we can mark her, for want of a better word, so others know she, or he, is not to be touched. It has to be taken into the body for the mark to be effective. Yeqon was clever in that he made sure he spilled outside; it was enough to let us know you were with another, but not enough to identify who."

"So when I was with Sam, he basically peed on me?" I asked, feeling slightly nauseous; there was something fundamentally wrong with these demons. Pen nodded, his eyes twinkling with humour at my terminology. "And scumbag of the century didn't *mark* me, which is why Sam thought it was Chaz?"

"Yes, both Chaz and I were not at the cottage that morning. Our absence was an unfortunate coincidence. Or was it?" Pen looked thoughtful. "What is his goal?" he wondered aloud.

"Who is he?" I asked quietly.

"He was one of the main ringleaders for the rebellion," Pen told me easily. "When we were cast out for wanting the same as humans, Yeqon was the one to encourage us to not only *watch* but enjoy the fruits earth gave us."

"That sounds like the old worldly way of saying he told you to get down and dirty with the locals," I mocked.

"Pretty much. Once we tasted the formerly forbidden fruit, we gorged." Pen's voice was thick with self-loathing. "We committed other sins, we taught the humans things only angels should know."

"Like what?"

"I taught them the art of writing, Chaz the way to read the clouds, our brother the courses of the moon, another the signs of the sun, another taught them to read the stars. My brothers taught them weapons, how to make shields, knives, how to fight using them, how to deliver a killing blow." Pen sighed. "And in doing so, we taught them how to break the commandments, heard of 'thou shalt not kill'?" Pen asked, and I nodded. "We gave them the weapons, and we taught them the act of war."

"Wow, and here was me thinking you were going to tell me that you told them what God looked like."

Pen laughed loudly. "You are funny." He smiled at me almost with fondness.

"So how many people are actually part angel?" I asked casually.

Pen lost his smile. "There are none."

"At all?" I asked in shock. "All that gorging on the fruit, and no little cherubs?"

Pen snorted at my terminology. "When we first fell, we did not know the consequences of our actions."

"No more wings?"

"Ha." Pen gave me an amused look. "Children born of a human and an angel, even one that has fallen, are called Nephilim."

"I know the term," I told him.

"Modern day interpretation casts the Nephilim as powerful half breeds." Pen frowned. "The Nephilim are monsters. Giants. They destroy everything, destruction is all they know, they sought to destroy this earth, and we fell to be part of humanity, not its destruction."

"So you killed your children?" I asked, slightly horrified. Zel was so adamant he didn't harm children, was this why?

"No, our Father sent the rain."

"Sent the rain?" I looked at him, and then I was on my feet. "Are you fucking kidding me?" I screeched. "Noah? And the Ark and the *flood*! Are you talking about the rain for forty days and forty nights?"

"It was needed."

"You've been here since the first book of the Bible?"

"I look good for my age, no?" Pen winked at me. He had no idea I was freaking out.

"You're *older than old*," I protested loudly. "You're not even *Twilight* old, you're *millennia* old."

"Age is relative."

I shook my head. "No, Pen, it really isn't. You're ancient." I stared at him in wonder. "Holy shit, I think my brain just broke."

"You accept we are demons with no issue, but I tell you we have walked this earth since it's conception, and you freak out."

I sank down on a pile of blankets. "Pen, I'm twenty-five years old…almost." My head was reeling. "You're a hundred million trillion billion years *older*."

"Slight exaggeration." Pen picked up my discarded sandwich and ate it. "You really do overreact in an extraordinary way." He drank some water from the bottle he had given me. "It's almost theatrical."

"I think I may be sick," I whispered.

"Why?"

"Because my brain is rejecting what you are telling me, at the same time as my body is rejecting *what* has touched it," I told him savagely.

"Star, it changes nothing."

"I think it does." I stared around the cave. "Pen…I'm not doing well with this."

"Hmm, I noticed." He leaned against the cave wall and closed his eyes.

"Are you going to sleep?" I demanded.

"Yip."

"What am I going to do?"

"I recommend sleeping," Pen deadpanned.

I paced the cave for a good hour. No one else came back, and my train of thought took a detour from the ancient *fallen angels* I was surrounded by to the fact that I wasn't currently surrounded by fallen angels. I had to call them demons. Every time I thought "angel," my brain immediately drew horns on Zel. Somehow, knowing they were demons didn't freak me out. Pen was right, I accepted their demon-ness? Was that a word? Regardless, I accepted them as demons. I had no issue making out with Sam the *demon*. Sam the angel? My brain farted in fear.

Eventually I lay down beside the fire and pulled blankets over me. I was still cold. I was in a cave, and although it was dry, I could hear the wind and smell the sea. I was never going to sleep in this cave.

I WOKE UP TO A WARM BODY TUCKING ME INTO THEIR SIDE. I recognised his scent, and it was another reminder of what I *hadn't* noticed when it mattered most. "Sam?" I asked sleepily.

"You're shivering and keeping the others awake," he said quietly. "Go to sleep."

I curled into him, but it wasn't enough. With a heavy sigh, Sam unbuttoned his jacket, and I was under it and revelling in his warmth within moments of him doing so. "I thought demons were supposed to be hotter," I murmured as I burrowed closer.

"I *am* hot," Sam snorted.

"Ridiculously vain demon," I murmured as my eyes closed, hoping his playful tone meant we were going to be okay.

"Unreasonable, annoying witch," he muttered back. "Sleep." I fell asleep smiling.

I woke up alone but warm. I stretched like a cat and then shrugged free of my blankets. Crossing the cave, I looked out at the North Sea and the rising sun. I looked down to the rocks below, and instead of contemplating how these caves were accessed previously, I leaned against the rock wall as I appreciated the view. When I heard sound behind me, I knew they had winked back.

"You're finally awake," Der spoke to me as he unloaded food from bags. I hurried forward, my eyes on the takeaway coffee cups.

"Mine." I reached forward making "grabby hands" gestures. I almost snatched the offered cup from Der, and then I was back at my spot on the opening of the cave, sipping coffee, watching the calm of the sea. As I stood, blocking out their murmured voices, I felt my elbow tingle. "Go away."

"Did you speak?" one of the demons asked me.

I didn't turn to look at the Druid, but I knew he stood beside me. "I'm having a rough few days, can you go back to wherever it was that you were?"

The cave was suddenly silent.

"You make a grave mistake," the old Druid told me sagely.

"I see what you did there," I joked as I looked at him out of the corner of my eye. "You're dead, grave mistake, I didn't think puns would be your thing."

"Foolish child," he hissed, and I finally turned to him. I tried to hide my shock.

"What happened to you?" I asked as I looked him over. Before, he had appeared as a man in his youth, now he was a shade of how he died. Old and withered, he stood, his clothes hanging on him like rags, his cheeks sunken, his skin like weathered paper.

"You moved my bones," he rasped beside me.

"Well, you shouldn't have put a curse on me," I replied sharply.

"A curse." He huffed in contempt. "I saved you, girl."

"From what?" I asked quietly. "What was I ever in danger of?" I shook my head in dismissal as I stared back out to the horizon. "Do you even know what powers I have?"

"Unbound, you are dangerous."

"Yeah, well, I'd say bound, I'm dangerous." My inner-self brushed against my power, and as it did yesterday, the pool swelled to greet me. The inner pool of tranquillity I was used to was now a raging stormy sea. I could feel it pulling at me, eager to immerse me within it.

"Even now you toy with it." Hamish's anger was unmistakable. "You let it pull you under, girl, and you *will not rise*."

"Rise where?"

"Untrained and ignorant," he spat in disgust.

"And whose fault is that?" I demanded equally angrily. "Yours!

You used blood magic on me, you old fool, no wonder I know nothing."

"Blood magic." Hamish showed me his yellowing teeth as he grinned, his teeth wide in his almost skeletal face. "It was the only way to keep *him* from coming for you, and now you let them in." Hamish was in my face, fury emanating off of him in waves. "You *sleep* with the very ones who would cut you down."

"You have no right to judge me," I growled at him.

"You *need* me. I can teach you, don't do this thing," he pleaded desperately. "You need me, witch."

"I need you not, old man." I scowled at him. "Your bones are all they need, and we have them."

"Do you?" He vanished.

I stood staring at the space he was in for a long moment before I turned to the six demons, who were watching me cautiously. "What?" I grumbled as I fully turned away from the cold October morning.

"It's something to see," Chaz said, his voice soft as always. "You standing, having a conversation with fresh air."

"She was arguing," Zel grunted. "She's always fucking arguing," he added with a disgruntled mutter. I poked my tongue out at him and revelled in his dark scowl.

"Who were you arguing with?" Sam asked me as he watched me from hooded eyes.

"You couldn't hear him?" I asked curiously. I sat down at the fire, reaching for a croissant and taking a bite.

"Not everything," Pen answered.

"Huh." I chewed thoughtfully. "But you could see *and* hear him the other day?"

"The Druid?" Sam asked. He was wearing a dark red chunky knit jumper today, which made his black hair look even darker, and his bronze skin looked so healthy I knew I looked like a milk bottle beside him.

"Yeah, Hamish came to warn me, taunt me and tell me I needed him," I told them as I took another bite. "Sad really," I mumbled around my food.

"What did he say?" Pen asked as he leaned forward with interest.

"Nothing much." I ignored three sceptical stares. "He bound me for my own good to save me, he didn't want me to break the bind, he can teach me to use what powers I do have, and…" I thought about it. "Oh yes, he teased about his bones."

"Teased?" Der asked as he looked to the cloth bag that held the Druid's bones.

"Yeah, it's nothing, he's dead and being spiteful."

"You are sure?" Chaz asked even as Der crossed the cave to get to the bones.

"Well, I said your bones are all we need and we have them, and he said *do you*. Then he poofed outta here."

"Poofed?" Sam asked me. His lips twitched, and I couldn't help but grin at him.

"Yeah, you know, like a puff of smoke. Poofed."

"Wouldn't it then be *puffed*?"

"No, that's silly and makes no sense." I stood, brushing the crumbs off my jeans. "Okay, I need a shower. Who's winking me home to get clean?"

"Winking?" Ros asked me with a huge grin.

"She means travelling," Pen supplied as he stood and held his hand out to me. "I have a place to get you clean."

"You do?" I asked interestedly. "Determined not to let me back to my cottage?" I baited him slyly.

"We may need to talk about that," Chaz said as he avoided my questioning stare.

"Why? What did you do?" I looked around at them all, but none of them would meet my stare. "Zel?" I demanded.

"It needed redecorating anyway." His bright blues eyes twinkled with malicious delight.

"Oh my God, you broke it, didn't you?" I demanded of Sam, who sat and then very slightly shrugged. "Are you kidding me?"

"We have a problem," Der spoke from the corner of the cave as he stared into the bag of bones.

"You're damn right we have a problem," I snapped as I scowled at Sam. "What did you do to my cottage?"

"We don't have all his bones," Der said as he came to stand beside me. "We need to get them all."

"Why? Haven't we got the big ones?" I asked stupidly. "Won't the main ones do?"

Der grinned at me through his beard and tousled my hair. "Need them all, twinkle."

"Twinkle?" I grimaced. "No."

"What?" Der laughed loudly.

Everything about Der was big. His laugh, his body, his *beard*, he was what Gran would have called a "larger than life" character. He would have looked perfectly at home on a "mountain men" calendar from Canada or somewhere, wearing an open flannel shirt, bare chest, holding his axe after chopping wood. "You're not calling me *twinkle*."

"Twinkle twinkle, little *Star*," Der sang playfully. "It suits you."

"I'm not answering to twinkle," I told him adamantly.

"Why? You answer to whore," Zel said with a savage grin, losing some of his glee when he caught Sam's glare.

"Drink more coffee, your demon is showing. At least pretend to be in touch with your humanity," I snapped at him. I turned back to Der. "Do we really need all his bones?"

"Yes," Sam said as he stood. "Show me," he instructed Der as he and Pen went over to the bag of bones.

I had finished my coffee and another croissant when they came back over and Der unceremoniously upturned the bag at my feet. Jerking back, I avoided the bones touching me, but I still noticed the ribcage, the skull, the big femurs. Hamish looked all there to me.

"Fingers, not toes," Der said grimly.

"No toes? But we have head, shoulders and knees," I quipped back, thinking I was hilarious but receiving six blank stares. "Forget it."

"His fingers are missing," Der explained slowly as if I was an idiot.

"Sucks to be Hamish."

"We need *all* his bones."

"I don't know what to tell you." I looked at them as I met the six hard looks. "What? I hardly have them in my poc—" I closed my eyes in realisation. "Eeew. *Eeew.* I can't believe it, no she wouldn't, oh she would. She did. It's a good job you're dead, Gran." I jumped to my feet. "Okay, I need to go back to my cottage."

"Why?" Sam asked me suspiciously.

"I know where his, ugh, this is disgusting, I know where his fingers are." I rubbed my hands over my jeans. "I need to shower. Ugh, I feel icky."

"What is *wrong* with you?" Zel asked me as he watched me with open aversion.

"So many things, my dastardly demon, so many, *many* things."

I STOOD in my bedroom and looked at the absolute devastation. My eyes tried to take it all in, but on each sweep of the room, I found more things to be dumbfounded about. The walls were covered in blood for one. Red wasn't really my colour for decoration. My pale blue walls would have attested to that had there been any pale blue left to see. My walls looked like I did when

Bonnie and Steven tossed buckets of red paint over me. They were coated, and I knew it wasn't paint.

It was blood. Which was just *wrong*.

The blood had dripped onto my dark grey carpet, staining it in darker patches. I tilted my head back and considered the ceiling. Blood splatter decorated there too. My room looked like a crime scene.

The dresser was cut clean in half. Like a giant sword had cleaved it in two. My wardrobe was smashed as if something heavy had landed on it, but it was the bed I kept returning to. My goose down duvet was ripped to shreds, the room was covered in feathers, the pillows tattered, the mattress torn into three sections, and the bed frame was merely nothing more than splinters.

"What?" I looked around again. "How?" I blinked as a feather fluttered slowly down. "When?" I looked at Chaz, who stood beside me, his head dipped, his chin resting on his chest. "What the *fuck* happened to my bedroom?" I asked clearly as the shock wore off.

"There was a slight misunderstanding," Chaz began.

"Slight?" I looked around again and picked my way over the debris on the floor. "Where the hell are my clothes?"

"They're there," Zel told me helpfully as he took a giant bite out of an apple as he leaned against my doorpost.

I followed his finger and looked at the wardrobe. Tilting my head, I could make out my clothes. My ripped and torn clothes. "Sam!" I screamed as I pushed past a laughing Zel and ran to the kitchen. I slammed my hands down on the kitchen table as I glared at him, and he met my glare with an indifference that ratcheted my anger up about ten levels beyond furious.

"You *shredded* my bedroom," I seethed at him as I felt the pool within me stir with anticipation. "Whose blood is on my walls?"

"Be grateful it isn't yours," he replied nonchalantly.

"Is it Yeqon's?" I demanded. "Are you freaking insane? Do I have *demon blood* on my walls?"

Sam scoffed and looked away from me as he tilted back on the chair, his stare on the garden outside.

"Don't you *dare* ignore me, you stubborn demon." I knew I was shouting in his face, and I didn't care. Sam shoved the seat back angrily as he stood.

"Don't I dare?" he roared back. "Don't I *dare*? I dare, witch, because you were *mine*."

"I'm not anyone's!" I shouted back at him. "And I told you and I told you and I *told* you again, I thought he was *you*."

"Well, that's alright then," Sam mocked me. "We're even."

"Even?" I demanded.

"As I watched him bleed on the bed you fucked him on, I imagined he was *you*," Sam told me coldly with a smirk as he turned to walk away from me.

"I didn't fuck him!" I screamed at him as tears threatened to spill. I always cried when I was angry, and Lord above, I was so incensed because he had destroyed my bedroom in a *temper tantrum*.

"But would you have stopped him?" Sam snarled, his eyes glowing green with anger. "No. You would have spread those legs for anyone who offered."

"Well, you offered and I said no, so maybe I *am* fussier than you think." I stood straight, my anger suddenly cold and hard within me as I met his fury with my own cold stare.

"I *did* offer. You suck dick well, but then whores always do." Sam showed me a lot of teeth as he smiled at me. "But then your actions reminded me why I don't fuck slutty and desperate."

The cold anger within me snapped. "I will kill you!" I launched myself forward at him. Strong hands grasped me, and I wrestled to get free of whichever one of his toadies held me. "Let me go." I struggled, and even as I did so, I felt it rising within me.

Take us, we are yours.

I shook my head to rid myself of the seductive whisper. Control. I needed control.

Star, we are yours. Take *us.*

"What's wrong with her *now*?" Zel asked, his glee evident as he stood to the side and watched the scene with delight.

I was caught fast in the arms of whoever held me as I felt it rising and rising within me. My head bowed as I struggled with the pulling and tugging inside. My emotions ran riot over me, through me, my blood raced in my veins, my body was shaking with anger. The cold, rigid anger I had formed at Sam braced itself for the rushing of power that surged to meet it.

My mum always told me that still waters run deep. I was about to dive deep, and my waters were no longer *still.* They crashed against the cold barriers I held around them. Containing them. Keeping them *in.*

I lifted my head and met his stare. Cold control spread across my limbs, and I effortlessly stepped out of the embrace of the one who held me.

"Whoa, what the hell happened to her eyes?"

"Witch." Sam took a step towards me. "Don't," he warned.

I smiled at the sinfully dark demon, who actually looked concerned for me. "Too late."

The world turned white.

CHAPTER 21

THE WIND TORE AT MY CLOTHES, I COULD FEEL IT IN MY *BONES*. The entire world was white, not covered in snow or anything explainable. I was in a forest, and the trees were white. White wood, white leaves, white berries. The grass was white. The sky was white.

The world had been bleached.

"Did I do this?" I asked out loud. The wind picked up, and I huddled against its force as leaves and debris swirled around me, creating a vortex that I stood in the middle of, crouching under the pressure of the wind. "Stop it!" I yelled.

The wind died.

I stood straight and turned slowly in a circle. I was in a desert. I had seen pictures of the white sands of the Caribbean. This was not that. This was sand turned white. Sand dune after sand dune rose and fell like frozen waves across the land under a sun that held no heat.

"Sam!" I yelled into the silence. There was no sound. I turned again. My feet made no sound on the sand. I jumped up and down on the spot. Nothing. "Sam!" I screamed.

A flutter caught my eye, and I turned quickly. It was gone. "Who's there?"

The wind picked up again, and once again I was crouching from the force of it. The cyclone travelled fast over the desert, and I braced myself as it enveloped me. I stood in the middle of it, staring upwards at the white cloudless sky.

"Where am I?"

Again the wind was gone, and I was on the edge of a cliff, looking down at a colourless sea. I could see the fish and sea animals clearly. I turned swiftly when I saw a shape that was too close to shark shape in the water below me. I stared out over plains of long white grass.

Another flutter, and I turned and came face to face with my gran. "Gran," I whispered as I fell forward and embraced her.

Gran hugged me back for a long time as I cried in her arms. "You're okay, lass, I got you now," she said as she soothed me.

Eventually, I stood back and rubbed my nose as I sniffled. There were more people now. The plains were full of them. They all stood immobile staring in the same direction.

"Where am I?"

"The Plains of the Dead."

"I don't want to be here," I told her with some alarm.

"Oh?" Gran looked around. "We better find someone to tell them then. I wonder who we can ask?"

"Funny. Honestly, I'm no longer in the land of the living, and you decide now's the time to be a comedian." I rolled my eyes at her as I looked around. "What are they staring at?" I asked quietly as I looked at the dead.

"Hmm?" Gran stopped chuckling. "Oh, they're really boring."

I looked at my gran in surprise. "What?"

"They are," she said defensively. "They stand there for eternity, waiting."

"Waiting for what?" I asked as my attention returned to the lifeless statues. "Wait, did you say eternity?"

"Give or take a millennium." Gran shrugged. "You want to stay here or move on?"

"Move on." I nodded firmly. The dead-kinda-alive-but-definitely-statue people were freaking me out. "Wait." I grabbed Gran's arm. "When you say move on, you don't mean like to here. *Spiritually.*"

"You're a breath of fresh air." My gran beamed at me. "I missed you so much."

"I miss you too," I said tearily.

"Oh stop crying, or I'll give you something to cry for," Gran scolded me. "Call the wind," Gran instructed me. "Come on, Pocahontas, I don't have all day."

"She *painted* with the colours of the wind, she didn't *call* the wind." I shook my head in despair. "You watched that movie with me a million times."

"Whatever, call the wind."

I was about to say *how* when I saw the mini tornado coming straight for me. "Brace yourself!"

Gran stood calmly in the eye of the storm and waggled her eyebrows at me. "You can stop now."

"Wind?" I called hesitantly. The wind disappeared. I was in a valley with high walls, thick white vegetation, scattered shrubs and trees and a beautiful crystalline waterfall that fell into a clear lake. "Wow."

"Pretty, isn't it?" Gran smiled as she walked leisurely towards the water. "This is my favourite place."

"It's beautiful." I looked around me in wonder as we walked together. "Is this, um…"

"If you say heaven, I will whack you so hard, lass, you'll be feeling it next week."

"I wasn't going to say that," I lied as I avoided eye contact with her. "Where am I?"

"This is the Land of the Souls." Gran sat down on a big white boulder. "But you knew that."

"Why haven't they moved on?" I asked quietly as I sat beside her. "They should be up or down by now, no?"

"Elevator broke. Repairman can't come until…Tuesday?"

"Are you going to be serious at all?" I demanded as I glowered at her. "I love you, and I love being able to see you, but can you tell me *why* I'm seeing you and how I got here?"

"You took a pretty good chunk out of that binding spell when you had your lovers' spat with your demon." Gran patted my hand in affection.

"I heard them." I remembered. "My powers, they spoke to me."

"Well, that's interesting." Gran looked at me speculatively. "Never heard that happening before."

"I don't want to be interesting."

"Too late, you're a natural at it." Gran grinned at me cheekily.

"Gran, please?"

She sighed long and loud. "Fine. I was just teasing. But you're right. Your demons are tearing my cottage apart trying to find you."

"My body isn't there?" I asked in alarm.

"Why would it be there when *you* are here?"

I stood abruptly. "Are you telling me I'm physically here?"

"You think it was your spirit?" Gran cocked her head as she considered me. "That's stupid thinking."

"What am I supposed to think?" I demanded in exasperation. "I *know* nothing."

"Well, you don't need to shout it to the world," Gran muttered. "Did you not learn when I passed, girl?"

"No. Mum sent me back to uni."

"Jean." My gran shook her head in sadness. "Stubborn as a mule, that one."

I looked at my gran in amusement. "Mm-hmm, I wonder where she gets it?"

"Hush you." Gran patted the stone, and I sat back down. "You were bound by that peacock Hamish and me. I didn't know he put a blood spell on you until it was too late. But…" Gran sighed. "It was for the best. Your powers are…wild. Unbound, you would have caused too much destruction."

"Then why am I being unbound now?" I asked in alarm.

"When you were a *child*," Gran emphasised. "As a child, you would have been destructive; as an adult, you can be taught."

"But then Hamish died." I nodded in understanding. "You died," I added sadly.

"Your mother promised me I would get you when you were twenty-one." She sighed heavily. "Old ticker got fed up waiting though."

"I'm sorry."

"Why? You didn't make me eat bacon and butter and all the other deliciously wonderful bad things that clogged me up." She looked me over. "Although looking at you, maybe you need some bacon and butter."

"No need to make it personal," I said with a smile as I nudged her.

"I told you to let them in," she admonished me.

"I did. I do readings, I listen to them, I pass on their messages," I protested.

"Parlour tricks," Gran scoffed. "I meant seances, Ouija boards, be the actual conduit you were supposed to be."

"A conduit?"

"Yes, you are the bridge."

"Bridge to where?" I asked apprehensively.

"Here." Gran looked up at the sky. "There, everywhere."

"Is that a serious answer?" I asked sceptically. "Or one of your funny things?"

"You can take a soul up, down or here." Gran was serious.

"*I'm* the elevator repairman?" I asked loudly.

"Kind of."

"But Sam said there are reapers, he said the reapers take souls."

"Oh, they do, but you can take them *from* the reapers." Gran winked at me. "Say you die—shut up and listen," she cut off my question. "Say you die. The reaper comes for you. He takes your soul from your still warm body, he carries it beyond the veil, and he drops it off." She scratched her chin as she thought about it.

"He's like the go-between, the middleman." She considered her next words. "Do you know how long you *wait* for someone to come get you once you've been dropped off?" I shook my head. "Eons," she answered.

"Eons?"

"Eons," she confirmed. "Yes, some pop right out of there in seconds, but most of them, the *so-sos*? The could-be-up, could-be-down ones? They spend *eons* waiting for their number to be called."

"Gran, is this…" I looked around. "Is this purgatory?"

"Mmm, not quite. Almost. It's like the next level up. Purgatory, you have to atone first. Ugh, talk about tedious."

"Have you been to purgatory?" I asked apprehensively.

"Don't be ridiculous, lass, I'm a witch."

"So?"

"I knew exactly where I was going. Now I just need to wait."

"For?"

"You, of course."

"What will I do?" I wasn't keeping up. My head hurt, and something was *pulling* at me.

"You can fast track souls." Gran looked delighted.

"I don't think that's for me to decide," I said hesitantly. "I think if there is an *up* and a *down*, someone may disagree with me interfering."

"Oh, don't be so square." Gran huffed in exasperation. "You cannot clear everyone, but you can fast track the ones the reapers know are going up or down."

"How?"

"I haven't figured that out yet," Gran admitted as she watched the waterfall.

"This is what my powers were bound for?" This didn't sound so bad.

"What?" Gran gave me her attention again. "Oh no, that's nothing."

Speak for yourself, Gran.

"No, you can also remove blood curses. Especially from certain princes of hell."

"Who is it?"

"Asmodeous."

"Never heard of him." That had to be a good thing, surely.

"Pft."

"Bad then? Wonderful."

"Have you ever heard of the seven circles of hell?" Gran asked.

"Um, vaguely."

"The seven deadly sins?"

"Yes! I know that."

"They're the same." Gran told me.

"What do you mean?"

"Each sin is a level of hell. Each level is ruled by a prince of hell." Gran patted my hand again. "And each prince is a complete and utter bastard."

"And Sam?" I asked with growing trepidation. "Is he a prince?"

"The Watcher?" Gran chuckled. "No, he and his fallen brethren are more soldiers but powerful in their own right."

"You call them Watchers," I mused.

"They are. They watched the world when they were in heaven, and they wanted what they should never have." Gran frowned. "Like the archangels that followed them, they coveted, and now they rule in hell for their sin."

"So the seven levels?" I brought her back to my current problem. I glanced at my surroundings. *One* of my more pressing problems, I should say.

"Asmodeous, he rules Lust."

"Oh." I was somewhat disappointed in my demons, lust was so…cliché.

"Your Watchers are not tied to any level," Gran assured me. "There are princes of hell, but the Watchers answer only to themselves. They orchestrated the fall. When Azazel fell like a star from heaven, their destiny was forged."

"Azazel fell first?" I whispered.

"You think a loyal soldier like Azazel would let his general fall into unknown territory?" Gran looked at me with a knowing eye.

"No, Zel would cut his arm off first."

Gran nodded in agreement.

"So, I cleanse a curse from Asmodeous, and then what?"

"Go home?" Gran shrugged carelessly. "Learn your necromancy. Be the bridge."

"This makes no sense," I said just as I doubled over. "Ow, shit," I hissed.

"Star?" Gran was rubbing my back in concern.

"It's pulling me," I groaned as I clutched at my stomach.

"What is?" Gran asked me with mounting panic.

"*Him*," I hissed. "Gran!" I screamed. The pull tightened, and then I was whooshing, there was no other word for it, I whooshed.

My back was on a cold floor. I opened my eyes and met green glowing ones. "Demon."

"Witch," Sam growled. "Where the fuck did you go?"

CHAPTER 22

"Away from you," I mumbled as I slowly got to my feet. I looked around and realised I was back in Dunnottar. "How am I here?" I looked around the large grassy area between the ruins and stared up at the old castle.

"How long have you been able to travel?" Pen asked curiously as he watched me carefully.

"I can't, I have no idea where I went or how I got there, but I know it hurt like a bitch being brought back." I levelled a glare at Sam, who stood impassively in front of me.

"Describe the hurt," Pen asked as he moved closer. He slowly walked around me and then leaned forward and *sniffed*. I saw Sam move also, almost as if he was walking in a counter circle to Pen.

"Whoa, that is *not* okay," I told Pen. "Boundaries, remember."

"You smell different," Pen mused as he looked over my head, at Sam I assumed, but since no one acknowledged him at all, Pen continued to watch me. "Chaz," Pen called.

Chaz stepped up to me and very slightly leaned inwards and inhaled. He gave a quick nod to Pen, and when Der and Ros also stepped forward, I stepped back.

"Sniff-a-thon can stop now."

One day, just *one* day, I'm going to be fully aware of my surroundings, so when I move to *avoid* someone, I don't end up being flush against the one thing I'm *definitely* avoiding. I could feel his heat from behind me, and although my reflex was to jump away, the message from my brain to my feet wasn't received.

His breath stirred my hair as he dipped his head to speak to me. "Little witch, where have you been?"

"London, to see the Queen," I snapped irritably.

"You smell of the dead," Sam continued as if I had never spoken at all. "Where have you been?"

I started to turn towards him when his hand shot out and stopped me. "What's the problem now?" I asked tiredly.

"Star." Chaz moved towards me slowly. "Star, you need to walk towards me."

"Why?" I asked suspiciously.

"Can you just do it, and I'll explain." Chaz sighed with exasperation, and as I took a step forward, the hand turned vice-like on my arm.

My eyes flew to Chaz's in alarm, and then the world *winked*.

I looked around frantically. I was on a large clifftop where long grass came to my knee. I could hear the water, whether sea or ocean, I didn't know, but it was crashing against the rocks below. The landscape stretched out before me, and in the dusk of night, I couldn't see any particular markers to indicate where I was.

The hand was still holding me, and suddenly I was pulled backwards into a chest. His arm came around my waist as I was pulled closer. His nose trailed along my jawline, and I inhaled his scent deeply—I would *never* make the mistake between them again. Sam's unique smell of sandalwood and citrus laced with smoke filled my senses.

"Witch," I heard him rumble gruffly as his arm pulled me even closer. It was a solid steel band around me, and I jerked slightly when his other hand tangled in my hair, tugging my head backwards. "Where did you go?"

"How about we start with where am I now?"

"My questions first." I felt his smile against my neck as his head nestled into my neck. "You travelled."

"I don't think I did," I argued. Why was I reacting to his touch like this, hadn't he destroyed my bedroom, called me names and lashed out at me in anger only hours ago?

"Do you know what happened to your eyes?" he asked as his lips traced my ear.

"Are you pulling the moves on me for answers?" I tried to escape and huffed in defeat against his immovable hold.

"You think I'm flirting?" Sam laughed lowly as he held me.

"No, I think you're seducing," I retorted angrily. "Which, considering what you think of me, is insulting not only to my body but my *intelligence*."

"Your body doesn't mind," Sam murmured as he moved his hand from my waist, and I daren't breathe as he inched closer to my breast. "Your body *sings* for me, little witch."

"Well, I bloody mind, demon!"

"Do you?" he asked, his voice silky and low, and as butterflies erupted within me, I wasn't sure who I wanted to punch more: him for being a Class A dick or me for reacting to the arsehole. "Your scent tells me differently."

"You people seriously need to stop sniffing me, I'm not a juicy bone for you to eat."

I was spun in his arms, and my hands flew up landing on his chest as I looked up at him, startled. Sam looked down at me, the low burning green glow of his eyes strangely enticing. "Demons, not people," he told me as his lips moved down to mine. "I do want to eat you." His eyes pulsed slightly as if I needed the reminder that he was a demon.

"Sam?" Uncertainty coursed through me as I looked up at him. *Do not lick your lips.* My teeth clamped down, nothing was getting in *or* out. "Where are we?"

"It isn't relevant." His lips hovered over mine enticingly. "Where were you?"

"Sam," I breathed as a featherlight kiss was pressed to the corner of my mouth.

"Tell me, because you smell of the dead," Sam said as his mouth moved down the column of my throat. "If I didn't know better, I'd say you were on the Plains of the Dead."

"Why would you think I'd been there?" I asked as I moved my head back *away* from his touch so I could look at him.

"You reek of loss," Sam told me as he recaptured me and brought me nearer to him. Images of the dead statues flashed in my mind, and I felt a sense of sorrow for them. Sam stood back and looked down at me coldly. "You travelled to the Land of the Souls?"

"Not intentionally," I admitted as I realised there was no point denying it. He could smell it on me, and they were, oh yeah, tele-flipping-pathic.

"You are so reckless," he growled at me as his eyes flared.

"I'm reckless?" I demanded angrily. "At least I didn't try to seduce someone to get them to talk to me!"

"You wouldn't know what me seducing you would feel like," Sam scoffed as he turned from me, his gaze wandering over the long grasslands.

"Excuse me? I've been on the receiving end of it, or is that something else you're conveniently forgetting?"

Sam laughed in derision. "That wasn't *seduction,* that was a clumsy *fumble.*"

"Well, my *clumsy* fumbling was enough to get you off," I countered waspishly. "I didn't hear any complaints."

"I didn't complain at your ministrations," Sam conceded. "You spreading your legs and letting someone else feast on your pussy within two days, *that* I objected to."

"Good God, how many fucking times do I need to go through this?" I yelled.

"There," Sam said softly as he stepped forward. "The level of anger you're at, hold onto it."

"What?" I asked in confusion.

"Witch, I need you angry, hold onto it," Sam warned as he reached out, and I jerked back reflexively. "That's it. More anger, little witch."

"I *am* angry, but I am also freaking out, what's happening?" I asked through gritted teeth as I felt the swell within me. "Sam! It's happening." I stared at him with mounting alarm.

"I know," he told me as he reached out tentatively. "You need to let me touch you."

"What? Why?" I asked fearfully as the waters sloshed within me.

"Because I need to come with you this time," Sam told me just as I *winked*.

We stood on the sand dunes, and I groaned as I looked around. "Oh, you have *got* to be kidding me!" I yelled at the white sky even as I saw the mini tornado heading straight for me.

"Are you okay?" Sam asked me distractedly as he looked around. "This is curious."

"Well, hold on, Dorothy, we ain't in Kansas anymore, and that cyclone has my name on it."

Sam snapped his head in the direction I was pointing to see the cyclone, and then we were within it. "Where is it taking us?' he asked curiously.

"Fuck knows, it moves me around like a demented transporter."

"You control it, witch." Sam's lips twitched in a smile. "Tell it to stop."

"Wind?"

We were at the waterfall. Sam looked around quickly and then at me. "Wind?" he mocked, even as he shook his head in bemusement as he headed to the waterfall.

"Have you been here before?" I asked quietly as I searched for Gran while I followed him.

"Yes, but it's never been *white*."

"What colour was it before?" I asked curiously as we both stared into the crystal-clear waters.

"Normal," he told me as he crouched and put his hand in the water. When he pulled it out, I literally saw the colour of his skin *drip* into the water.

"What the actual—"

"You're doing this," Sam said as he stood, cutting me off. "Penemue will be begging you to take him here," he told me dryly. "Don't do it, he and Chaz will never leave."

"That would be a problem," I muttered. I looked around and then mimicked Sam and plunged my hand into the water. He didn't try to stop me, just watched with a raised eyebrow. I withdrew my hand and was disappointed I looked normal. "Why am I different?" I asked as I looked between my hand and his, which was slowly regaining its colour.

"I'm sure your mother has been asking that question all your life." Sam smirked at me as he headed to Gran's boulder. He sat down on it with an easy familiarity as he looked around, his eyes taking in everything whilst he said nothing.

"How do you know this place?" I asked curiously as I followed him.

"This is called the Waterfall of Solitude," Sam told me as he gestured to the waterfall. "I think the answer's in the title."

"But you're not alone."

"Well spotted." Sam's mouth hooked up in his familiar smirk. "You were here last time?"

"Yes, one of the places. I was here with Gran." I looked away from him as I stared at the waterfall. "I wasn't alone then either."

"Your gran is dead. You were here with a spirit, while you are human." He pointed at himself. "I'm a demon, you're human."

"So if I was here with my mum, for example, that wouldn't be allowed?"

"Well, no, but for many reasons more than two humans," Sam

answered as he leaned back on his hands as he appraised me. "Your eyes went white, then your irises glowed blue."

"I glowed?" I asked excitedly. "Like you do?"

"Yes, but trust me, witch. You're nothing like me." He stood and held his hand out. "Can you take us back, or do I need to do it?"

"I don't know how I did this the first time, I may kill us."

"I'm immortal." Sam shrugged uninterestedly. "Good luck with that."

"You're *immortal?*"

"This is what you're going to struggle with?" he asked me as he made a *come here* motion with his hand.

"Why can't you die?" I demanded peevishly. "That's so unfair."

"The sentiment for my well-being is heartfelt, thank you."

"Shut up and take me back." I elbowed him in the ribs for good measure.

We *winked*. I was back at Dunnottar Castle. The others were in the old chapel, waiting patiently.

"Fear or anger?" Pen immediately asked.

Sam huffed a laugh as he took a place beside the opposite wall. "With her? Anger."

"Obviously," Ros said as he beamed at me with almost...pride.

"Tea?" Chaz said with a smile as he passed me a mug.

"This is my mug," I said accusingly.

"Would you rather it was a stranger's?" Der asked me curiously. "Does it make you angry? Sad?"

"Okay, you have to stop all waiting for me to react," I said as I took a drink of tea. "So, we're just winking in and out of my cottage now?"

"You need to stop calling it winking," Ros said good-naturedly. "Sounds weird."

"Well, I whooshed earlier, why not wink now?" I shrugged as I looked around and decided that the floor looked clean enough. I sat down, leaning against the wall tiredly.

"Tired?" Chaz asked me softly.

"I am." I nodded as I closed my eyes.

"So what did you say to make her lose it?" Zel asked Sam.

My eyes snapped open as I met his amused look. "Don't you dare," I warned him even as realisation bloomed within me. "You *baited* me? On purpose?"

He winked. Not as in travelling, but an actual smug, self-satisfied wink. "I referred to her indiscretions with our brother, Yeqon."

"You were nowhere near as polite," I growled at him. "And for the record, *never* refer to my lady parts as a pussy again." Chaz choked on his tea as Ros roared with laughter.

"Will I say vagina?" Sam asked wickedly, his eyes hooded and dark, and I felt a thrill of excitement as he looked at me.

"No, because I'm not thirteen." My face was getting redder as I pulled my attention away from him.

"Crumpet?" Der offered.

"No! Oh my God, this isn't a suggestion box!" Would this mortification never end?

"Hairy box?" Ros offered speculatively.

"Meat taco?" Der high-fived Ros as they both grinned like idiots.

"Stench trench."

My look was deadly. "Stench trench?" I asked sourly. "Really, Zel? *Really?*" I stood abruptly. "You're all immature, small-minded little *shits*." I stormed out of the chapel and made my way in the dark to the Countess's bedroom. I could hear them laughing louder as more vulgar suggestions were bandied between them.

The castle was horrifically spooky in the dark, and I stood hesitantly at the bottom of the short stairs to the upper floor. I screamed when the hand touched my elbow.

"Well, if there are any dead sleeping here, you just woke them," Pen said with amusement as he moved past me. "Come on, follow me."

We climbed the short stairway, and I entered the Countess's bedroom. Making my way to the window, I stared out over the calm North Sea. "It's a beautiful night," I said as I looked up at the moon. "Not ready yet?"

"No. We found the fingers," Pen supplied as he stood at the other window. "Did you know?"

"What? That my *prop* rune stones were actually a Druid's finger bones?" I gave a sarcastic snort. "Nope, have you learned nothing, demon? I know shit."

"You know more than you think you do," Pen said quietly as he considered me. "Your powers are growing, the spell to unbind you may actually not be needed."

"Hamish will be delighted I don't need to crush his bones," I said, feeling a sense of relief.

"Well, about that…"

"He's already dust?" I guessed with a grimace.

"Basically."

"Well, that explains why he isn't here." I turned away from the view and went over to my corner from the previous night I was here. "Am I staying here?"

"We haven't had time to fix your bedroom, but I will make sure that we do," Pen assured me.

"Wouldn't expect you to fix it," I told him as I prepared to curl up in a ball on the stone.

"You're going to freeze." Pen caught my arm. "Did you forget the cave?"

"Was hoping for a blanket, not going to lie." I grinned up at him, avoiding the fact I *had* forgotten about the cave. My brain was short-circuiting; I no longer remembered where I was the night before. I needed to sleep.

"Such a stubborn thing for being so slight." Pen took us to the cave and then led me across the floor to the pile of blankets.

"I'm five seven," I argued as I pulled apart the blankets and lay down.

"I'm delighted for you."

My light laugh carried in the night. "You demons are a pain in my arse, you know that, don't you?"

"Arse is acceptable terminology?" Pen teased.

"Oh shut up." I closed my eyes as heat flooded my cheeks. I heard him move, and then he was lying down beside me, moving me, placing me against his side. "What are you doing?" I asked softly.

"Keeping you warm, Star, nothing more," Pen assured me.

I closed my eyes, fighting the happy smile that threatened to spread across my face so easily. They weren't *all* bad, these demons. "Thank you," I whispered into his side. "Night."

CHAPTER 23

I SLEPT SO WELL ON THE STONE FLOOR OF THE CAVE I WONDERED IF it was the blankets, the rustic setting or the fact I had been exhausted. I then chuckled at myself as I looked around the *rustic setting* of my cave. I slept in a cave, there was nothing rustic about it. I was alone again, I noticed as I stood and stretched. Yawning, I wandered over to the cave opening and looked out over the North Sea. The sea was choppy today and looked absolutely freezing. The water was that dark grey-blue colour which was mirrored in the sky above. Heavy storm clouds sat thick in the sky, and I doubted the power of the blood moon tonight.

Looking around the cave, I wondered if I would spend another night here, or would I actually get to go home? *Why wait?* I looked around one more time. There were definitely no demons here. I could travel. Kind of. Almost. Maybe?

Bracing myself, I closed my eyes and…nothing. What was I supposed to do? Think of home? Click my heels? Twitch my nose? I scratched my head. I closed my eyes again and thought *home*. Opening one eye, I still stood in the cave. Huh.

Sam said to the others that I needed to be angry. I *did* spend most of my life in a constant state of agitation, could I make myself angry? I pinched myself. Nope. All that did was make me yelp in pain and no doubt bruise me.

Think angry thoughts? The complete opposite of how to fly, I mused. I really needed to stop watching Disney movies.

Angry thoughts, okay, let's do this. Sam. Mild irritation flared within me. Despite his angry words and his heavy-handed treatment, I understood why he was pissed. If the shoe were on the opposite foot, I would have gutted him if he did this with Abby, after being with me in the toilets, or even the front seat of my van the night before. He had slept beside me, and I hadn't noticed he wasn't the man I kissed the next morning. Not man, demon. Male. Whatever, *him*. So yeah, he may have destroyed my bedroom and tore all my clothes up and flung me through the air, but was his anger unfounded? Not really.

So Sam didn't make me angry. Huh. I toyed with my jumper. I needed a demon to be mad at. Zel. He popped into my brain unbidden. I ran through several scenarios where Zel pissed me off. He was either protecting Sam or he was just being his naturally dry mean self.

Zel didn't make me angry either.

I was a complete snowflake. None of the demons made me angry. I reacted to Sam, *in the moment*, but when I was rational and adult—cue brain snort—about it, I could see both sides of the argument.

Who else pissed me off without even trying? Ruairidh. The fact his name popped into my head unbidden made my eyes open in surprise. He made me mad? He was sleeping with Abby. Did that make me mad, or was I jealous? I thought about it, hard. Nope, that pissed me off big time.

I felt the waters stir and grinned. I then dredged up the Bonnie incident and the time he had come to St Andrews to "talk" but then never did anything about it once I was home and no longer sleeping with anyone. Sam was right, he had kept me warming as a placeholder for when he ran out of options.

Oh my God, I was his *backup* plan. I paced the cave as my powers churned deep within me, and I thought about my *best* friend Ruairidh. He *was* my best friend, he was a good friend, but he was a spineless shit when it came to women…to *me*. Sam was right. Ruairidh knew I cared for him, liked him as more than a friend, and he didn't let me down gently, or address it, or acknowledge it. He *kept me hanging*.

My powers rose higher, and I reached out to them. *Home.*

I winked, travelled, whatever. I was in my front room, and I was so surprised I managed it I flopped down on my couch in relief. Almost immediately I was on my feet, making sure all of me travelled and I hadn't left anything significant behind. Was that possible? Freaked out at the idea of only half of me turning up, I ran my hands over myself once more. Definitely whole.

Shower. I needed one so badly. I headed to my bedroom and once again took in the devastation of my room. Fine, I could see why he would be upset, but seriously? This? He was an arsehole. My nose wrinkled at the drying blood on the walls even as I rummaged through my torn clothing to find something I could wear. Finding nothing, I went back to the kitchen and found clean clothes folded on top of my dryer. Grabbing jeans, a T-shirt and a long cardigan, I headed back to the bedroom. I ignored the chaos as I locked the en suite behind me and ran the shower. I was so happy to brush my teeth I did it twice.

Leaving a pile of clothes on the floor, I took a long hot shower. I was rinsing out the conditioner when I felt the cold air whoosh into my bathroom. I carried on rinsing my hair as I worried which one was behind the curtain. Grabbing my body wash, I tried to pretend they weren't there. Finally, when the silence was too much, I popped my head out from behind the shower curtain.

"Hey."

"What are you doing?" Sam asked me, even as his jaw clenched tight.

"Taking a shower." I produced my body puff, full of soap suds. "See? Soapy."

"I will fucking *drown* you one of these days," he swore as he closed his eyes, and his lips moved.

"Are you counting to ten?" I asked, genuinely curious, but swallowed hard when he glared so intensely at me that I felt myself pale.

"Kitchen. Five minutes." He stormed out.

"Well okay then," I mimicked his tone. "Bossy bastard." I finished my shower and got dressed. My hairdryer was under who knew what in my bedroom, so I braided my wet hair, and after rooting around and finding clean socks, I went to the kitchen.

Sam and Ros sat at the kitchen table. Ros grinned at me with a conspirator's wink before he schooled his features when Sam shifted his stare from me to Ros.

"What did you think you were doing?"

"We went over this," I said as I filled the kettle. "I had a shower, which honestly, I don't need to even draw you a picture, you were in there." I looked at him and then turned away with a hidden smile. "You're being redundant."

Ros coughed out a laugh and nodded when I asked if he wanted coffee.

"You took my mugs, but you didn't bring them back?" I said with a sigh as I looked at the empty cupboard.

"Dishwasher," Ros supplied helpfully as he pointed to the dishwasher.

"Oh, thanks." I made three mugs of coffee and then stood and waited for either his eruption or his indifference. The room was so cold it was hard to say which way the demon would react.

"How did you do it?" Ros asked me, obviously as fed up with the tension as I was.

"I made myself angry," I answered honestly. "I felt the powers rise, and I used them."

"What pissed you off this time?" Ros asked with a good-natured grin.

"Men," I told him with an easy smile.

"Yeah, that'll do it." Ros stroked his beard as his eyes twinkled with laughter.

"I'm getting better," I said as I drank my coffee. "But, you know, just in case"—my eyes flicked to Sam before returning to Ros—"can I, um, leave anything, like behind or something, if I do it?"

"Like your coat?" Ros asked with a frown.

"She means can she splice," Sam said as his eyes finally rested on me.

"Oh." Ros wasn't laughing anymore. "Well, yes. But it's unlikely."

"How unlikely?" Alarm was mounting within me.

"Seventy, maybe seventy-five percent."

"Oh my God!" My horror must have shown on my face, because Ros was at my side rubbing my arm in what I think he thought was a soothing manner, but in reality was just rubbing my flesh off the bone.

"You need to be taught." Sam's voice was heavy with contempt.

"Well, I don't have a teacher."

"Chaz has offered."

"You're okay with that?" I asked dubiously.

"Why wouldn't I be?" He leaned back in his seat. "Would you prefer Zel do it?"

No, I would prefer you do it, you sanctimonious shithead.

"Most definitely not," I said instead. "Zel would encourage my *splicing.*"

"I'm going to teach you how to fight," Ros said eagerly. "Der too."

"Why do I need to know how to fight?" I asked as my alarm rushed back.

"The Scavengers have accepted a higher bid." Sam's cold voice brought chills down my spine. "If you were to take note of your surroundings instead of walking around fucking oblivious, you would notice the fog has returned." He nodded to the garden. "We haven't much time, get what you need."

"You ripped all my clothes up," I muttered sullenly as I pulled on a pair of boots.

"So, travelling light?" Sam asked facetiously. "Excellent." He grabbed my arm, and we were back in the cave where he instantly dropped my arm.

"She used anger at *men* to travel," he told Chaz. His tone dripped with scorn, and I narrowed my eyes on his back. "Her nature is to forgive too easily," he carried on, despite the fact I was *right* there. "Anger won't sustain the energy for long. She needs to be taught and taught fast."

"Pen will aid me," Chaz said as he looked at me with a smile. "There's no one we cannot teach," he added encouragingly.

"You've met *her* though," Zel grumbled as he lay back on *my* blanket pile, his eyes closed.

"A challenge then." Pen grinned as he stood. "How exciting."

The three of us travelled to a large deserted field. "Where are we?" I asked as I looked around.

"Where and when you are *now* is irrelevant for this exercise," Chaz told me as he bound his hair in his sexy manbun. "Where you are going, that's the lesson."

"You want me to go back to the cave?" I nodded in under-standing.

"Yes." Chaz beamed at me.

"Okay." I shrugged and closed my eyes. I thought of Ruairidh again, and the anger from earlier was now more a muted irrita-tion. I recalled in graphic detail Bonnie telling me how she took Ruairidh's virginity and that she had asked him afterwards if I would mind, and he had *allegedly* said, "Star? Star who?" I felt a surge of anger, but it didn't so much as cause a ripple in my pool.

"I think he's right," I admitted in defeat.

"Anger gone?" Pen asked casually.

"Yeah, well, anger at Ruairidh is gone." I closed my eyes again. "Zel pisses me off every moment, I'll think of him."

I waited. I thought *really* hard of all the horrid things Zel had done and still…zip.

"Okay, anger may not work."

"That's a good thing," Chaz said, dropping down to sit on the grass. "It's a strong emotion, true, but it burns too brightly. It saps your energy."

"How about fear?" Pen asked, and suddenly a huge great white shark was suspended in front of me. I screamed and winked.

I was still screaming when I opened my eyes and looked at the four amused demons even as I tried to stop my shaking.

Pen and Chaz were beside me, and I punched Pen so hard I think I broke my hand. He didn't so much as move, and that ignited my anger more. "Arsehole!"

"Fear works," Chaz said dryly. "Not sure of its practicalities though," he murmured under his breath as Pen rubbed his jaw.

"Is she hysterical?" Zel asked curiously as he watched me hyperventilate in front of them.

"Star?" Chaz asked as he reached out to touch me, and I stepped back in fear and anger.

"Why is she traumatised?" Sam asked in annoyance.

"I may have underestimated her *irrational fear*," Pen admitted.

"Sharks?" Ros laughed. "But she's dry?"

"I didn't send her *to* the sharks."

"Oh." Ros started to laugh. "I would have loved to have seen that."

"Dickhead," I snapped.

Sam stood and walked over to me and took my arm. "Let's try this again."

We were back in the field, and I clung to him as I looked around for the shark. "Where did it go?"

"Hopefully back in the ocean." Sam smirked as he looked down at me. "It makes no sense for you to be scared of them, you're hardly going to come across one in the Highlands."

"Hence why it is called an *irrational* fear."

"You're absurd."

"You should have seen its teeth," I whispered as I tried to calm my shaking hands.

"Sorry," Pen said from behind us. "I didn't realise it was such a strong fear."

Sam tensed beside me, and then the others spun too. Scavengers were advancing on us. "Is this a fear test," I asked warily as I watched them.

"No, this is an attack."

"Well," I said, placing my hand on Sam's arm. "I'm ready, wink me."

"You really do need to stop calling it that," Sam said as he looked down at me, his forest green eyes flickering once with amusement. "Only we have a problem."

"Only one?" I commented snarkily.

"If we run, they can follow us. I don't fancy being in the cave with them, do you?" He acknowledged my vigorous head shaking. "If we go back to the cottage, same problem." He took a step away from me, and his twin swords of flame appeared in his hands. "Sometimes," he said with grim satisfaction, "a message needs to be sent."

"You're going to fight?" I whispered in realisation.

"I need to let some pent-up aggression out," Sam said with a straight face as he watched the Scavengers.

"Why aren't you calling for the others?" I asked worriedly as I saw Pen and Chaz both arm themselves.

"You go fetch them."

"What?" I stared at him.

"Hurry along, witch, they're not content to wait, and the others need the exercise," Sam told me as he nodded to the advancing Scavengers.

I could feel my power, and I looked between the three of them. "I swear, if this is a test…"

"*Today* would be nice," Sam growled.

"Fine." I travelled. In the cave, I quickly filled the others in. Zel was gone before I even finished, Der and Ros not long after. I stood in the cave and looked around. I reached for my power, and it was sleeping again. Excellent. Now what did I do? I sat down to wait and wondered how pissed they would be I hadn't returned.

CHAPTER 24

I WOKE UP TO THE SOUND OF THE RAIN. THE WIND WAS WHISTLING through the cave, and I was shivering. The cave was in darkness, and I knew I was alone. I hadn't expected to fall asleep, and as I got to my feet unsteadily, my brain finally made the connection with my body that travelling took my energy. I needed to build up my stamina. I wondered if that was the reason why I needed to learn how to fight.

A healthier me maybe meant a more energetic me? It was a wonder they hadn't given me a meal plan yet. Maybe they didn't know what that was. Mental note to self, do *not* mention meal plans.

Stumbling, I made my way over to the entrance of the cave and looked out. I hastily stepped back again as the wind was high, the rain almost horizontal as it fell, and the sea was stormy. Pale moonlight flickered on the cave walls, the thundery clouds chasing themselves across the sky.

I had no light in the cave. The others would make a fire, but there wasn't one burning just now, which told me they hadn't come back. *Where were they?* I reached for my power and felt its warm caress as I touched it softly. Did I have enough to travel? But then, I didn't know where they were. I could go home? Fix my bedroom. See if Gran had any books in the cottage that may actually aid me with what I needed to do. Picking up a blanket, I folded it and held it close. I'd need an extra layer when I got to the cottage while I waited for the heating to warm the house up.

I closed my eyes and thought of home. Arriving in my kitchen, I screamed when the presence brushed against me. Quickly realising it was only Hound, I scolded the hellhound for a good minute before he got fed up and walked away from me.

"Bloody stupid mutt," I muttered as I switched the light on and flicked on the timer for the heating. It was mid-October, and some days were still mild, so my heating didn't go on its regular programmed settings until after the clocks changed and the temperature dropped.

I was home for two hours and was in my bedroom, grumbling as I cleaned it, when Zel found me.

"You know you're a witch, right?" he asked me as he propped himself against the door.

"So you keep reminding me," I answered glibly.

"Your magic can do this."

I looked up at him in surprise and then at the room. "It can?"

"Why do you think we need you for the spell?"

"My charming personality?" I suggested. My grin grew as his scowl got worse. "You should try to smile more, Azazel. You're a very attractive male, but you're so grumpy all the time."

"Are you flirting with me?" He looked so horrified at the thought that it made me giggle.

"No, dumbass, I'm trying to be *nice* to you; us fighting all the time wears me out," I admitted with a sigh. "Okay, you need me for the spell, which I can't read by the way, and you need me because of my blood."

"Correct." Zel nodded even as he frowned. "But you could be full of juicy blood and not be any use for the spell because you need to be a witch, a *strong* witch."

"I tell you to be nicer, and you counter with *full of juicy blood*. I mean, seriously, can you see why I struggle?"

"I was being nice," he grumbled as he frowned at me. "And as always, you missed the point."

"No, I heard you. Forgive my sensibilities that my whole entire being felt repulsed at the blood reference." I rolled my eyes at him before I looked around the bedroom. "Okay, so I have zero reference for this, I can't read the spell, and I can't really tap into my power, so how do I fix the room?"

Zel actually smiled at me. "This is why you're a strong witch. You list all the reasons why you can't do something, and instead of saying I can't, you say let's do it."

"But you said I could do it," I said self-consciously.

"Because you can," he told me as he came further into the room, closing the door behind him. "You need to focus. Chaz and Pen are…good at some things, but I'm better."

"Cocky much?" I jibed good-naturedly. He actually huffed out a laugh. Was this really Zel? I thought in wonder, and then remembering my incident with Yeqon, I felt a sliver of trepidation. "You are *you*, aren't you? You aren't someone else?"

"Do you think these scars can be replicated?" Zel asked me, his face hard.

"How did you get them?" I asked quietly. "If I'm allowed to ask."

"Combat." He beamed. Actually beamed. "In the great rebellion, I was captured, and these were given to me as a mark for my treason against our Father."

"Who did that to you?" I asked as I looked at them more closely. They were deep, and although a scar was usually puckered and uneven, they ran in perfect synchronisation, deep grooves into his skin.

"Gabriel, he's such a prick, you'd hate him," Zel told me conversationally as he moved aside a piece of the dresser easily.

"Aren't angels, um, good?"

"No, most of them are annoying, self-righteous zealots."

Wow, I had no reply to that. "Did they hurt? Your scars."

He touched his hands to his face. "I bled for twenty years," he said as he glanced back at me. "Took another fifty years after that for my sight to return. But freedom comes at a price, and my pain was my price."

"Christ, Zel, you're really making me not want to go upstairs when I die."

Zel laughed out loud. "You don't get to go to heaven." He shook his head as he chuckled.

"What? Why?"

"You're a witch. Your blood marked your ticket downwards as soon as the first woman in your line picked up a book on magic." Zel started to gather my clothes. "Now, do you want to learn this or not?"

"I'm hell bound?" I demanded angrily.

"Course you are, anything with *extra* abilities are. Why do you think all the fun stuff happens downstairs?"

"I don't get to see the pearly gates?" It's not every day you're told you're going to hell; he'd need to give me a minute to process.

"Overrated. Plus, they're more bronze than pearl and break more often than not. We used to just prop them open," Zel recalled before he gave me his full attention. "Are you honestly surprised?"

"A little," I murmured.

"Oh." He looked uncomfortable. "Should we do this later?"

"Are you considering my feelings?" I asked suspiciously. "Because I can't be having that. You being nice is already a mind fuck." I caught the narrowing of his eyes and hastily added. "I'm *not* complaining, I like it!"

"Do you want to learn the spell?"

"Yes, please."

"Okay." He made a *come here* motion, and I crossed over the room to him. "The spell you need to do for the blood curse is written in Enochian."

"What's that then?"

"The language of Angels," he said, and I stared at him wide-eyed, causing him to smile slightly. "Are you so arrogant to think that *English* was the language of the first people?"

"I've never thought of it," I admitted. "I mean, I know it wouldn't be, because I remember reading something years ago that said *all* languages are merely dialects of the first spoken words, and as men moved and travelled over the continents, the dialects of that language became a new language of that new community or colony. Common English is basically a bastardisation of multiple languages all melded together."

"Exactly." Zel nodded in approval. "And even *that* English has been further butchered into this slang that you speak in now."

"You seem pretty fluent in slang," I mocked him gently.

"I have to make sure I don't stand out." He shrugged. I swallowed my snort when I saw he was serious. "You cannot read Enochian." He waved his hand up and down my body as if my ineptness at reading the language of *Angels* was my fault, and he returned to his lesson. "But, as a witch, you can cheat."

"There's a cheat sheet for spells?"

"There's a cheat for everything," Zel told me with contempt. "Witches are the masters at cutting corners."

"You really don't like them," I commented as his frown returned.

"Lazy and inherently cunning," Zel said with a grimace. "Usually backstabbing and selfish too. Everything is about power, who has more, who has less, how to get more, their drive for power makes the worst tyrants in history seem humane."

"My gran wasn't like that," I said softly. "My mum isn't."

"Not all are power hungry bitches," Zel conceded, but it was obvious it pained him to do so.

"How do I cheat then?" I asked grudgingly. "And by doing so, aren't you making me into the very thing you despise?"

"I am." Zel nodded. "But I don't like you much anyway, so

once the spell is cast, we go our separate ways, and I'm sure I'll never come across you downstairs."

"Wow, Zel, what a salesman you are."

"Are you going to complain?" Zel demanded impatiently.

"No," I mumbled sullenly. "Cheat me."

"Okay, you need to sit."

"The floor's got demon blood on it," I protested.

"Just sit on the fucking floor and stop whining."

"Fine!" I snapped as I thumped down onto the floor. Gracefully, he sank down across from me, crossing his legs as he did so.

As he sat across from me and closed his eyes, he held his hands out palm upward. "Hands."

"Legs."

One eye popped open, and a crystal blue eye looked back at me in annoyance. "Hands," Zel growled.

It was so easy to push his buttons, but knowing not to push *too* far, I reached out towards him. Cool hands encircled mine. His rich, dark skin accentuated my pasty whiteness, and I envied his beautiful skin tone. His long graceful fingers held my hands gently. "You have beautiful hands, Zel," I said as my fingers curled around his wrists.

"Thank you," he murmured, and I saw the bronze flush of his cheeks. "Now concentrate." Smiling inwardly that Zel and I were actually being nice to each other, I did as he said. "You can feel your power, yes?" he asked.

"Yes, it's there."

"Describe it."

"I think of it as a pool," I admitted self-consciously. "It's as if it's contained within a well within me, and the water usually lies still and out of reach, but then I've never reached for it before."

"That's very descriptive." Zel sounded encouraged. "What happened to the water when you were angry or scared and you travelled?"

"Choppy times," I answered firmly. "It was like the North Sea when I woke earlier, choppy, wild, surging."

"Excellent," Zel said, slightly enthusiastic. "Your eyes better still be closed."

I hastily shut my eyes in case he caught me. "Yip."

"Your heart rate increased, liar."

"You're such a freak," I muttered. "Why are my eyes closed?"

"Because you're concentrating," Zel reprimanded me. "Now, I want you to find the well."

I concentrated and reached the waters easily, their inky blackness almost welcoming me. "Done."

"Now, step into it."

My eyes flew open. "What?"

"Eyes *closed*."

I shut my eyes. "What?"

"Witch, imagine you are standing beside the water, dip your foot in."

"But I'm not standing beside it, it's inside me," I protested.

"It's not a well filled with water either, yet you imagine it inside you so easily," Zel rebuked me quietly.

Oh, well, when he put it like that. "What am I wearing?"

"I don't give a fuck if you're naked, witch, *dip* your damn toe," he growled.

Arsehole. I imagined myself in a full-length ballgown. I had never worn a ballgown in my life, but I was decked out in a blood red ballgown with a high neckline and backless. It came complete with tulle and crystal accents. My long blonde hair was in an elegant twist, and I just knew I had smoky eyeliner and ruby lips. Lifting my skirts, I dipped my toe into the black waters.

"Oh."

"Cold or warm?" Zel asked me softly.

"Warm." I smiled, stepping further in. "Soothing?"

"Don't go further, witch, just your toe," Zel warned.

"More foot than toe," I admitted.

"Take your foot out."

"But—"

Zel was beside me at my pool. He was in his black tunic and leathers, but they were *more*. Armoured shoulder plates accentuated muscles, as the tunic was stretched tightly over his chest and shoulders. A host of weapons decorated his body: knives, daggers, was that *rope*? I looked at him and met his clear blue eyes. "How?"

"We're touching, so we are connected." He looked down at his clothing. "Nice," he complimented me. His eyes ran over me appreciatively. "More formal than I would have thought for you."

"I don't know where it came from," I admitted. "I've never worn this in my life."

"Suits you."

"You just complimented me. Again."

"No one else witnessed it." He grinned at me. He looked around. "Why is it so dark? Make it lighter."

"I can make it lighter?" I asked even as the area brightened. "Oh wow, look at that," I said in wonder. "It's not a well, it's a proper pool." I leaned forward and studied the water.

Zel looked around. "We can work with this." He walked over to the "wall" that wasn't a wall obviously, as this was happening in my head. "I'm going to draw a symbol on your hand, you will replicate it on this wall."

"What is it?"

"It means Awakening," Zel told me as I felt his finger trace a pattern on my hand. I felt the swirls, and when he did it again, my skin glowed lightly.

"My skin is blue?"

"Your magic is reaching for it, your tone is blue." Zel's eyes met mine. "Interesting." He nodded down to the symbol glowing faintly but fading.

I drew it on the wall, but I got it wrong. "Missing the swirliness of the loops," I murmured as I held my hand out impatiently. "Again."

Zel drew the beautiful symbol again, and my skin flared blue. Instinctively, I stepped forward and placed the back of my hand to the wall. "Go." A flash of blue, and the symbol was enlarged onto the wall. I heard the bubbling water behind me and turned. My pool was no longer black, but a beautiful turquoise blue. "Zel, look."

"I see it, witch, I see." He was staring at me, and I glanced at him in question.

"Will I dip back into the pool?"

"No, you've done enough. Time to go." I felt a tug, and my eyes opened to meet Zel's.

"That was awesome." I beamed at him even as I noted I was in jeans and my cardigan.

"You did well."

"Um, thank you." I smiled at him shyly. "Now what?"

Zel stood fluidly as he studied me closely. "I reckon you have five minutes."

"Five minutes for what?" I asked as I stood.

"Clean the room," Zel instructed.

"How?"

"Don't care." He shrugged. "Reach for the pool, do *not* go into the water."

I went back to my now pretty tranquil spot and looked around. The symbol that Zel had shown me pulsed slightly on the wall. Transfixed, I walked over to it, and my fingers traced lightly over the wall. A rush of words formed in my head, words I didn't know but at the same time, I *knew* them.

"Restore." I spoke loudly. When I opened my eyes, my room

was repaired. "Zel? Did I do this?" I asked hopefully, feeling a rush of excitement.

"It was you," he confirmed as he moved forward. "And there you go," he said softly as he caught my fall just as I slipped into unconsciousness.

CHAPTER 25

I WOKE UP IN MY BED COMPLETELY RESTED. HOUND LAY ACROSS THE doorway, and I was pleased to see sunshine outside my window. Tossing back my duvet, I marvelled at the room. I did this. I recreated my room with *magic*.

I was a witch.

I giggled as I looked down at my pyjamas and lost my smile. I was in pyjamas. I felt like I had made a breakthrough with Zel last night, but undressing me? A step too far. I reached for my power and was delighted it was still turquoise and tranquil. I was so happy. I didn't want him to know I was happy though, so I tried to hide my smile. Hound stared at me as I approached him.

"Morning," I greeted. Hound stood and met me at eye level. With a dismissive sniff, he walked past me and lay in the patch of sunlight on my floor. "You have more cat in you than dog," I muttered. The angry growl I received made me hastily leave the room, but still Hound's grumpiness couldn't stop me smiling.

In the kitchen sat three demons, the back door was open, and the other three were outside. From a quick glance out the window, they looked to be fighting...I really hoped that was training.

"Morning," I greeted Pen, Chaz and Ros. The three of them had plates overflowing with food, and I looked back out the window just as Sam savagely struck Zel with a roundhouse kick before slashing at him with his sword. "Are they having fun, or do we need to intervene?" I asked cautiously as I made my way over to the door.

"They're fine," Ros assured me as he chewed his breakfast. "Come, break your fast."

Instead, I went to the coffee pot. This was the first time I was getting Zel's "superior" coffee. I took a tentative sip before I added milk. Hmmm. I liked it. I took another sip. I liked it a lot. The universe was against me in my quest to dislike Zel on principle. "Who put me to bed?" I asked casually.

"Sam," three voices all said at once.

Stinking liberty-taking demon. I was going to have words with this male. *Strong* words.

Taking my cup with me, I went back to the doorway. Der lifted a hand in greeting, but the other two were too engrossed in what looked like to me a kicking the shit out of each other contest. With swords.

"Heard you did well," Der's voice carried over the garden, and he looked pleased for me. "Have you eaten?" he asked, and I shook my head even as I winced as Zel punched Sam firmly in the jaw. The weapons were thrown to the side, and now they were just having a brawl in my opinion. "Go eat, we're almost finished."

Hesitating, I watched the two demons. They were obviously enjoying themselves, and I, in particular, was enjoying the feast they were presenting me with. Both shirtless, both sweating, both wearing grins of satisfaction as they circled each other throwing jabs and punches. Sam wore black sweatpants, whereas Zel was in grey shorts. Sam's golden skin shone with sweat; it was my first time seeing him shirtless, and I prayed it wouldn't be the last. He had thick black tribal looking tattoos on his upper chest and shoulders ending in what looked like black points that spanned across his shoulders and halfway down his arms. His forearms were clear of tattoos as were his hands. He ducked away from Zel's advance and spun, presenting his back to me. I think I may have drooled. His back was tattoo free apart from the tribal markings that flowed a little down from his shoulders. Watching the muscles of his back move as he fought made my mouth salivate. I wanted to lick him—I wasn't even ashamed of the thought

—when he spun back around, and my eyes greedily drank in his perfect abs. I wanted to lick every groove on his body. *Hot damn, he was fine.*

I heard Sam grunt as Zel landed another blow, and I just as equally lapped up Zel's masculine perfection as well. Muscles upon muscles rippled as he moved and fought, and I am pretty sure the term "arm porn" was phrased after some lucky lady saw Zel shirtless. Those biceps needed their own Instagram page. Zel's back had multiple scars across the expanse of his upper body, and I wondered if when they maimed his face, they whipped him as well. My love for the heavenly angels was rapidly diminishing.

"Star," Pen said quietly from behind me, "you're projecting your thoughts quite clearly."

"Huh?" I asked him distractedly as my eyes returned to the glorious display of *male* in front of me.

"We can hear you," Der said to me with amusement. He stepped into my line of vision. "You want to make it a three-some?" His eyebrows waggled at me mischievously as he went to pull his T-shirt off.

What? *Shit!*

I instantly closed my eyes and whirled around and hastened back into the kitchen. Chaz was trying to hide his smile, but Ros was grinning openly as he finished his breakfast. He pulled his T-shirt up, showing me rock hard abs. "Want to lick me too?"

My face was burning, and I wanted to hide, but the absurdity of it all made me grin, and as Ros showed me more of his impressive physique with a playful wink, I started to laugh. Soon, I was doubled over laughing at being caught being a lech. "Well, if you wore more clothes and didn't all look like Chippendale models, I may not be so distracted." I winked at Ros, who laughed loudly.

The Viking-like demon stood and patted my bum as he

passed me to go outside. "Any time you want to take me for a test drive, little lady, you let me know."

Giggling, I sat down at the table and reached for the toast they had…made? I really hoped they weren't appropriating our breakfast illegally. I looked up as the shadow fell over the table.

Sam looked down on me. His face was stone and his eyes hard. He was still shirtless and, dear baby Jesus, did he know how low those sweatpants sat on his hips? "You won't be riding any of my brothers," he growled as he drank from a bottle of water. "You've already *tested* one too many."

It seemed Pen and Chaz suddenly remembered they needed to be in the garden as they both hightailed it out of the kitchen, closing the door behind them.

I fought the sigh, but in reality, I wanted to hit him with the butter dish on the table. I forced down the urge to snap at him. "Morning," I greeted. Mum always said it cost nothing to have manners. I wish she was in this kitchen right this minute, because it was costing me a great deal to be pleasant to the arrogant prick in front of me.

"Zel says he broke through your thick skull, and you have begun your Awakening."

Thick skull? "And I'm done." I stood abruptly, grabbing my toast and my coffee cup. "Going for a shower, and when I come back, you can be back in the cave. I think it's more suited for your personality anyway."

I stalked angrily towards my bedroom and kicked the door shut behind me. Hound was gone, and with my toast hanging from my mouth, and balancing my coffee cup, I climbed back under my duvet. Settling the covers around me, I lay slouched against my headboard as I munched my toast. I should have taken two slices. I was hungry. I finished it in three bites and washed it down with Zel's tasty coffee. It was uncalled for that someone who looked as delicious as Sam could be a giant A-hole.

As I stared out my window, I had flashes of them both training outside and sighed with satisfaction. He may be grumpy and rude, but he looked nice, and that was something at least, as long as he didn't speak.

Speak of the devil, Sam walked into my bedroom without knocking, completely ignoring my cry of protest as he turned and closed the door. Sitting on the chair, he looked around the room. "Zel says you visualise your power as a pool," he started.

"Hello!"

He paused and looked me over. He waited and was quite obviously biting his tongue from his sarcastic reply. I glowered at him while he remained patiently waiting, and they said *I* was the obstinate one.

"You cannot come in here without knocking and then just sit there," I complained, trying so hard to keep the frustration from my voice at the same time as regretting the fact he had taken the time to pull on a black T-shirt.

"Why?" He canted his head to the side as he considered me. "You're not doing anything, and after behaving like a brat, I have no choice."

"A brat?" I asked as I tossed the covers back. "I'm not a brat," I bit out as I stood, my hands on my hips.

His lips twitched with amusement as he watched me, his eyes clearly telling me I was proving his point.

"You're so overbearing!" I cried. "You say mean things, you *keep* undressing me, and you act like I'm a complete inconvenience, yet you follow me *everywhere*."

Sam stood fluidly and crossed the room, stopping mere centimetres from me. "You done?"

"No—"

He kissed me, and I resisted for a good five seconds before I melted into him. *How had I ever thought that Yeqon was him?* I fleetingly thought before I heard Sam's unhappy grumble as he pulled me closer. Sam's kiss was possessive and insistent just as much as it was soft and toe-curling. It was perfect. I kissed him back with equal enthusiasm, and much like the night in the bar, I was soon wrapped around him as his mouth moved over mine and his hands travelled freely over my body. Together we sank onto the bed, and I moaned when he nudged my legs apart before settling in between my thighs comfortably.

I could feel him pressing against me, and I cursed my thin cotton pyjama bottoms and his sweatpants. His hands were on my pyjama top and pulling it off over my head in one swift move. "What are you doing?" I gasped as I arched under his touch as he covered my breasts with a gentle touch. My breasts weren't big, no more than a handful, but as his head dipped to capture a nipple in his mouth, it was clear Sam wasn't complaining.

"I'm undressing you," he mocked as his mouth moved slowly over to my other breast.

"You're a complete dick," I grumbled. I gasped when his teeth lightly nipped my sensitive flesh.

"You don't seem to mind," he murmured as his mouth caught mine again, and he pressed his hips into mine, rubbing his substantial length against me.

"No, it's good, being a dick can be good," I agreed as my hands travelled over his back and then under his shirt. "Off," I instructed, and Sam pulled his T-shirt off, tossing it to the floor before his mouth was on mine again and his tongue duelled with mine. My legs were wrapped around him, and I was very conscious that my hips were rolling under him of their own accord.

Sam moved down my body, his hands resting lightly on my pyjama bottoms. He looked up at me, and his eyes pulsed lightly with desire. "Tell me to stop."

"No," I whispered as I shyly met his gaze. I felt an almost erotic thrill when his eyes blazed green. I heard the tear as he pulled the pyjamas roughly from my body, and didn't care because Sam was devouring me in a way Yeqon never had. My hands were tangled in his thick black hair, and I was only aware of sublime sensation coursing through me. His tongue was inside me, and his thumb brushed my nub gently in rhythm with his tongue as it moved, licking, sucking, rolling over me. "Sam," I moaned even as I tightened my hold. "Sam, you're going to make me—"

"Come," he growled as his mouth moved away from me for a moment to speak. "I want to taste your come on my tongue."

That was all I needed, his voice was thick with lust as his tongue moved out of me and up to my nub as two long fingers slid smoothly inside me. It was going to be my tipping point. As he kept stroking inside me, I felt the orgasm start at my toes. *"Sam!"* Somehow he switched his mouth and fingers back without missing a stroke and his thumb flicked against me, sending me into blissful oblivion. My head tilted backwards as my back arched, and my hands grabbed the headboard behind me as I succumbed to the pleasure racing through my body as I rode out the wave.

"Fuck me, you taste like nectar," Sam groaned before he took one more long lick of my core. "I could fucking eat you all day." He dipped his head back between my legs, his tongue lightly stroking through my wetness. Abruptly he stood and pushed his sweatpants down, and his grin was wicked when my eyes widened. "Want to lick?" he teased as he kicked his sweatpants to the side. "Keep them open," he commanded as he sank back onto the bed.

"My legs?" I asked distractedly as I followed the movement of his lower body as he returned to his previous position.

Sam snorted at my question as his fingers slid back inside me. "Your eyes," he told me with his sexy smirk. He pushed my legs wider apart, and the hunger in his eyes as he rocked back on his heels to appreciate my body replaced any feeling of self-consciousness I had at being so exposed to him. "So fucking innocent," he said as he nudged his dick softly against me.

This is going to hurt, my mind screamed at me while my body told it to stop bitching. "Sam?" I tensed slightly as I felt him at my entrance. "I don't think—"

"Agreed," he said as he kissed up my body. "You don't think, but we can talk about that later." He moved inside another inch or two, and I bit my lip as I felt my lower body struggle to accommodate his size. "Just relax," he murmured as his mouth covered mine. His hips moved forward, and my cry of being overly stretched was drowned in his kiss. Sam tensed and waited, and I felt my heartbeat racing in my ears. His kisses never stopped, and gently he started to rock into my body. "That's it," he encouraged. His mouth was on my breast again, and his tongue traced over my nipple. He adjusted his weight slightly, and then his thumb was brushing over my nub. My hips moved to meet his, and he groaned in approval as he sank deeply into me.

"Sam." My moan was half sigh, half pleading. "I need you to move." I sighed with satisfaction as he did as he was told. My legs wrapped around him, and my fingers tangled in his hair as I pulled him down to meet my kiss. "Fuck," I moaned when he started to move his hips in earnest as he kept a steady rhythm, and for a long time we simply enjoyed the feel of one another.

Suddenly, he was on his knees, pulling my body up with him as his hands grabbed my hips, and his green glowing eyes captured mine. "You feel like sin," he told me as he moved his hips faster.

"Is that bad?" I whispered as my fingers dug into his forearms.

"So *fucking* good," he admitted as his head dropped onto his chest, and he pulled me harder into his body. "You were made for me," he growled before he flipped me around and was pulling my hips up and pushing my shoulders down. How was I fuller in this position? Sam's hand was in my hair, pulling my head back and lifting my body off the bed. "That's it," he encouraged me, pulling me up straighter as his hips drove relentlessly into me. "Like that, oh fuck...that's it." His teeth were in my shoulder, one hand on my hip, the other around my waist in a hold I couldn't get out of even had I wanted to. I didn't want to. My legs were splayed on either side of his thighs, and the only thing holding me up was Sam as he pushed up into me with deep powerful thrusts.

"Sam," I warned as my head fell back onto his shoulder.

"I know," he spoke into my skin as his lips grazed against the back of my neck. "Fuck, I can't hold back anymore," he said roughly as he pushed me back down to the mattress, and my hands wrapped around my wooden headboard, but with the sudden change in angle, I cried out as wave after wave of pleasure crashed over me. His movements picked up speed, and my orgasm caused me to scream for him as I continued to clench around him.

"More," he commanded as he lifted my body and turned me onto my back, never leaving my body. Sam raised my leg and wrapped it around him as he moved relentlessly inside me. His head dipped to look at where we were joined, and as he watched himself plunging into me, I saw him bite his lip. He was so sexy I almost came again just watching *him* watching *us*. Raising his head with a low growl, he met my half-lidded look. "*Fuck*," he hissed, and then his mouth was on mine, his tongue stroking against mine. My legs wrapped tightly around him as my final orgasm took control of my body. One of his hands slid under my back as his other propped himself up over me, and still he kept moving, his pace never lessening. He tore his mouth away from mine as he roared, his whole back bowed, and his head was thrown back as his own release poured from him.

We lay tangled in each other's arms for a long time in silence.

Sam's head was on my chest, one arm flung possessively over my hips as my hand trailed through the damp locks of his hair.

"We should move," I suggested as my eyes refused to open.

"Shower," Sam agreed. "You need to be ready for tonight."

My eyes flew open. "It's tonight?"

"Yes," he said as he moved his head off me and sat up. I watched him shake his head as if to clear the cobwebs of sluggishness, while he stretched. "Fuck, woman," he said, grinning as he stood, "I knew you would be good."

"Just good?" I looked at him, and I did feel sexy when he looked down at me, his eyes roving over my body slowly.

Sam bent and kissed me. My arms wrapped around his neck, and when he straightened, he took me with him. I was on my knees, our mouths still fused together when his strong arms picked me up, my legs wrapping around him, as he walked us into my en suite. That afternoon, I had shower sex for the first time in my life, and I had absolutely no complaints.

"GLAD YOU COULD JOIN US," Zel commented dryly when Sam travelled us to Dunnottar Castle. I blushed scarlet while Sam simply ignored him. We were in the quad area of the grounds, with the castle behind us and the chapel in front. Open fields were on one side, and the ruined wall of the tower to the other.

"Are we ready?" Sam asked the others as he cast a watchful gaze over them.

"Almost set," Pen confirmed as he stepped up to me with a smile. "You good?"

I nodded shyly. It was a bit disconcerting knowing that they all knew what Sam and I had been doing for most of the day.

"The length of time they've been gone?" Der joked with a knowing smile. "I'd say she was better than *good*."

"Brother," Sam's voice held a warning note in it as he cast a sharp glance Der's way. "That's enough."

Der mumbled an apology, and I turned away trying to hide my smile. I'd been unsure how Sam would react to the others and their comments. I wasn't so naïve to think that there wouldn't be *something* said, but I hadn't been sure if he would let them tease me. It seemed teasing was off the table, and that made the butterflies I had with Sam swirl happily in my tummy.

"Star," Chaz said as he approached me, "when the moon is at its most powerful, we will begin the unbinding. As soon as you are unbound, we will give you the spell. With Zel's help yesterday and your newly unbound power, you should be able to read the spell. Are you ready?"

I looked at Chaz, and I nodded, feeling slightly overwhelmed. I hadn't realised I was doing a two-for-one show tonight. I felt Sam step up behind me. "Are you sure?" he asked me softly, and I leaned back into him for a moment, savouring his strength, as his hand ran soothingly down my arm.

"Let's do this," I said with a confidence I hadn't been feeling, but as I looked over my shoulder and up at Sam, I knew I could do it.

"Get it ready, brother," Sam ordered as he stepped away from me, barking out orders to the others.

I could do this, I told myself as I mentally prepared. *Couldn't I?*

CHAPTER 26

I WATCHED THEM PREPARE, AND AFTER SEVERAL MINUTES, I thought it only prudent that I ask *what* they were doing. I was the one being unbound, what were they preparing for?

Chaz and Pen were using what looked like a pestle and mortar to grind herbs and weird looking spiky white flowers. I decided they were the safer option to approach as Der and Ros built a huge bonfire, which they assured me no one else could see. I found it hard to believe since we were on top of a big ass cliff, but felt it better not to argue with them. Zel and Sam spoke together on the other side of the grounds as they checked weapons. Why we needed weapons, I didn't know. I was leading up to that question though.

"Hi," I greeted the two safer demons. Both looked up at me with the same polite smile. "Can I help?" I asked as I watched Chaz sprinkle a fine powder into his stone mortar.

"Not just now," he said and flicked his eyes to Pen.

"You should get comfortable," Pen told me as he looked me over.

I was wearing jeans and a purple hoodie under my thick black double-breasted woollen coat. "I am comfortable," I told them as I sat down beside them.

"Did Sam see your clothes?" Chaz asked casually.

"Yes, he was with me when I got dressed," I answered easily even as my cheeks reddened at what I had just confirmed, and I saw Chaz wince at my easy tone.

Pen looked over at Sam and Zel, and frowned. "One moment." He stood and made his way over to them.

"Are you okay?" I asked Chaz quietly as I plucked a blade of grass from the ground and studied it in the dying afternoon light.

"Of course, Star," he replied as he crushed more leafy things together. "Why wouldn't I be?"

"I don't know, I just want to make sure you aren't sore with me," I admitted as I looked around the castle ruins and studiously avoided eye contact.

"I don't understand, sore?"

"Oh, I mean mad at me." I sighed. "No, not mad, it means put out. Upset."

"Oh." Chaz blinked in surprise. "Why would I be upset?"

"Um…" I felt like an idiot. Chaz and I had a connection, yes, but it was friendship. Okay, I had contemplated flirting with him, but if I was completely honest, the only demon who had held my attention the whole time had been Sam. From the time we were buried together, the attraction had been there. Even before then, if I was honest. It had always been Sam, well, except when it was Yeqon. I heard the loud snap and looked over to find glowing green eyes stare back at me. *Oops.* Smiling, I turned my attention back to Chaz. He was watching me with a sad smile as he looked between the two of us.

"You are beautiful, inside and out," Chaz told me. "And I would have been honoured had you picked me." He looked over at Sam with a faraway look in his eyes. "But you were not meant for me."

"Huh." I plucked another blade of grass and looked back over at Sam, who was once again talking to Zel, their heads bent together. Pen had moved over to Der and Ros and seemed to be deep in conversation with them. "Funny you say that," I mused.

"How so?" Chaz asked as he sprinkled more powder into his bowl.

"My gran, when she passed, she came to me at St Andrews," I told him. "I was with Ruairidh, and I knew she had gone." I swallowed the lump in my throat. "And I remember I took his hand, and she looked at it and said he wasn't meant for me." I looked once more at Sam, who was watching me across the space. "She said *he is not your destiny. Let him go, Star, a much darker one waits for you.*" I turned back to the blue-eyed male across from me. "Is he my darker, Chaz?" I asked softly.

"You should start to prepare, we do this at dusk." Pen sat back down beside me and handed me a bundle. "You need to change."

Standing, I unfurled the bundle, and a long white dress dropped to the grass as I held it in front of me. "Getting strong vibes of Kate Bush telling Heathcliff she's come home," I murmured as I studied the dress. I saw their blank faces. "Too much 'Wuthering Heights' and not enough clifftop in October. You get me?"

"You won't be cold when the ritual starts," Pen told me confidently.

"Ritual?" My brain stumbled slightly, but I pushed past it. "And until the *ritual?*"

"You have a coat," Sam said as he wrapped his arms around me, "and me to keep you warm." He turned me in his arms. "Come, I'll help you change." I ignored Zel's disgusted snort of contempt and Ros's muttered *yeah, right.*

I followed Sam back into the castle, and he led me to the Brewery area. It was fully enclosed and made me skittish because of the plaque outside it about the "ghostly hauntings" which, considering I could see the dead, was stupid. My head snapped up and around.

"What is it?" Sam asked as he produced a torch from thin air, it seemed.

"There are no spirits here," I said as I looked around and pulled inwards slightly. "Not one."

"It is not uncommon for spirits to avoid places," Sam said as he shrugged.

"But that plaque tells of at least three ghosts, so where is the woman in green plaid, where is the deerhound, where is the soldier? Where are *any* of the soldiers burned in the church?" I chewed the inside of my lip as I considered it. "There is nothing, this place is void." I looked at Sam. "Zel said this place is soaked in the blood of traitors, enemies, innocents, where are they?"

"They must have moved on." Sam shrugged again. His finger trailed slowly along my jaw. "It is not for you to worry about just now." He looked at me as his eyes glowed slightly in the torch-light. "Okay?"

I nodded even as I sighed. He kissed me softly and then with more urgency. The torch was laid down in the old brewing vat, which was a circle indentation on the floor where they used to brew the castle's ale. The torch flared, and soon we had our own low-level lighting as Sam's hands pushed my coat open and off, catching it seamlessly before it fell to the ground. My hoodie was pulled over my head, and I gasped into his mouth when he lifted me before I was pressed against the wall. My hair was in a messy bun, which I was grateful for as my head rested against the wall while Sam's hands made short work of my jeans.

"Sam," I protested as he pushed my jeans down. "Should we be doing this?"

"Absolutely." He nodded as his lips kissed their way down my throat.

"Aren't we busy?" I asked just before my whimper mewled out of me as his strong fingers moved my underwear aside and he pushed them inside me. His fingers were perfection as he strummed my body like I was his instrument.

"I am *definitely* busy," he agreed, and I caught his smirk before he was on his knees before me, his tongue moving through my folds.

"Oh shit," I groaned as my hands twisted in his hair. "This is so inappropriate," I murmured as he pulled my underwear down and, lifting my leg, placed it over his shoulder. I felt his smile just before he lapped at my core. "Mmm more," I encouraged him as his fingers picked up their pace. The wall scraped my back as I rubbed myself against his mouth, greedy for the sensations he created within me.

Swiftly he stood, and even as he picked me up, he was loosening his own clothes. Sam lifted me higher against the wall, and then I was being lowered *onto* him. "Oh fuck," I moaned as he filled me and instantly started moving his hips. My head lolled backwards as I clung onto his shoulders. Sam was teasing my breasts as he fucked me hard against the wall, and all I could do was hold on. My arms looped around his neck, and my legs curled around his waist as he somehow got deeper and deeper within me.

"This is insane," I whispered before I felt my orgasm rising. My nails dug into his shoulder blades while he swallowed my cries as I came undone for him. Sam caught me as I staggered when he let me down, and with a gentle push on my shoulders, I was on my knees, my tongue moving over him eagerly as he encouraged me to take more of him into my mouth.

"More," he whispered in the dimly lit room, looking down at me with stark hunger in his eyes as he pushed at the back of my throat. His hand caught my chin, and I tilted my head back slightly, allowing more of him in. His eyes flared bright green as I worked his length, my hand keeping rhythm, stroking him, as he thrust into my eager mouth. "So fucking good at this," he whispered as his head tilted back. Sam's hand loosened my bun only to catch most of my hair as it fell free in his hand. "I need to dictate the pace now," he warned me, and I nodded as I braced my hands against his strong thighs. Thank God he was holding my head steady, otherwise he would have broken my neck or knocked me over completely. He was almost violent in his thrusts, but it was so hot, watching his face twist in pleasure, knowing I was the one making him lose control, that I didn't complain, and then he suddenly stopped and spilled in my mouth. His groan echoed in the chamber, and I continued to lick him gently while he softened. He dropped his head against the wall as he recovered, his breathing heavy, as he ran his hand through my hair.

Tentatively, I drew my head back and tapped his thigh. "Just realised my knees are sore," I admitted awkwardly. Sam helped me up, and I studied my grazed knees. "Do you think there's dirt in them?" I worried as I watched Sam straighten his clothes.

"I have a salve I can rub on your knees and your back."

"My back?" I twisted my head to see, but I'm not an owl and my neck only allows so much movement. "Is it bad?"

"No," Sam assured me as he held out the dress to me. "Put this on. I'll tend to your scrapes outside."

I held the dress up dubiously and then with a resigned sigh, I looked for my underwear.

"They need to stay off." He was looking at me, and I hesitated slightly at his expression. "I think I stood on them," he told me. "They're best left where they are."

"Oh." I bit my lip. "Not sure this dress allows for commando," I said as I looked at the floaty white skirt. "A strong breeze, and the others will be up close and personal with my lady parts."

Sam's hand snatched out and grabbed the dress, using it to pull me closer. "Only I get to be up close and personal with any part of you," he growled possessively.

"Well, I wasn't offering a gang bang," I snapped as I shrugged out of his hold. "Settle, petal."

"What does that even mean?" he asked me in frustration.

"It means calm the fuck down," I told him waspishly. I shrugged the stupid dress on. "I hate this already."

"Your bra needs to come off."

"Excuse me?"

"It has metal in it; your clothing has to be natural." He held his hand out. "Trust me, you don't fuck with spells."

"I may as well be naked!" I protested, but his scowl stopped the rest of my words. With a disgruntled mumble, I unhooked and wiggled out of my bra under the confines of the dress. "Happy?"

"Happi*er*, wouldn't say I was happy."

Well okay then.

As we made our way back to the others, I had no idea what I looked like, but I avoided Pen's look as he passed behind me. My hair hung loose over my shoulders, I knew my lips were swollen from his kisses and *other* things, my legs were still weak from being wrapped around him, and my knees were scuffed. On top of all that, I was in a dress that sacrificial virgins wore in horror movies.

I stopped dead on the grass as I looked around and down at myself. I was dressed like a lamb for the slaughter, and the demons were preparing for a fight. This was more than me unlocking a spell. "You fucking bastard," I whispered in dismay.

Sam turned and looked at me, one eyebrow raised. "Witch?"

"You fucking tricky bastard!" I yelled at him. My wild glare took them all in, only half looked guilty. "You had sex with me all day so I would have your fucking *seed* in me!"

"You didn't complain," Sam said coolly as he crossed his arms over his chest as he watched me. "Do you scent her?" he asked the others casually. They all nodded. "Perfect." His smile was colder than the sea behind me as he watched me.

I met Zel's gaze, and the scarred demon did not look away from me. "I'm already unbound, aren't I?"

"For two nights now," he confirmed.

I shook my head as I refused to make further eye contact with any of them. I felt a tear slip free and wiped it away angrily. They didn't get to see my tears. "Why?" I tilted my head back and looked up into a clear sky. The sun was setting in the west, the red and pink hues spread across the sky even as the moon waited to rise fully, and I could see it was already tinted with red. Some stars were already in the sky, eager to come out. "What was the point?"

"You needed to be marked," Sam told me bluntly.

"I'm not an animal." My eyes snapped to his in fury. His eyes glowed in the dimming light. "You heartless—"

"*Demon*," Sam finished my sentence as he took a step forward in irritation. "I am a demon. *We* are demons. You keep forgetting."

"Samyaza?"

I turned to the newcomer. He was tall, slender, his skin was a deep golden brown, thick chestnut curls rested on his head, and amber eyes fixed on mine. "Is this the morsel you offer me?" He inhaled deeply. "You tasted my witch," he scolded playfully before his eyes narrowed in anger. "You did more than *taste*."

It was very weird that he was discussing me as if I was a sample platter and stranger still that he had a smooth, slow American drawl. It was exactly as I imagined a gentleman from the Deep South would sound. Only it was clear he was no gentle-man, despite his three-piece burgundy suit with crisp white dress shirt and shiny black shoes. He even had a black cane, and I saw Pen lick his lips as he watched the cane tap impatiently on the grass.

"She is the witch who can clear your blood curse," Sam informed him, his words hard. "I did more than taste," he confirmed with a self-satisfied smirk. "I told you a long time ago, she is not for you."

"And you think she is for *you*?" The demon laughed into the cool of the evening as he stepped towards me but hesitated. "You place her in a protection circle? From me?" He cast a sly look at me before his attention was back on Sam. "Or protection from you?"

I was in a circle? I glanced down and realised that I was indeed in a circle. The weird spiky flowers and the powder had formed a solid barrier, and I realised Pen hadn't been creeping behind me, avoiding my post-sex state, he had been *sealing* me in. Oh my God, I realised with dismay that I was encircled in Hamish. *That* was the powder Chaz kept adding in. I was going to be sick. Maybe this was a retelling of an old horror movie after all.

"She can undo the curse. Let her do the spell, return Araqiel to us, then go, Asmodeous." Sam's look was full of contempt for the prince of hell who stood before us.

"The witch needs to bleed," Asmodeous hissed as he glared at me. "Her bitch of an ancestor cursed me, and I have her burning in oil daily, but this one will bleed as well."

"She will not." Sam's voice was loud and clear. I was almost, *almost* glad he was on my side. "Witch." His eyes flicked to mine. "The spell's in your pocket."

Of course it was. Arsehole. I hoped he could hear my thoughts now. Reaching into my pocket, my fingers brushed the animal hide. As I withdrew it from my pocket, the Scavengers arrived in full force.

"You brought friends?" Sam deadpanned.

"More than *friends*." Asmodeous grinned evilly. "I brought *brothers*."

Yeqon and two others walked out from amongst the Scavengers. "Star, you don't smell as sweet," he greeted me jovially. "I fear you have lost your delicious taste," he mocked.

"Has everyone fucked the whore?" Asmodeous sneered as he glared at me.

"Fuck you." I'd finally found my voice. "Fuck all of you." I reached for my powers, and my eyes flew to Zel's in outrage. "You *bound* them?"

"You need to do the spell," he told me firmly as he looked at me steadily.

"This spell?" I held it up in front of me as they all watched. Asmodeous took a step forward. "Fuck your spell." With a strength born of fury, I tore it in two. A strong burst of wind erupted around me, and I let the ripped hide go. It whipped into the air once, twice, three times, and then it flew over the edge of the cliff. "Go find another witch." I held Sam's carefully controlled stare with my angry one. "I'm done with demons."

"Kill her," Asmodeous snarled.

CHAPTER 27

THE SCAVENGERS THREW THEMSELVES FORWARD, AND MY SIX—NO, not mine—*the* six demons that I was used to, took up their defensive positions. Not around me, I noted. They were as wary of the circle as Asmodeous and the Scavengers seemed to be.

Could they get in? More importantly, could I get out?

I looked around me as fear and anger mixed within me, and a cry had me looking up. The battle was in full flow, I couldn't comprehend how fast it had moved, and I stood transfixed as I watched the six demons fight as one. As they had before, they took my breath away in their beautiful savagery. Their clothing had changed, I hadn't even seen it happen. All wore their black tunics, and as I had *dressed* Zel at my pool, they had armoured plates over their tunics. The leather trousers had many leg holsters housing weapons, and as they each fought with their weapons of fire, they were as spectacular as they were daunting. All six had their hoods up, and only from getting to know them over the last few days was I able to identify them as they fought.

Last few days? I blinked. Had it even been a week since my whole life was turned upside down? This time last week, I was happily working as a freelance accountant and doing simple readings for paying customers in the evening.

Now? Now, I was watching a battle of demon against demon while I stood helplessly in a protective circle. I still wasn't sure if the protection was for me. *Gran.* I closed my eyes and *pulled.* Nothing. I felt tears of frustration well behind my closed lids.

"You can step out at any time, witch." Asmodeous was beside me, carefully walking the circle as he watched me like a cat watches a mouse. "Come out and play with me, Star," he taunted.

"I think I'm okay here," I answered even as my throat dried with fear. Sam and the others were demons, and yes, they were scary when I met them, but this was a prince of hell, and he was more than scary. Even within the circle, I could feel the evil pulse within him. His amber eyes roamed over me, and as the wind moulded the stupid white dress to my body, Asmodeous's eyes flared with appreciation.

"I can see why Samyaza was tempted," he told me as his head canted to the side. "Yeqon tells me you taste like the nectar of heaven." Asmodeous leaned forward slightly and inhaled deeply. "It's been a long time since I tasted the heavenly honey, witch." His amber eyes glowed brightly. "I *hunger* for it."

"And it will be a long time to never before you *taste* me," I told him firmly. There was something seriously wrong with these demons. "I'm not coming out." I glanced to the six demons. "And they won't let you in."

Asmodeous scoffed. "The Watchers think they are immune to the hierarchy of hell." His chestnut curls blew slightly in the breeze. "They are deluded. I will cut them all down before I am finished with them for this betrayal."

"They are immortal," I snapped. "You cannot beat them."

"They cannot die, but oh, my little witch." His breath whistled between his teeth as he folded his hands and rested them under his chin as he looked at me with a hooded look. "They *bleed*, they *suffer*, and their pain is *intoxicating*."

Fear for them rose within me as I looked over, and I saw Ros in battle with one of the demons Yeqon had come with. Were they not the same? Weren't they all Watchers? Ros took a heavy blow to his arm, and I heard him cry out. My worry grew for their well-being, but my anger at their trickery fought it.

"What was the trade?" I asked as my eyes followed Sam.

"The spell to break my curse for a brother." Asmodeous tossed it out there as he continued to prowl outside my circle.

"Just a spell," I asked quietly as Zel ducked and brought his short sword up into the gut of a Scavenger. I turned as the Scavenger's insides splattered onto the grass.

"You want to know if it was the complete package deal?" Asmodeous asked me with a sly smile. "It was."

My attention switched to him. *No*, they wouldn't. Again my internal rage fought me, but I *had* to believe they wouldn't hang me out to dry. I had had sex with him, my mind screamed. Image after image of Sam moving in me, over me, under me, flashed into my head. I remembered his moans, his whispered words, his complete possessiveness as we moved as one. That couldn't be faked. Could it?

"You're just a fuck, witch," he said crudely. "Like all the many, *many* fucks he's had before and the thousands that will come after you." Asmodeous laughed into the darkening night. "He will have forgotten you before he's even sinking his cock into the next willing slut."

My jaw clenched as I felt his words like a punch in the gut. My look returned to Sam, and I watched him cut a path through the Scavengers to get to me. I saw his green eyes burning with fury as he caught my look, and even in the chaos that raged around us, I felt our connection. It gave me strength. *He* gave me strength. I turned back to Asmodeous.

"There have been many before me," I acknowledged despite the surge of jealousy. "There will be more after me," I said, feeling the pang of sadness as I glanced back at my demon. "But for now? For now, I am his and he *is* mine."

Asmodeous threw his head back and laughed loudly into the night. I didn't care about Asmodeous, I cared about Sam, and I saw the brief smile as he heard my words, it was all I needed.

"Fuck off back to hell, Prince, I won't help you." I met his angry stare with my own. "My ancestor cursed you for a reason, and I sure as hell won't break it." I looked him over with scorn.

"You burn her every day in oil? And still she does not lift the curse?" I shook my head. "And neither will I."

Asmodeous stepped closer to the circle. "You cannot stay in here, witch. You will come out, and there is nowhere on this earth that you can hide from me. I will find you, and I will cut you to pieces and feed you to your Watchers. I will make you suffer worse than any before you," he promised me as his eyes burned with fury, and I realised his amber glow came from flames burning in his eyes.

His eyes burned with the flames of hell. *Holy fuck, what was I doing refusing a prince of hell?*

Obstinate and stubborn, they called me. Smiling widely at the demon whose hate for me was tangible, I turned my back on him. "Go away, little prince, there's nothing for you here."

His roar of fury echoed in the night air just as the wind picked up and the storm clouds raced across the empty sky. I called the wind and the rain, and as I did, I felt my power rush up to meet me. I closed my eyes in relief as I felt it coursing through my veins again. When I opened them, the threat was gone and I was staring at six bedraggled and slightly injured demons. Soldiers. Watchers.

Yeqon and the two Watchers with him stood to the side, and he watched me carefully. His dark blue eyes flicked over me as he looked between me and Sam. Sam held his stare for a long time before Yeqon nodded slightly. "You play a dangerous game," he said softly.

"I do?" I questioned him.

Yeqon smiled briefly at me before he turned to the others. "This does not get us Araqiel back," he snapped angrily at Sam.

"And siding with *him* does?" Zel snarled back. "We have to think smart, not act with stupidity."

"Brother fighting brother is not the way," Chaz spoke quietly as he looked to the sky, his gaze on the clouds. "There is still so much to be done," he sighed as he looked back at his brothers. "Araqiel needs to be free, we need him, but we need to be careful about what we are willing to sacrifice."

"Is that me?" I asked cautiously. Three *threes* looked at me as one. Holy shit, I was still in deep shit. "The sacrifice, I mean. I'm not on board with that."

Der grunted out a laugh as he flexed his shoulder. "I could have done without the play-by-play porn show as I was fighting." He grinned at me. "But appreciate you sharing."

"What?" My eyes were as wide as saucers.

"We need to teach you to school your thoughts," Pen told me in amusement as he unstrapped his shoulder plates. "What the fuck did you hit me with, Bara?" he asked one of the new ones.

"My mighty sword," the new one answered. He hefted the biggest sword I had ever seen as he grinned. His shoulder-length brown hair styled in loose waves softened his square jaw. Deep brown eyes ran over me. "Thought you'd be prettier."

"Thought you would fight with your brothers, not against them," I snapped back. *Dick.*

Ros snorted in amusement even as Bara bristled. "She just says what we're all thinking." Ros stroked his short blond beard as he looked at me. "I think you're plenty pretty," he added with a wink.

"Are you coming out?" Sam asked me impatiently.

"Nope."

"No?" His full attention was on me. "What do you mean *no*?"

"It's the opposite of yes," I told him with a scowl. "I'm not coming out until you *all* tell me what the fuck is going on." I folded my arms across my chest.

"She swears a lot," the last demon I didn't know spoke. "It's jarring."

"They swear all the time," I protested with an angry point at my demons.

"They are male," he answered simply.

Oh hell he did not. "I beg your pardon?"

"Granted." He beamed at me, and I had the feeling he would have patted my head in appreciation had he been able to reach me.

"*Sam!*" I demanded tersely. "Which idiot brother is *this*?"

Sam's eyes had closed briefly when his *brother* had spoken. He looked at me now in resignation. "This is Suriel. He is fluent in the art, of course, of the moon." Sam's voice had a warning undertone.

I ignored it. "It seems he has the *art* of chauvinistic pig mastered."

"She's delightful." Bara grinned at me. "Completely untaught and wild." He turned to Yeqon. "She taste as good?"

Before I protested, Sam had punched his brother out. I felt a surge of appreciation for him. "*All* of you will stop talking about *anyone* tasting her," he growled as he looked at them all. He looked towards me, and I saw amusement in his eyes as he caught me nodding emphatically at his words. "You," he spoke to me. "Out."

I stopped nodding, and I tilted my head to the side as I looked at Sam and then the rest of them. "No."

"Star?" Pen caught my attention. "Why are you not coming out?"

"Why?" I looked at them all in disbelief. "Because about an hour ago, you tricked me into this damn circle, you were going to give me to a *prince* of hell, he"—I pointed at Sam—"tricked me into having sex with him, and you *all* betrayed me with your lies."

"When did I trick you into having sex?" Sam demanded as he unbuckled his shoulder plate, rubbing his shoulder underneath. "You hardly tripped and fell on my dick, witch."

I heard Chaz's *oh no*, I heard Ros's delighted *here we go*, and I heard Zel's snort of derision. I heard them, but I couldn't believe the audacity of this demon in front of me.

"Was that wise?" Pen murmured to Sam in rebuke.

I should've ignored him. "Tripped and *fell* on your dick!" Yeah, there was no way I was letting that pass. "You seduced me, you arrogant prick!"

"I did not seduce you," Sam growled. "You threw yourself at me."

My head reeled back in shock. "Threw myself at you? At *you?*" I looked around wildly, my gaze landing on Chaz, who had been pulling his hair into his manbun and looked at me startled when my eyes narrowed on him. "Him!" I pointed at Chaz as my glare returned to Sam. "If I was going to throw myself at anyone, it was *him.*" I carried on, recklessly ignoring Sam's low growl. "But you, *you* stopped me. *You* kissed *me. You* threw yourself at *me*. You came into *my* bedroom, you made every single move on me."

"You mean when I had you screaming on the end of my dick and begging for more?" Sam bit back crudely.

"I was begging for you to *stop*," I lied as embarrassment and anger flooded my cheeks. I poked Sam in the chest as I stepped up to him. "You're a complete wanker."

"Got you." His eyes glowed with triumph, and I realised I had stepped outside my circle. His strong arms caught me from behind as I turned and tried to run back inside the circle. He held me against his chest. "Now, now, little witch, you know you like it when I'm rough," he whispered into my ear as he rumbled with laughter.

"She's passionate at least," Bara commented to the others as he watched me struggle futilely in Sam's hold.

"Completely unaware of her surroundings," Zel criticised as he gave me a dismissive glare. "Reacts before she thinks. She's a danger to herself and everyone around her, stupidly reckless."

"We can work on it," Pen assured me with a comforting smile.

"We can?" I asked dubiously as I fell in defeat against Sam as his arm tightened across my waist.

"Absolutely." Chaz nodded emphatically. "Anything can be taught," he said with a warm smile.

Maybe Zel was right, this was the third time Sam had made me react to his taunting, and I fell for it every damn time. "What if Zel is right and I'm unteachable?" I asked self-consciously.

"Can't teach stupid," Zel muttered.

"I'm not stupid!" I snapped at the surly demon.

"Then you can be taught," Bara said with an encouraging smile. "You're lucky, we are very good teachers."

"Aren't you the enemy?" I asked cautiously. "I mean, you were *just* fighting each other."

"Opposite sides of the same goal." Yeqon spoke dismissively. "We want the same thing, our brother free of Asmodeous."

"And I was merely what? A fun *fuck you* to Sam?"

"The swearing is excessive," Suriel said sadly to Chaz.

"She grows on you, in a few days you won't even notice it." He clapped his brother on the shoulder as he walked over to join Pen and Der.

Yeqon watched their exchange before turning his attention back to Sam and me. He gave an unconcerned shrug. "I did not know it ran so deep," he said to Sam with a slight bow of his head.

"Now you know," Sam answered as his arm tightened around me.

"Now I know."

"Know what?" I asked Sam in confusion as Yeqon too joined the others. Sam spun me in his arms, and I looked up at him warily, his green eyes glowing softly.

He dipped his head to mine, his lips brushing mine softly. "Knows you're mine."

"Am I?" My uncertainty must have been evident, and his eyes dimmed slightly as his finger traced across my lips.

"Most definitely." He kissed me hard, and tentatively I returned his kiss before he became more demanding, obviously impatient with my hesitation.

The course of the evening flashed through my mind, and I remembered the strength I felt when I recognised our connection. The strength I got from Sam made me banish a prince of hell back to the underground. My arms wound around his neck as my mouth opened to return his kiss, and I heard his groan of approval as his arms tightened around me.

Yes, he was a complete overbearing dick, but for now, I was his and he was mine.

Epilogue

"WE SHOULD RETURN TO YOUR COTTAGE," SAM TOLD ME AS HE pulled his head back and looked down at me.

"Why the dress?" I asked as I reluctantly stepped out of his hold, looking around to see that the others were gone.

"You look good in a dress," Sam teased as he picked up his shoulder plate. "You look better out of it, to be fair." His eyes flared with lust, and I stepped away from him with a smile, my hand held up in warning.

"No." I laughed as he pouted in disappointment. "I think I have had enough outdoor sex, don't you?"

"No." He shook his head as he grinned at me.

I laughed out loud and looked up at the sky. It was fully dark now, and the blood moon hung heavy in the sky. I lost my smile as I gazed at it.

"What is it?" Sam asked me softly as he watched me.

"Was everything a trick?" I asked him. My eyes stayed rooted to the moon, scared in case his expression told me too much. Who was I kidding? This was *Sam*, the man had the poker face of champions.

"Not everything," Sam conceded. "I genuinely never expected you to destroy the spell and throw it away for one," he admitted sombrely. "I may be immortal, but my damn heart almost stopped."

I grinned at him as I giggled. "I think Asmodeous had a stroke."

"I think we *all* had a stroke," he told me with a wry smile.

"Why didn't you tell me you were putting me in a protective circle?" I asked as I scuffed my boot across the grass.

"You react better when you are unsuspecting. It was a gamble your anger would be enough." He winked at me. "But we should know not to underestimate your temper."

"Right, fear or anger," I murmured as I looked at the castle under the blood moon. "I was definitely terrified and furious at the same time, I should have remembered."

"We can discuss this back at the cottage," Sam reminded me.

"Are they all there?" I asked reluctantly. "Yeqon annoys me."

Sam laughed out loud. I watched his eyes dance with pleasure as his rich laugh warmed the night. "Yeqon annoys us all, but he is a necessary evil," he told me as he reached for my hand.

We travelled and I was in my bedroom. Sam tugged my hand and pulled me towards the door. "They are waiting."

"You pulling me *out* of the bedroom is new," I remarked saucily as I followed him.

Sam's head turned, and I saw his brief reconsideration as he looked towards the bed, and then he shook his head grudgingly. "Later."

"Confident, aren't you," I teased as I walked past him towards the kitchen. "Got so much more eye candy to look at now." I yelped when he smacked my bum, hard.

"No looking," he growled as he pulled me against him. "No calling my brothers *candy*."

"You're no fun," I whispered as I stood on tiptoes and brushed his lips with mine.

"I'm all the fun you need." His teeth caught my bottom lip, and he bit gently. "Want me to show you?"

"I thought that was for later?" I asked huskily as my hand boldly caressed against the front of his leathers, and his eyes darkened with want.

"It is!" Ros shouted from the kitchen. "Please stop, you're making me horny."

Blushing, I dropped back onto my feet as my head rested

against Sam's chest and I giggled in embarrassment. "How soon can I learn to keep my thoughts to myself?" I asked desperately.

"It's called Shielding," Sam said as he walked ahead of me. "We'll make sure you learn that first."

Nodding, I followed him. My kitchen was overflowing with demons. "I have more rooms in the house," I told them dryly as I regarded them all.

"Here is closer to outside," Der told me as he opened the back door to the garden beyond.

As they spoke amongst themselves and they all drank my whisky, which I wasn't sure how they had found, I sat on Sam's lap, my head resting on his shoulder tiredly.

I tuned them out slightly when Ros and Der decided to challenge Bara and Suriel to combat. Six demons spilled out of my kitchen to my back garden as they wrestled. For the first time since meeting the Watchers, I gave a prayer of thanks for the fact I looked out onto fields and had no neighbours. Absently, I scratched at my arm and looked down at the mark.

"Will they still come?" I asked Sam as I brought his attention to it. "The Scavengers?"

"Oh, that." Yeqon reached over, and his hand brushed along my arm. The mark was removed.

"You did this?" I demanded angrily.

"They were cloaking you, I needed to find you." He sipped his drink. "It was nothing."

"It was *something* to me," I snapped at him angrily. Yeqon merely shrugged, and standing, he joined the others outside.

"Arsehole," I muttered as I got off Sam's lap. "You've finished all my whisky," I reprimanded Sam and Zel, who stayed within the kitchen. "I'll get more."

I walked through to the living room, and crouching down, I opened my "drinks cupboard," which translated to a shelf at the bottom of my bookshelf where I kept my stash of booze. I was tired. Kicking off my boots, I sat on my couch, tucking my feet underneath me. I could hear the others and their loud laughter as they enjoyed the evening. My eyes closed in weariness. There was so much to learn. *So* much to learn, and I was scared of what was to come. My elbow itched.

"Lass, my cottage is overrun," Gran said to me, and my eyes popped open in surprise.

"Gran!" I exclaimed happily as I jumped up and embraced her. "How are you here?"

"There are three *threes* in my home, even the veil cannot keep me from the defilement on the soil," she scolded me as she looked around. "You fixed the leak?"

"Huh?" I looked at the corner of the room. "Yes, got the gutter repaired." I shook my head to clear it. "I didn't do the spell, Gran," I told her excitedly as I pulled her with me to sit on the couch. "I sent Asmodeous back to hell."

Gran nodded thoughtfully as she patted my hand. "Yes, we know."

"We?" I asked in confusion. "Who's we?"

"Every soul burning in hell at his fury," she told me with a sad smile. "You angered him good."

"Oh." My excitement at seeing my gran was diminishing. "Did I do the wrong thing?" I asked worriedly.

"Only you can answer that," Gran told me evasively. "Get that book." She pointed to the bookshelf.

Looking between it and her, I nodded and brought the book over to her. "*Scotland and the Celts: A History,*" I read. "I'm confused."

"Open the book and stop when I say."

I did as I was told, and I flicked through the pages until my gran said stop. "What do you see?"

"A tree? The tree of life?" I told her as I looked at the tree. It was a well-known Celtic symbol.

"Do you know why the tree of life is special?" Gran asked me.

I thought about it and frowned as I did so. "No, actually, I don't."

"The tree is said to connect that which is above to what is below," Gran told me as her fingers hovered over the symbol. "It is said that the tree connects the world of man to heaven." She looked at me. "Or that it connects *us all*. Connecting everything to each other."

"I like that one better," I admitted, my voice a whisper as I studied the tree. "Which one is it though?"

"Turn the book around," Gran told me. I did so, and I stared at the tree. It was exactly the same. The roots of the tree were now the leaves, and the leaves were now the roots. "That which was underground is now above, and what was above is now below," Gran said softly.

"The roots become the branches," I realised as I stared at it, and a cold shiver of fear ran down my spine.

"And the branches reach for the sky."

"The sky from where they already fell," I murmured in understanding.

"And as they fell, they burned across the sky in a glow of stars and dusk," Gran whispered to me. "You are in too deep, my lass, you need to find a way out. The tree is all that can save you from him now."

"Gran?" I looked away from the book to look at Gran, but she was gone. Instead, Sam stood in the doorway, his eyes shuttered as he looked at the book in my hands. "Sam." I gulped and hastily closed the book.

"Bit late for reading," he said as he leaned casually against the doorway.

"Yeah." I stood quickly, dropping the book face down on the couch. "You're right, I think I should go to bed."

"Do you?" He assessed me coolly; his eyes ran over me before he held my stare. "Why is your heart racing, witch?"

"Exhaustion?" I punted wildly in the dark.

"Hmm." His look was hooded as he held his hand out to me. "Come," he instructed.

Find the tree, Gran whispered in my ear. Hesitantly, I reached out and tried not to flinch when Sam's fingers curled around mine. He pulled me to the kitchen and through the kitchen door to the garden outside.

A circle of Watchers waited for me, all donned in their hooded tunics, weapons of flame at their sides. Their heads were bowed, but I saw eight variations of blue and brown glowing eyes as they watched us.

"Sam?" I looked at him as fear clutched at my throat. Sam led me into the circle and stepped back, leaving me barefooted on the grass in this stupid white dress, which offered no protection from the cold October night.

The blood moon shone above me, and I was startled to see how red it was.

"Some believe that it's red because it mirrors the sun," Pen's voice throbbed with power. "That the earth's air molecules scatter out the blue light, leaving the remainder to reflect on the moon's surface with a glow of red from the sun."

"Others believe that the blood moon comes with evil intent." I recognised Der's voice and turned my head to look at him. In the darkness with their hoods up, their heads bowed, *all* of their eyes glowing with power, I couldn't tell who was who.

"Which one is it?" I asked, my voice hoarse in the night.

"Which one do you want it to be?" Sam asked me, his voice was easily recognisable.

"I'm hoping not the evil intent?" I hedged, wanting this to be one of their weird pranks. Like when Pen dropped a great white shark in front of me. *Fun times.*

"What do you see?" Chaz spoke across the night.

"You lot scaring the shit out of me?" I bit out tersely as I searched the faces of those in front of me.

"Tell us what you *see*." Chaz's voice was hard, something it had never been before.

I turned slowly as I looked at their forms. "I see nine demons —" I heard the dissatisfied rumble, and I corrected myself. "Nine *Watchers*, hooded, weapons drawn, eyes glowing with power as they watch me."

"Is that all?"

I wasn't sure if that was Ros, but I turned slowly again. What was I missing? As I peered into the darkness, the spirits walked forward, encircling the Watchers. "The dead are here." I wasn't sure if this was good or bad. I hoped good. I searched the souls for Gran, but it seemed she was missing.

"And?" I didn't care who spoke as I turned again.

For the third time. I had turned full circle, three times. *Shit.*

Red eyes blazed suddenly in the night as Hound walked towards me as he made his way through the throngs of the dead.

"Hound," I said with relief.

"What do you *see*?" someone asked me again.

"I told you!" I said as fear rattled my bones. "Watchers, spirits and Hound."

"Witch, what do you see?" Zel spoke clearly into the night.

Were they deaf? "I see Watchers, dead people and a hellhound," I snapped angrily at them all.

Sam was in front of me. I would know those eyes anywhere, even as his face was cast in darkness. "A blood moon means a sacrifice," he told me quietly. His hand cupped my face gently as his other held my arm. "Witch, what do you see?"

I was away to punch him when suddenly my eyes flew to Hound, and my step back caused Sam to tighten his hold. "No," I whispered.

"Yes," his voice was firm and sure. "Tell me."

"I see a hellhound." My voice was a dry broken whisper as tears began to flow down my cheeks. I was back at the cemetery on the very first night the Watchers came for me. *To see a hellhound meant death,* I remembered as I thought back with fear to the night I met them. Hound stepped closer, and his eyes blazed brighter as his jaw opened and his fangs glistened in the red of the moonlight.

A dagger or a knife was pressed under my breast, and I looked up at Sam in panic. His forehead rested against mine briefly before his lips brushed my forehead.

"I will see you burn in hell," I seethed at him as he pulled me closer.

"I'll be waiting." He slid the blade smoothly into my body, and I cried out in agony as I felt it pierce my heart.

Sam stepped back as I fell to the ground, and I watched the white dress turn red as my blood stained the fabric as it flowed out of me and onto the grass below me. I looked up at the hellhound that now stood over me. Massive jaws descended on me even as I flung my arms up to protect myself.

Darkness enveloped me as my screams were swallowed in the night, and I died at the hand of the Watchers, under the glowing red of the blood moon, as a hellhound carried my soul to hell.

Acknowledgments

There are a few people I would like to thank for their help in getting this book into your hands.

Anna, the cover for this series is AWESOME. I love it. This is my first non person cover and it blew me away when you showed me it. Thank you for sharing your amazing talent with me.

Amber, Julie, Katy & Renee, girls you were my little rocks throughout this book. This was a step away from the norm for me and I cannot express how much your words of encouragement boosts my confidence. I say "words of encouragement" but it's more demands for more with shouty capitals. Either way…I love you all for your continuous support.

My editor, Helayna, does a marvellous job on commas and whatnot, but she also needs a mention because she's a supportive friend and I can bounce ideas off her as we're editing.

Renee, also gets another hug in words, because she fell in love with this story in the first chapter. It's a very humble thing to be told by someone that you wrote their favourite ever book. I don't think she understood at the time, the enormity of that sentence or the impact of her words when she told me. So I'm putting it in writing for everyone to see - ARE YOU FREAKING KIDDING ME!? I wrote your most favourite ever book? I have no other words - except THANK YOU! I love you, and I really hope I continue the momentum into Book 2 (no pressure on me at all…).

My mum gets a special thanks because she loved this book so much. She loves all my books (I'm very lucky), but she laughed throughout this one and is waiting (im)patiently for me to write Book 2, so she can see a certain demon get his comeuppance. She's also the best mum a girl can have, and I don't say enough how grateful I am that she's mine. Love you mama x

Mr. M…ten full length books written since I started writing in August 2018. Thank you for putting up with me. Thank you for listening to all the book things, for the emotional support you give me and the unwavering confidence you have in my ability to tell a good story. Everything I do is for you.

And finally, to my readers. Thank you from the bottom of my heart for continuing to pick up my books and lose yourself in the pages of a world I have created, it's an amazing gift that you give me each and every time you read my words.

Love Eve x

About the Author

Eve L. Mitchell is a USA Today Bestselling author who writes contemporary romance and urban fantasy.

Being an avid reader from a young age, Eve still considers herself to be a reader first. She believes there is nothing better than getting that new book either on your e-reader or in your hands, and the fact she may bring that excitement to a fellow reader, fills her with wonder. She writes under a pen name because otherwise her Secret Agent status will be revoked.

Eve lives in the North East of Scotland, with her three coffee machines and her significant other, Mr. M. She enjoys NFL Football, music and having long conversations with the voices in her head, which sometimes turn into the stories she writes.

If you want to keep up to date with all things Eve, to be the first to hear about updates from Eve sign up for her newsletter.

All the books; both fantasy and contemporary:
https://bit.ly/Evesnewsletter
Just contemporary romance book news:
https://bit.ly/Evesromancenewsletter
Just Fantasy books news:
https://bit.ly/Evesfantasynewsletter

Connect with all things Eve here: https://bit.ly/Eveslinks

Creatures of evil roam the shadows - the Drakhyn. They may look like humans, but their taloned hands and razor-sharp teeth serve one purpose only; killing.

A Sentinel's purpose is to patrol and protect. They are highly trained soldiers with superior skills and abilities. Whether they be Vampyres, Lycan, Castors or gifted Akrhyn, their purpose is the same; hunt the Drakhyn and rid the world of their evil presence.

GET THE SERIES
WWW.EVELMITCHELL.COM

FROM BOOK 1:

They hunted me down.
Six demons who believe I can cast a spell to lift a blood curse.
But I'm merely a clairvoyant who can summon the dead.

Being thrust into the world of demons is terrifying, intimidating, alluring…
Their leader refuses to believe I cannot understand the spell.
He's infuriating—but there is something about him that calls to me.
An attraction that scares me.

GET THE SERIES
WWW.EVELMITCHELL.COM

FROM BOOK 1: You'd think the universe would toss me a break after the year I'd had.

I made a plan, one that would give me a fresh start in a new town where no one knew me.
It should have been simple, but nothing is ever as easy as it should be when starting over.
New town, new school, and a new life. It sounded easy enough, or I'd thought it had.

It wasn't.

GET THE SERIES
WWW.EVELMITCHELL.COM

FROM BOOK 1: I knew the moment I saw Aiden that he was the kind of man who would break a woman's heart. With his looks he could grace the cover of any book or magazine.

Even as I got to know him, his hard no nonsense attitude was alluring. He was as captivating as he was intense. My pulse raced and my stomach fluttered when I was near him. Having his attention was as intoxicating as it was overwhelming.

Yes, Aiden would break a woman's heart. If she let him.

Maybe, even if she didn't.

GET THE SERIES
WWW.EVELMITCHELL.COM